Elaine had thought he no longer loved her—that love had been burned away by bitterness and sorrow—but the look he gave her made her heart race.

Gazing into his eyes, which looked dark and bottomless this morning, she felt a spasm of desire. Her mouth felt dry and her tongue moved over her lips as she tried to control the sudden leap of excitement. For one precious moment she had seen something in his eyes— something that reminded her of the youth that had left her to fight for his ideals.

She felt light-headed and almost swayed towards him. It seemed to her that his mouth softened, and she longed to kiss him, to be held in those strong arms as she'd been held so many years ago—but she had been a child then, and now the woman she had become longed for more.

AUTHOR NOTE

When brave men set out to fight for their King and Christianity they knew they were leaving their homes, their families and their sweethearts for years. It wasn't possible for them to come home on leave, as our wonderful soldiers do today; it would be years before they saw their homeland again. Wives and sweethearts were often left wondering if they would ever see the man they loved again in this life, while a young son might grow to manhood in his father's absence. Little wonder, then, that a girl's uncle might seek to marry her to a rich and powerful man, bidding her to forget the man she loved.

This is the story of Elaine, who was determined to stay faithful to her love, but when Zander returned he was not the same. Could she ever hope to find the love they had lost?

I hope you enjoy this book as much as I enjoyed writing it.

Prologue

'Please don't go,' the girl cried and clung to the young man in desperation. 'Don't leave me, Zander. If you go, I think I shall die of a broken heart. I cannot bear it if you leave me.' She loved him so much and her life would seem empty without him.

Zander was tall and strong, but still a youth, being no more than seventeen years of age. He bent his head to drop a kiss on the girl's fair hair, hiding the pain her entreaty caused him.

'I must go, my dearest heart,' he whispered, his throat catching with emotion. 'You know I love you and shall until the day I die—but my father was murdered and most of his lands have been sold to pay debts. My mother has gone to a nunnery to weep for him, but I must avenge his death. To become strong enough to demand justice for my father, I must join the crusade and become a knight. Only then may I avenge my family and claim you as my bride.'

She gazed up at him, her eyes as blue as the summer sky above them, her pale hair wild about her face. Somewhere a meadowlark sang, but she did not hear its sweet song. All she knew was that the person she loved most in all the world was going away and she might never see him again. She tugged at his simple short tunic, her face strained with grief.

'What shall I do if you are killed?' she asked pitifully. 'How can you leave me so?'

'You are not alone, Elaine. Your father loves you dearly and will care for you. If I am killed, then you must forget you ever knew me.'

'I shall never forget you,' she vowed passionately. 'You are the only man I shall ever love.'

'You are but fourteen,' Zander said and smiled tenderly. His hair was the colour of night and his eyes grey with a silver light in their depths. She thought him beautiful, his sweet singing voice a romantic delight, for he sang songs of love to her and played with her in the meadows all the summer long, making her chains of daisies. 'I do truly love you, but your father would not let us wed. He has promised

Anne Herries lives in Cambridgeshire, where she is fond of watching wildlife and spoils the birds and squirrels that are frequent visitors to her garden. Anne loves to write about the beauty of nature, and sometimes puts a little into her books, although they are mostly about love and romance. She writes for her own enjoyment, and to give pleasure to her readers. Anne is a winner of the Romantic Novelists' Association Romance Prize. She invites readers to contact her on her website: www.lindasole.co.uk

that if I return a knight with a fortune I have won for my valour, then he will look kindly on us, but until then I can offer you nothing.'

'I care for nothing but you…' What would all the gold in Christendom matter if he were killed and did not return to claim her?

'I will not take my wife to a hovel and expect her to live like a pauper.' Zander's mouth hardened, his eyes becoming flinty. 'I must go, Elaine. When my quest is over I shall come for you.'

'And if I am wed?' she demanded, her head high, eyes bright with pride. He had refused her and she would not beg for his favours.

'Then I shall wish you happy and go away.'

'You do not love me as I love you…' She turned away, hurt and angry because he would not listen, but he caught her arm, swinging her back to face him. Then he bent his head, his mouth taking hers in a kiss of possession that told of the man he would be one day—a kiss that had her near swooning for love of him. 'Zander, forgive me…I love you…'

'And I you.' He touched her cheek with his fingertips. 'Take care, my beloved. I shall dream of you—and I swear that one day I shall come back to claim you.'

So saying, he pushed her gently from him

and left her standing there as he mounted his horse and rode away. Elaine stared after him, tears trickling down her cheeks. She loved him so desperately and she was afraid that he would never return.

Chapter One

The knight stood in the middle of the field of carnage and looked about him at the dead and dying. Friends and enemies lay side by side, united in death, as they could never be in life. He had come here to this land called the Holy Land as a young man, filled with zeal and a burning desire to carry the Cross and bring the true faith to the heathen. All he had found was a terrible despair born of grief, pain and the disillusionment that comes from discovering that the king he had followed could on occasion be as cruel and unjust as the Saracen enemy. Indeed, at times the enemy seemed to be more merciful than the Christian knights who slaughtered prisoners without mercy.

As he found the youth he searched for amongst

the fallen, Zander de Bricasse felt his sorrow deepen to the point where it became almost unbearable. The boy was a newcomer, fresh from his village in England where he had been recruited to fight the king's wars—just as Zander had been five years earlier. *He* had fought so many terrible battles and survived, but this lad Tom had died in the first brief moments of his first encounter with the enemy. His mother and sweetheart would wait hopefully for a letter or a message that he was safe and well, but they would wait in vain. Tom would never go home.

Zander scooped the boy into his arms and carried him away from the stench of blood, the heat and the dust. He could not take the lad home to his mother, but he would bury him with honour in a place of peace that he knew of and he would send word to England of his brave death in battle. And then what would he do?

Zander felt his cheeks wet and knew that he was crying—crying for a boy he hardly knew. Or was he crying for the boy he had once been and a life he'd known so many long years ago? Into his mind came the picture of a beautiful young girl and the promise he'd made her to return and marry her once he'd made his fortune and avenged his father's cruel death.

Depositing his precious burden in the shade

of an olive tree by a pool that never dried no matter how hard the hot sun beat down on the land, Zander began to dig the grave that must hold Tom's body. He would pray that the boy's soul went to heaven—but where was heaven and where hell? Surely if there was a hell it was here in this terrible sun-drenched land.

Zander was no longer sure if either existed. As he worked, his tears dried and his resolve grew. He was done with this war and the cause he'd thought so just. He was not sure that he even believed in God anymore. Perhaps the heathens were right in their beliefs and his people were wrong to try to impose their religion.

It no longer mattered to Zander. He felt empty, drained of all emotion but pity for the waste of life. All he wanted now was to go home and find peace.

Would Elaine still be waiting for him—or would she have married long ago? He knew that he must return to England, to the home and the village of his birth. He was ready to seek the revenge that must be his—and then to claim the woman he loved.

As he rose from his knees after saying the words of prayer that the boy Tom deserved, Zander heard a yell from behind him. He whirled round even as the huge Saracen charged, sword

in hand, arm raised to strike. Four others followed, sharp scimitars raised. Zander was un-
prepared, his sword abandoned for the spade
to dig his friend's grave. He saw it lying beneath a tree—but could he reach it before they
cut him down?

Zander knew a moment of despair. 'Forgive
me, Elaine,' he murmured, and it seemed that
soon his blood too would stain this place of
peace.

'You will do as you are told, Elaine.' Lord
Marcus Howarth glared at his beautiful niece.
'Your father indulged you and allowed you to
stay at home and wait for the return of a man
who may already lie dead in Jerusalem. Now
your father is dead and I am master here. The
Earl of Newark has asked for you in marriage
and I see no reason to refuse his offer. He is a
powerful man and your marriage would make
us stronger here at Howarth.'

'Please, I beg you, sir,' Elaine Howarth cried.
'Do not force me to this marriage. I dislike the
earl and my heart belongs to Zander. If he is
dead, I would rather go to a convent and spend
my life in prayer. I gave him my word that I
would wait when he left to follow the king and
I shall not break it.' Her blue eyes flashed defi-

ance at him. 'I refuse this marriage. No matter what you say I shall not wed a man I despise—nor shall I break my word to Zander.'

'Indeed?' Lord Howarth towered over her. A tall thickset man, he was the very opposite of her gentle father, for whom she was still in mourning. 'We shall see about that, lady.'

The late master of Howarth Castle would never have forced his only daughter to marry a man she despised. He had married Elaine's mother for love and mourned her sincerely when she died in childbirth some seven years after her daughter's birth. Her babe had survived but a few hours after her and the then Lord Howarth had wept as he buried his son's tiny body with its mother. He had loved his wife too well and would not take another, though it meant his brother would succeed him. He had his daughter and that must suffice.

'Marcus is a just man,' her father had told Elaine as he lay dying earlier that year. 'You must follow his advice, my dearest child, for if you do not he may grow angry. My brother is honest, but he is not the most patient of men and he likes to be obeyed.'

Elaine had kissed her father's cheek and told him not to worry for her, but she had not given her promise. She had never liked her uncle and knew that he thought her spoiled and too proud. His wife Margaret was quick to obey him; indeed, she tried to anticipate her husband's every whim and was clearly afraid of displeasing him. Elaine could not go to her aunt for help because she would tell her it was her duty to obey her uncle.

'I am an heiress in my own right,' Elaine said, looking at her uncle boldly. He was tall and strong and could break her with his hands if he chose, but she doubted that he would stoop to violence. She supposed that in his own way he was the honourable man his brother had thought him, but he believed that he knew what was best for her—for the family. 'If you will not allow me to wait here for Zander's return, allow me to go to my dower lands. I can live there and be no trouble to you, my lord.'

'Foolish girl!' Her uncle looked at her in exasperation. 'How long do you imagine you would be permitted to remain there without my protection? Your beauty—your wealth—makes you a target for every rogue baron in the country. Within six months you would find yourself a prisoner of some penniless knight and forced to wed him because he had disparaged you. I am offering you a match that will bring you prestige and wealth. Newark is a favourite with

Prince John and will take you to court, where your beauty will be appreciated. You will have beautiful clothes, jewels and a respected name as his wife. Come, Elaine, give me your word and I shall send for him and the betrothal may be in a few days.'

'No...' Her heart raced as she saw the fury spark in his eyes, but her chin jutted and her head went higher. 'My word is given to Zander—'

'A landless knight who can offer you nothing! Your father told him he must prove himself before you could wed—and what did he do? He took the Cross and went to the Holy Land. Had he stayed here and won honours from Prince John, you might have been wed long since.'

Elaine bit her lip. In her heart she felt much as her uncle did, for she'd wept bitter tears night after night when Zander had left, but she knew that the man she loved would never have sought honour at Prince John's court. He would think the prince corrupt and despise the way he imposed fines and taxes on a people struggling to survive despite poor harvests and the poverty that so many endured.

There was no point in telling her uncle that she did not wish to go to the prince's court. All Elaine wanted was to be chatelaine of her own home. The dower lands that had come to her through her mother were fertile and situated on the borders between England and Wales, a distance of almost a hundred miles. If she left her uncle's protection she knew that she would become a target for unscrupulous knights, who might snatch her and force her to wed them for the sake of her fortune.

'Please, Uncle, for the love you bore my father, grant me a few more months. If Zander does not return by…the Eve of Christ's Mass, I will accept my fate and marry the man of your choice.'

Lord Howarth stared at her in silence for several minutes and Elaine feared that he meant to impose his will. Rather than submit, she would run away, but she knew that if she did she might find herself in more danger. Unless she had an escort of armed men she might be kidnapped and either held to ransom or married against her will. Her best option was to wait for Zander's return, but it seemed that her uncle was impatient for her marriage. She knew that she was well beyond the normal age for marriage, which for girls of her lineage was often arranged by their twelfth birthday. Yet she would rather live as a spinster than marry a man she despised.

Why did it matter to her uncle whom she

married? Surely he had nothing to gain either way—and yet perhaps he would rather the earl was a friend than an enemy. If Newark was angered, it might mean that he would try to take by force what he could not get another way.

Howarth's gaze narrowed. 'You will give me your solemn word, Elaine? If this rogue you've set your heart on does not return by the Eve of Christ's birth, you will marry the earl?'

'If it is your wish, sir, yes.' She crossed her fingers behind her back for nothing would make her marry that evil man. Somehow she would contrive to get away and seek sanctuary in a convent.

Her uncle inclined his head. 'Then I shall grant your wish. It is but two and a half months away. I am not such a hard man that I would force you just to please myself, niece—but this is for your own good. If you delay much longer, the chance will pass you by and you may have no choice but to retire to a nunnery.'

She would much prefer that to a marriage she did not like, but she said nothing of defiance, pretending to a calm she did not feel.

'I thank you for your patience, Uncle.' She lowered her head demurely so that he should not see the flash of temper in her eyes. Rather than marry a man she despised she *would* retire to a nunnery—or, if driven to it, she would take her own life. There were poisons that were quick, though they caused terrible pain, but she would endure even that rather than submit to Newark. The way he looked at Elaine made her cringe inside and his thick lips made her shiver with disgust at the thought they might touch hers.

'Very well, my word is given. Go to your aunt now and see if you may help her. She was feeling poorly earlier and your skill with herbs may ease her.'

Elaine inclined her head. She had already tended her aunt, for the poor lady suffered with terrible headaches and lay prostrate on her couch. There was no point in telling her uncle that her aunt was now resting. He might visit her to investigate when all that gentle lady needed was a little peace.

Leaving her uncle's private chamber, Elaine walked through the great hall. The room was always filled with knights and servants going about their business. In winter and even on summer days a huge log fire was kept burning in the hearth, for the stone walls and high vaulted roof made it cold. Sunlight seldom penetrated the tiny slitted windows and it was often dark. Outside it was a glorious autumn day, but in the castle there were dark corners until the torches were lit.

Her dower lands did not boast a stout castle such as this one, merely a manor house, but it was much lighter and the deep windowsills made a perfect place to sit and look out at the gardens and fields that surrounded her mother's home. She had spent many happy days there in childhood and wished that she might go there now, but her uncle was right. Without a husband to protect her she would be vulnerable and at the mercy of ruthless barons.

'My lady, will you walk?' Marion, her companion and faithful servant, came up to her, a basket over her arm. 'We need herbs for the kitchens. I go to the woods. Will it pleasure you to come with me?'

'Yes, why not?' Elaine was already wearing her cloak, for she had intended to walk in the grounds of the castle, but on such a pleasant autumn day it would be enjoyable to go further. 'Shall we take Bertrand with us?'

'Bertrand waits for me in the courtyard,' Marion said. 'He said that I should not go alone to the woods for he heard of a band of marauding bandits in the area. We have always been safe on your father's land, but...' She glanced over her shoulder. 'Lord Howarth does not send out patrols as often as did your father, lady.'

'My uncle believes that his name is sufficient to deter those who would come against him. His neighbours are on good terms with him and I think we must be safe enough—but I am happy to have Bertrand with us.'

Bertrand had been courting her lady-in-waiting for some months now. He was a soft-spoken man, tall, strong and pleasant in manner, but somewhat diffident in the presence of ladies. Although he had shown some preference for Marion, he had not asked for her. It would be a good chance for the pair to spend a little time together. Elaine would wander a little ahead of them, giving them the opportunity to speak what was in their hearts if they so chose. If they should ask for her permission to wed, she would give it, but she hoped that Marion would not leave her service, for she loved her as a sister.

She wished with all her heart that Zander had returned to England so that he might accompany them to the woods and a little smile touched her lips as she remembered all the times she'd walked in her father's woods with the young knight before he'd left for the Holy Land.

'*You know that I love you, Elaine? You know*

that I would not leave you if there were another way?'

'Yes, I know.' Elaine had smiled up into his grey eyes. He was so handsome with his proud noble features, his mouth soft and seductive, his brows fine and dark. Hair the colour of ebony had fallen across his brow and she'd reached up to brush it away. *'Please promise to come back safely, Zander. I do not care if you bring riches. When I am eighteen my mother's dower lands become mine. They are all we need to live in peace and happiness together.'*

Zander had reached for her, pulling her close to him. His mouth was sweet on hers as he kissed her lingeringly and with such tenderness that it brought tears to her eyes.

'Know that I shall never love another woman, Elaine. If I do not return for you, it will be because I lie dead in the Holy Land.'

'No! You must not die, for I could not bear it. Must you go? I wish you would not. Seek honours at court and in time my father will relent.'

'I must take the Cross and follow the king. Richard seeks to convert the heathen or drive them from God's Holy City. Only when Jerusalem is ours may we consider our duty done. And then I shall avenge my father...'

'Supposing you never manage to capture Jerusalem?'

'If I feel the cause hopeless I shall return— but we are right. God is with us and we must prevail for we undertake His work.'

'But you leave me behind and break my heart? How can you talk of love and hurt me so?'

Elaine felt the tears on her cheeks. Zander had kissed her deeply with such tenderness that she had not doubted his love. His cause was just and she could not in all conscience have prevented him from leaving.

She dashed her tears away. Her memories were precious and she treasured them. Zander had gone because he believed the king's cause just and because it was the only way he could earn honours and return a rich knight. All her entreaties had not deterred him and so she'd watched him ride away. The years had been long since then and she had grieved for the love that might have been. While her father lived she had waited patiently, but now her soul cried out to the man she loved.

'Where are you, Zander?' she whispered as she followed a few steps behind her serving woman to the courtyard, where the burly groom waited. 'Please return to me. I beg you, do not desert me.'

Raising her head, Elaine forced a smile to her lips as she passed through the courtyard. No one must realise that she was close to tears. Only a weak woman cried. Elaine was strong. She had won a promise from her uncle and she had more than two months of freedom before she must think about becoming the Earl of Newark's bride.

'When do we attack the castle?' Stronmar looked at his lord, the Earl of Newark, as he walked into the hall where the scene was one of preparation for war. 'All is ready, you have only to give the word, my lord.'

'Howarth is a fool,' the earl growled. 'He told me that his niece would be mine at Christ's Mass if I waited in patience, but a man should not be ruled by a woman's whims. He should force her to obey him. There is no reason to wait.'

'You do not need to wait. Howarth neglects to send out patrols and believes the rumours of a band of marauding bandits on his land are merely that. He has no idea that we have been the ones attacking travellers and burning the isolated cottages. We leave none to tell the tale.'

'You have done well,' the earl said and smiled thinly. 'Had the lady agreed to the marriage I might have spared her uncle, but I shall not be thwarted. I want her and her lands—but she is Howarth's heir. When her uncle dies she will be twice the heiress she is now, for besides the castle he has other manors in the north.'

Stronmar grinned, revealing a row of rotten teeth. He was an unfortunate-looking man, his features heavy and ugly, the stench of his breath worse than a latrine. His one redeeming feature was his loyalty to the earl and he would die for the lord who had rescued him when as a young lad he had lain close to starvation after his parents had both died from a terrible fever. The harvests had rotted in the fields that year, for a pestilence had killed most of the villagers. He, too, would have died had the lord not ordered him taken up and carried to his castle, where Stronmar had grown strong and tall as the years passed.

'The lady will be yours, my lord. Give the word and we shall ride for the castle this very day. The fools will not suspect an attack and we may take them with scarcely a fight.'

'Then we ride at once,' the earl said. 'I see no reason to wait when I may have the lady now. Once I have bedded her she will beg me to marry her. A woman must be shown who is the master or a man is nothing in his own home.'

'The Lady Elaine is too proud for her own good.'

The earl nodded, his thick lips curving in a sneer. 'Pride such as hers must be curbed, and methinks I shall find it amusing to teach the wench a lesson she will not forget. Besides, I need an heir, for my wives gave me only daughters.'

'We have gathered herbs and berries enough,' Elaine said. Their baskets were filled and the day was drawing to its close. Enjoying the unseasonably warm sunshine and the freedom of being away from the castle, they had strayed a long way from her home in search of berries, herbs and nuts to fill the deep panniers that Bertrand had attached to the pack horse. He was riding his own stout horse while the ladies had ridden Elaine's palfrey. 'I think we should go home now.'

'Yes, my lady.' Marion smiled at her. 'Your uncle may grow worried and send out men to search for you if we do not return before nightfall.'

'I would not have him think we had run away.' Elaine thanked the groom as he put first her, and then her lady, up on the palfrey. Marion rode pillion behind her, as was the custom for a serving woman, though for some of the day she'd ridden with Bertrand so that the palfrey should not tire of carrying them both.

The little party turned in the direction that would lead them home. They had laughed, talked and danced in the clearing as they gathered their rich harvest and now they were tired, ready for the food and drink that awaited them at the castle. Marion had brought some bread, cheese and a flagon of ale, which they'd shared, as well as feasting on the ripe blackberries that grew in abundance in the woods. Yet even so their thoughts had turned to the supper that would await them and Bertrand apologised for his rumbling stomach.

'Do not apologise,' Elaine said and laughed. 'I think we shall all eat well this night, for there is roasting pig as well as pigeon and capon.'

Her mouth watered at the thought and she realised that she, too, was hungry. It was at that moment that she caught the smell of burning and her nose wrinkled at the stench.

'Someone has set a fire,' she said, 'but I think…'

The words died unspoken, for as they crested the rise they saw the pall of dark smoke hanging over the castle and smelled the awful stench.

'There has been a fire,' Marion cried. 'The keep stands, but the smoke is thick. What can have happened?'

'The castle has been attacked,' Bertrand said and brought his horse and the pack pony to a standstill. 'We must go no further, my lady. You should take shelter over there in the empty barn we passed this morning. I shall leave the horses with you and go on to see what has happened.'

'You should not go alone,' Marion said and then blushed at her forwardness. 'What will happen to us if you should be killed?'

'Do not fear for me, dear heart,' Bertrand said and smiled at her. 'I know how to remain hidden and survey the lie of the land. If my lady's uncle was attacked in his castle, it must have been a strong force. This was not the work of a band of marauding bandits.'

'No, I think you are right,' Elaine said and shivered. 'We shall do as you ask, Bertrand, but please take care. Marion is right. Without you we should be vulnerable and an easy prey for whoever has done this thing.'

'You may trust me—I shall not let you down,' Bertrand said. 'Stay hidden until you hear my call.' He made the sound of an owl hooting. 'As soon as I know how things stand

I shall return, my lady. Whatever happens now, I shall protect you both with my life.'

'I know and I thank God that you were with us,' Elaine said and shivered. 'I do not know who has done this wicked thing—but I fear for my aunt and uncle and all our people.'

'Stay hidden,' Bertrand bade them and gave the reins of the horses to Elaine and Marion. 'I shall discover all I can and return to you as quickly as I may.'

He set off at a run, heading towards the castle as the dark gathered about them and the only light was from the red glow that hung over what Elaine guessed to be some outbuildings. She thought that the great hall and the keep still stood, so whoever had attacked the castle had not intended to destroy it, but merely to capture it.

She could only hope that they had been as considerate of the people. The thought of her aunt and uncle lying dead in the castle caught at her heart and brought tears to her eyes. No matter that she'd resisted her uncle's demands for her marriage, she cared for him and her aunt in her way and prayed that they still lived.

'Come, my lady,' Marion said. 'We must do as Bertrand told us and take shelter. Whoever attacked the castle may pass this way and we should be easy prey.'

'Yes.' A little shudder went through her. Had she not gone foraging with Marion she might even now be dead or a prisoner of whoever had attacked her uncle's castle.

Chapter Two

'Tell me where your niece is, woman, or you will join your husband in an early grave.' The Earl of Newark glared at the woman his men had dragged from her chamber and brought to him in the great hall. The remains of his supper lay strewn on the table, for he had ordered the food served even while the stain of his victim's blood remained on his hands. 'Tell me where she went and I shall spare you.'

'If I knew I would tell you,' the poor lady cried, wringing her hands in distress as she looked about and saw bodies still lying where they had fallen. Some of her husband's people had tried to defend him and for that they had lost their lives. 'Forgive me, sir. I lay sleeping when she left the castle and have no knowledge of her whereabouts.'

The earl drew back his mailed fist and struck her a blow that sent her to her knees. She stayed where he had put her, head bowed, weeping with fear and grief.

'Stop that snivelling, woman,' he growled. 'If you are hiding her, it will be the worse for you.'

'I beg you, lord, do not strike my lady again.' One of the pages ran forward. 'I saw the Lady Elaine go riding with her serving woman and the groom Bertrand earlier. They have not yet returned to the castle.'

The earl's eyes narrowed as he looked at the young page. The boy was slight, but stood proudly before him. He would have felled him, but something in the youth's manner stayed his hand.

'You speak the truth?'

'I swear it on my life, lord.'

Newark nodded. 'Very well, I believe you. If she took nothing with her, she must return. We shall send out men to find her and bring her back.' He frowned as the page reached the side of his weeping mistress. 'Yes, take her away out of my sight.'

As the countess staggered to her feet, he held up his hand. 'Leave the castle in the morning.

You may take your clothes and chattels with you—but the silver and gold remains. If you try to cheat me, I shall kill you.'

The countess bowed her head, making no protest as other servants came forwards to lead her away. She could return to her brother and sister-in-law, who would give her a home. She would not linger until the morning, for she could not wait to leave this place—and she would not stay even to see her husband buried. She would grieve for him, but in her heart she knew that her grief would not last long for he had not been a loving husband. She must thank God that the earl had seen fit to spare her. Whether her brother would take revenge for what had happened remained to be seen.

Allowing her servants to lead her away, the countess wondered what had become of her niece. If she could warn her to stay away from the castle, she would do so, but, since she had no idea where the girl had gone she could do nothing. For all she knew Elaine had taken flight to her dower lands. Yet it seemed she had taken nothing with her so it was more likely that she had merely gone riding, as the page claimed. It was a mercy that she had not been in the castle when the earl attacked them, but no doubt he would have her one way or the other.

Weeping, the countess ordered the packing of her things, secretly hiding a few of her jewels about her person. The earl had too much on his mind to order her searched and she did not intend to leave with nothing. She would take what she dared and leave swiftly, before he changed his mind.

She thought of Elaine's jewels, but decided it was not worth the risk of trying to steal them away. The earl had ordered a watch kept on the girl's chambers and any attempt to spirit away her things would meet with a sharp punishment.

Elaine must just make the most of her freedom if she could and perhaps reach her dower lands, though now that her uncle was dead there was no one to protect her even there. The countess could do nothing to help her, for she must throw herself on her brother's charity and hope that he would take her in.

'Listen...' Elaine touched Marion's hand as she heard the owl hooting. 'I am sure that is Bertrand. He has returned at last.'

'I knew he would not let us down.' Marion rose joyfully as the barn door opened and a shadowy figure entered. 'Bertrand, is that you?'

'Yes, dear heart,' Bertrand said and moved to catch her in his arms, holding her close for a moment before turning to Elaine. 'Ill news, my lady. The Earl of Newark took the castle by a trick for he came under the guise of friendship. Your uncle was foully slain and your aunt mistreated before being told to leave the castle.'

'My uncle dead?' Elaine gasped. Her hand flew to her mouth—despite her recent argument with him, she honoured both him and her aunt. He was her father's brother and, though stern, she knew that he cared what became of her. 'And my aunt?'

'Told to leave with her goods and chattels, but not the silver or jewels.'

'Newark intends to have it all. Why could my uncle not see him for the villain he is?' Elaine asked, a little sob in her voice. 'Had I wed him he would not have rested until my uncle was in his grave. We dare not return to the castle. Somehow we must try to reach my dower lands—but I have no money with me. We have nothing but the clothes we wear and the food we gathered.'

'We have a little more,' Bertrand said. 'Your chamber was guarded, my lady. I fear I was able to take nothing of yours, but it was easy to enter Marion's chamber. I have brought some clothing, which you may share, also some silver and pewter that I managed to snatch. I have a little coin of my own and a few of my own things.'

'Yes, Marion's clothing will fit me and it may be best if I change before we begin our journey. If I pass as your sister and Marion your wife, we may escape detection and be safer.'

'Yes, my lady, that is true,' Bertrand agreed. 'I am sorry I could not bring your jewels.'

'I wear the silver cross and chain my father gave me beneath my gown always,' Elaine said and smiled. 'Nothing else matters but our lives. If we can reach my dower lands, we can recruit more men to defend us—though I fear the earl will try to stop us before we reach safety.'

'Once he realises that you do not intend to return to the castle he is sure to scour the countryside for us,' Bertrand said. 'Yet if his men ignore a yeoman and his wife and sister they may pass by without noticing us.'

'I shall be careful to cover my head and face if we are questioned.' Elaine looked at him gravely. 'You know that you both risk much by accompanying me. If the earl captures us, you may suffer for helping me to escape.'

'I would never desert you,' Marion declared instantly. 'We love you, my lady.'

'Yes, I know it and I thank you. I pray that

we shall reach my dower lands safely. Once there we can at least try to defend ourselves.'

'At least you were not in the castle when he took it,' Bertrand said. 'We have the advantage for he will not know where to look. I know you must both be tired, but we ought to leave soon. If we ride through the night, we may get ahead of them.'

'Will the earl not send men to your dower lands?' Marion asked.

'We must try to get there first,' Bertrand said grimly. 'Yet we should not go directly south, as he would expect. We shall ride to the east and then double back and that way hope to avoid his patrols. If we are fortunate, he will not send men out until the morning and by then we shall be well ahead of them.'

'But our horses have carried us all day…'

'I have brought fresh ones,' Bertrand said. 'We should turn your palfrey loose, my lady. If it returns to the castle seeking its stable, the earl's men may waste time searching for you.'

'They might think I was thrown.' Elaine smiled. 'You have done well, Bertrand. I think we should ride now and continue through the night. We may rest for a little time when we have put some leagues between the castle and us.'

* * *

'You are weary, my friend,' the dark-skinned servant watched as his master dismounted. 'Allow me to see to the horses this night. You were sick for so long and you have not yet recovered your strength.'

'I should have died had it not been for you,' the knight replied and smiled. In the moonlight his face might have looked handsome to a casual observer, for the deep red welt that marred half of it was hardly noticeable because of his hood of mail. The scar ran from the corner of his left eye to his chin and was still painful to the touch even after many months of healing herbs and lotions applied by the faithful Janvier. 'Had you and your family not taken me in that day…'

Janvier smiled, his teeth gleaming white against the dusk of his skin. 'You forget that you saved mine and my whole family when the Christian knights rampaged after Saladin's men wreaked vengeance on them for the murder of the Moslem prisoners.'

'Do not remind me of our shame,' the knight replied wearily. 'I grow better every day, Janvier, but I will admit that I am tired this night.

If we rest for a few hours in the morning, I shall feel much better.'

'You should go home to your family, my lord.'

'I have duties to perform before I may rest,' Zander replied. 'Tom's body lies in a place of peace, but his family knows naught of what happened to him. First I must speak with his family, tell them he died bravely and was buried with honour—and then I must seek out the lady of whom I told you.'

'You will ask her to wed you?'

'No, not yet, for I must also seek revenge for my father, but if she has not married I shall pledge myself to her, as her protector and her servant—if she wishes it.'

Zander touched the red welt on his cheek. The pain was less now than it had been when it was first inflicted. He'd lain for weeks in a fever and afterwards he'd been too ill to remember who or where he was. It was Janvier who had carried him back to his home and helped to care for him as he raved and cried out in his agony, Janvier who had insisted on accompanying him to England, when he recovered enough to travel.

'Do you think any woman would wish to marry me now?' he asked, a touch of bitterness in his voice. 'Even if she remains unwed, I cannot ask such a sacrifice of her.'

'If she loves you, it will be no sacrifice. You should at least ask her, my lord. If she has waited all these years, it is your duty to offer her the chance to be your wife.'

'Perhaps...' A sigh was on his lips. 'I dare say she forgot me long ago. She was beautiful, Janvier. Why should she wait for me?' He pushed the grief from his mind. 'We must rest now, my friend, for we have a long way to travel yet.'

'You push yourself too hard.'

'No, I am better now, merely unused to riding for long periods. If I do not make an effort, I shall never recover my strength. A man who cannot defend himself has no place in this world of ours, Janvier. I went to the wars because I thought our cause was just—and I hoped to win honours and wealth. I won both—but what profit a man if he gain the whole world, but lose his faith and his belief in his fellow man?'

'You are the most honourable knight I know,' Janvier said and grinned.

'And you the best friend a man ever had. I do not know what lies ahead—but I shall make a life for us both here somewhere in this land or another if I prove unwelcome here.'

'Inshallah,' Janvier genuflected. 'What Allah wills shall be. Whether it be your Christian god or mine, we are in His hands.'

'Yes, it is so, though sometimes I wonder if God is but a comforting myth we humans invented for our own purposes.'

'You are weary, my lord. Rest and eat. As your strength returns so will your faith.'

'If I knew how to pray, I would pray you were right.'

Zander inclined his head and sat down on the blanket his servant had placed for him beneath a sheltering oak. The weather was mild enough, but after the heat of foreign lands he was shivering. He hugged his cloak about him and hoped that it was not a return of the fever that had plagued him for so many months.

He must avenge his father's death. The knight who had had him killed for daring to remonstrate at the way he had caught and beaten a runaway servant, raping the man's wife and daughter, was a beast who deserved only death. Zander would seek revenge for his father—and for the others the Earl of Newark had brutalised and murdered.

Yet all he truly longed for with his body and his heart was to seek out Elaine and offer her his service. Once he'd hoped for so much more, but now his hopes were ruined—what woman could love a man such as he?

Chapter Three

Hidden by the thickness of the trees and the undergrowth in which they had taken refuge at the sound of horns and approaching horses, Elaine held Marion's hand. Bertrand had taken the horses on a little, fearing that they might snicker and betray the presence of the two women.

The sound of horses, jingling harness and voices grew louder. The Earl of Newark's men had gathered in the clearing and were looking for signs.

'Three horses went this way, my lord,' one of them cried. 'See where the undergrowth is flattened. 'They must have gone this way.'

'We cannot be far behind now,' Stronmar said. 'If we ride hard, we shall find them within the hour. We must find her, for the earl is anxious she should become his bride.'

Marion's hand was trembling. Elaine held it fast, putting a finger to her lips as they heard the sound of the horses riding away.

'That man,' Elaine whispered. 'I know him. It is rumoured that he is Newark's son, born of a peasant woman—and he is even more evil than his father.'

'If they catch Bertrand, they will kill him...' Marion looked at her fearfully.

'You must not doubt him. He has kept us safe for two days now.' Elaine's heart was racing but she raised her head proudly. 'Come, we must do as Bertrand told us and make our way across the river. We shall meet back at the mill he spoke of earlier and then it is but another day or so to my dower lands.'

'Supposing the earl has sent men to your home?'

'We must meet that possibility when we come to it,' Elaine said. 'It seems that they wasted some time in looking for me when my palfrey returned. Bertrand has taken them on a detour and he will return with just two horses, sending the other careering off by itself. Hopefully, the earl's men will follow it for long enough to get us safe to Sweetbriars.'

'Even if we reach your home the earl may attack.'

'Yes, I know.' Elaine's face was pale but determined. 'I can only pray—' She broke off as they heard the sound of voices. She tensed, listening hard. Newark's men or someone else?

'I think there are only a few.' Marion parted the bushes carefully and looked. 'Two men ride this way, my lady—a knight, I think, and a servant. The servant's skin is dark.'

'Let me see…' Elaine peered through the bushes and then drew back. 'The knight's head and much of his face is covered by his chainmail, but the servant wears strange clothes— the clothes of a Saracen, I think.'

'Then we must try to avoid them,' Marion said. 'They may be some of the Earl's men.'

Elaine was about to agree, when she saw the servant look at his master anxiously and the knight suddenly slipped unconscious from the saddle.

'The knight is ill,' Elaine cried and, before her companion could stop her, she had left the safety of the trees and was running towards them. The servant had dismounted and was securing the horses to a branch, but Elaine was on her knees and bending over the knight in concern. 'Sir Knight, I think you are ill,' she said and touched his gloved hand. His eyes were closed, but he moaned faintly and opened them and she felt an odd tingle down her spine. His eyes seemed familiar, but his skin was almost as dark as his servant's and she could not have seen him before.

'My master has been very ill,' the servant said and bent over him, lifting him in his arms as he came to his senses. 'I am able to care for him. Do not disturb yourself, lady.'

'I would help you if I can,' Elaine said. 'I have some skill with herbs and could make you a tisane to restore his strength.'

'Give me the herbs and leave us,' the servant said. 'My master would not wish to trouble you.'

'Nay, Janvier,' the knight said weakly. 'Do not treat a lady so scurvily.' His eyes narrowed as he rose to his feet with Janvier's help. 'What do you here, mistress? Are you alone?'

'My brother and his wife are nearby,' Elaine replied, relieved as she saw Bertrand leading the horses towards them. He had made his detour and was on his way to meet them at the appointed place.

The knight nodded, looking at her oddly. 'These are dangerous times to travel, mistress.

What is your name and where your destination?'

Elaine hesitated. Should she tell him her story? He was ill and something in his eyes made her feel that she could trust him—but in her precarious situation she must be cautious.'

'We travel to the lands of our lady,' she replied. 'My lady is in some danger and we are vowed to help her if we can.'

'Will you tell me her name?' the knight asked and now he was standing alone without the help of his servant. 'It might be that we could travel together. It is safer to travel in numbers.'

'My lady's name...' Elaine faltered. She wanted to tell him the truth, but Marion was shaking her head. It was perhaps too soon to trust the knight, for he might lead them straight to the earl's men.

'Her name is the Lady Philippa of Earlsmere,' she said, the lie coming awkwardly to her tongue. 'We travel south-west, sir...to the lands of the Marches, between Wales and England.'

'Then bear us company for a little time until we must go our separate ways,' the knight said. 'I think perhaps you are in some trouble, mistress. Although my strength is not yet what it should be, my servant and I would protect you if we could.'

Elaine wavered. Ought she to take this knight at his word? Even as she hesitated, Marion gave her another warning look.

'You are kind, sir, but we travel alone,' she said. 'I shall give your squire the herbs, which must be steeped in hot water for six hours, and half a cup of the mixture drunk twice a day. Their healing properties will help you to regain your strength, sir.'

'I thank you,' the knight said. He laid a hand on Janvier's arm and the servant held back whatever he had meant to say.

Elaine gave the servant the herbs, then allowed Bertrand to help her mount one horse while Marion rode pillion behind him.

'You took a risk,' Marion said as they rode away. 'It might have been a trap.'

'The knight has been very ill,' Elaine said. 'I believe we should have been safe with him, but it was best to be cautious.'

She was conscious of an odd feeling of loss as they rode away. His eyes had said something to her, but she was not sure why they had made her heart race. Her instincts had told her she could trust him, but perhaps Marion was right. He was a stranger and as such could not be trusted once he knew her true identity.

'The earl's men have been misled,' Bertrand said. 'Yet it will not be long before they discover their mistake and come after us once more. We must put as much distance between us as possible.'

Zander sat silent, lost in his thoughts and unsure of his own feelings.

'Something lays heavy on your mind,' Janvier said. 'You have seemed strange since the stranger came to your aid.'

'It was she,' Zander said. 'She would not tell me her true name and yet, though she is older and a little changed, I know it was Elaine Howarth.'

'The lady to whom you gave your promise?'

'Yes. She did not know me, Janvier—or she did not wish to acknowledge it. Either way...' He shook his head. 'Yet she was dressed as a yeoman's sister. Why was she in disguise—and where was she going?'

'Perhaps she merely bears a likeness to your lady?'

'I was not certain enough to reveal myself,' Zander said. 'I would prefer to be stronger before I offer her my service—and I must still avenge my father.'

'You must regain your strength before you can think of revenge.'

'Yes.' Zander nodded. 'I feel better now. I think it was merely tiredness that made me fall from my horse—but I should like you to make up the brew she told us of, Janvier. I will try her cure and see if it improves my health.'

'Do you trust her?' Janvier said. 'If she concealed her identity, she lied to you.'

'Yes, and I believe she is in some trouble. We shall follow where they lead, my friend, a little behind and see what transpires.'

'I thought you wished to avenge your father?'

'I do—but if the lady is going where I think she must be, I shall not be so very far from Newark's lands. He has many manors and one of them lies only a few leagues distant from Sweetbriars.'

'If you would risk your life for her, she must be special to you, my lord?'

'I would give my life for hers willingly. I am determined to follow the route they took. We are but half an hour behind them; their horses are of the common sort and will not bear them as swiftly as our destriers. We should catch them before nightfall, but we shall watch them from a distance. I would know more of where they go and why before I reveal myself to her.'

'We shall rest here for a while by the stream,' Bertrand said and dismounted. He helped Marion down and then went to assist Elaine. 'We are sheltered in this hollow and the horses can go no further until they rest for a while.'

Elaine looked about her. They had not seen the stream until they crested the rise. Perhaps the earl's men would ride by if they came this way.

'We have no choice,' she said. 'The horses are weary and so are we. We must eat and drink and so must our horses, for we should be lost without them.'

'I will take them to the shallow edge to let them drink,' Bertrand said. 'Rest there beneath the tree, lady. Marion will bring you food—and there is water to drink from the well we passed.'

'Marion must rest before she prepares our food,' Elaine replied. 'Later, we will prepare the meal together.'

'That would not be fitting, my lady,' Marion said.

'It would appear odd if I did nothing while you two worked,' Elaine said with a smile. 'I am supposed to be your equal, Marion, not your lady. Come, sit and rest beside me, and then we shall prepare the food together.'

'Do as your lady bids you,' Bertrand said and led the horses to the edge of the stream, where they began to drink thirstily.

Elaine was deep in thought when Marion sat on the blanket beside her and rested her back against the tree. She had not been able to put from her mind the thought of the knight who had been so exhausted that he fell from his horse. She wondered if he had been to the Holy Land and whether he had been injured there. His servant was most likely a Moor or a Saracen, though how could it be that he had chosen to serve a Christian knight? Elaine was certain the knight must be one of those who had taken the Cross and followed King Richard on his crusade. Why else would his skin be so dark that he looked like a Saracen?

What was it about his eyes that seemed so familiar? She puzzled over it in her mind but, though the answer seemed close, it lay behind a curtain of mist. She could never have met him, for surely she would remember?

Zander looked down from the rise on the man and two women as they began to load their belongings on to the packhorse. Then the man came to help the woman who claimed to be his sister up to her horse before seeing to his wife. There was something reverential about the way he assisted his sister—but of course that was merely a disguise.

The lady was a lady, not a person of the yeoman class. He'd known when he heard her voice and as time passed grew more certain that she was Elaine Howarth—the woman he had pledged to return and marry. Her face had been a little brown for she'd always had a true English-rose complexion—but mayhap she had stained it with walnut juice. Some of the knights had used that ruse when trying to infiltrate the Saracen's camp.

His thoughts led him to the same conclusion; she and her companions were hiding from someone—someone who meant them harm. Zander watched the two horses and their riders move away and then let his horse wander down to the water's edge. They had ridden hard and could afford to let their quarry go on a little. It had been easy enough to discover their route, for they had stopped in a nearby village to take water from the well and buy bread and cheese.

Why would Elaine choose to ride with so few escorts? She must know that she was at the mercy of unscrupulous men. Even with her face

stained she was lovely—and there were many
that would want her dower lands. Why would
her father allow it?

Perhaps her father had died and she was at
the mercy of some unscrupulous guardian.

Of course! The solution came to him in a
flash. She was hiding from someone who
wished to force her into marriage and take her
fortune for himself.

Zander frowned. She needed his protection,
but she had refused to trust a stranger, fearing
that she would be led into a trap. He must either reveal himself to her—which he was reluctant to do yet—or he must follow behind and
watch over her.

He was not yet strong enough to fight for
her himself, though Janvier would do his best
if asked to lend his protection. Zander knew
that when he sought revenge on his enemy he
would need strong men to fight for him. He
must recruit them—and they would soon be
at the estate of his uncle, his mother's brother,
Sir Roderick Harvey. There they would find
friends, but if he stayed with them he might
lose sight of Elaine.

'You must follow the lady and her companions,' he told Janvier as he brought food and
wine from their packhorse. 'This night I shall

stay with my uncle and follow in the morning with all the men I can muster.'

'Leave you to travel alone?' Janvier looked at him uneasily. 'If you should faint again...'

'I shall not, for I feel a little better. Give me some of Elaine's herbs and I will brew them this night.'

Janvier frowned. 'You place much trust in a lady who would not trust you with her name or destination.'

'I know where she goes. We have been heading steadily south-west all day. She means to try to reach her dower lands. I fear that rogues are pursuing her.'

'It is your wish that I follow and do what I can to protect them?'

'For the love you bear me, protect her whom I love if you can,' Zander said. 'In the morning we shall follow and in good time I dare say we shall come up with you.'

'I am only one man, perhaps against many. Yet I will seek to do as you ask, my lord.'

Zander frowned—he did not wish to lose his friend. 'I think if this man desires her in marriage he will not seek to harm, only to capture—it may be best if you simply follow and observe. Should she fall prey to some rogue's perfidy, follow her to see where he takes her and then come for me. I shall not be long behind you.'

Janvier nodded. He lifted his flask and drank deeply. 'If I believed it possible, I would help her, my lord—but I shall do as you order me.'

Zander nodded. The two men clasped hands and set off in their different ways. Zander's head was aching again, but he ignored it, determined to reach his uncle's house before nightfall. His mother's brother would do all he could to supply him with men he could trust—good fighting men who would stand by him.

He had thought to wait until he reached his father's lands, but now he had no choice. If Elaine was in danger, he must protect her somehow.

Elaine glanced over her shoulder. She had an odd feeling that they had been followed from first light, when they left the barn that had sheltered them from the night. A willing farmer had supplied food and a place to rest after Bertrand gave him most of their money. She touched the silver cross that hung beneath her tunic. It was precious to her, but they would soon need more funds; she must sacrifice the necklace, if need be. Her friends had already done much for her and she could not ask them to go hungry when she had the means to ease their predicament.

Looking round again, she thought she saw a man riding a horse, but he was hidden in the trees that bordered the track on which they rode. Her spine tingled and yet she did not feel that the presence of her shadow was menacing.

When a little later they left the woods behind, she caught sight of the man again, and this time she knew him. He was the knight's servant.

Was the knight with him—and why was he following her?

Elaine was considering whether she should stop and let him come up with her, then demand an explanation or tell Bertrand and try to throw him off. Before she could decide, she heard a shout from ahead and suddenly saw a party of six horsemen bearing down on them. They wore the yellow-and-black colours of the Earl of Newark and Bertrand signalled to her to ride away into the trees.

'You must hide, lady,' he said. 'We shall go another way and hope to draw them off. From this distance they cannot see us clearly. Go back into the woods and hide. If we escape them, we shall return to look for you—if we do not…you must go on alone somehow.'

'You risk your lives for me.'

'Waste no time in regrets—go now, my lady, before they come up with us and see you.'

Reluctantly, Elaine turned back into the woods. Her throat hurt and she was close to tears. Her darling Marion and Bertrand had already done too much for her. For a moment she was tempted to turn back and let the earl's men take her rather than risk the lives of her servants. Yet she knew that Bertrand would never stand by and see her captured. She must hope that they managed to outrun the earl's soldiers.

Leading her horse further into the woods, she dismounted and sat down on a fallen tree. Bending her head, she covered her face, feeling close to tears. If they did not return, how would she ever manage to reach her home?

'Your friend is a brave man, lady.'

Elaine's head came up as she heard the man's voice and knew it for that of the knight's servant.

'You have been following us,' she said. 'You are alone—where is your master? Is he ill?'

'My lord went to the house of his uncle to recruit men to ride with us,' Janvier said. 'He sent me to watch over you, for he feared that you were in danger.'

'Yes, I am,' Elaine said. She saw with blinding clarity that she no longer had an option: she must trust the knight and his squire. 'I am pursued by the Earl of Newark, because he wishes to capture me and force me to be his wife. I am…heiress to some lands he covets because they run close to his own. My father would never listen to his offers to buy the land and now he seeks to take them for himself.'

'Come, lady, mount your horse and let me take you to my lord. He cannot be far behind us now. Once you have his escort you will be safe—we should give our lives to protect you.'

Elaine hesitated. Her instinct had been to trust the knight, but Marion had warned her to hide her identity from him. Now that she had confessed part of her story, she would tell the knight the whole when they reached him.

Hearing some voices back the way she had come, Elaine lost no time in mounting her horse and following Janvier back through the trees. For a while it seemed as though the voices were following them, but then Janvier pulled her along a narrow track that led close to a dangerous ravine. Her nerves jangling, she allowed

him to lead her horse, closing her eyes and re-
fusing to look down.

'We are safe now, lady. I saw this track earlier, but most would not notice it. I think we can
rest now for a little.'

'Thank you.' Elaine allowed him to help her
down. She sank onto the blanket he placed for
her and leaned back against a tree. Tears were
very close, but she refused to shed them, though
she could not help thinking of Marion and Bertrand.

'Your friends may have managed to give
them the slip. It is clear that the earl split his
forces to follow you—perhaps this will save
them.'

'Yes, perhaps,' Elaine said and took the bread
and cheese he offered, breaking small pieces to
eat. 'You, too, could have died if they caught
us.'

'There were no more than three. I am a match
for them,' Janvier said. 'I thought it best to lead
you to safety if I could, but had it been necessary I should have given my life to save you.'

'Why?' Elaine looked at him in wonder. 'You
do not know me—why would you risk so much
for me?'

Janvier shook his head. 'It is my lord who
would keep you safe. He is the most honour-

able knight in Christendom—and he would not see any woman fall prey to the man who pursues you.'

'You have heard of the Earl of Newark?'

'Yes—but I shall say no more. You must learn what else you need to from my lord.'

Elaine nodded. 'I am ready to go on, sir. I would meet with your lord before nightfall if 'tis possible.'

'Come then, lady,' Janvier said. 'For I think he is close behind us.'

Chapter Four

'I am glad to be of service to you,' Sir Roderick said as he clasped Zander's hands. 'I honour you for all you have suffered in the Lord's cause, and my men will serve you faithfully for as long as you need them.'

'When I secure my father's keep I shall employ more and send them back to you.'

A shadow passed across his uncle's face. 'I fear there is little there to reclaim, Zander. The lands were small, as you know, for your father fell into debt and forfeited some acres. His keep is nought but a mouldering ruin.'

'Then I shall restore it and build a fine manor house,' Zander said. 'I have won both honours and a fortune, Uncle. I shall restore the name of my father and bring his lands back into good heart so that there is food and a place to live for those that are still loyal.'

'Then go with my blessing and may the peace of God be upon you, Nephew.'

'My soul can never be at peace until I avenge my father,' Zander replied, but he smiled and clasped his uncle's hand. 'I thank you for your help and now I must go, for I fear my lady is in great danger.'

He mounted his horse, signalled to the men his uncle had assigned to him, and set off at a canter from the moated manor house. It was a secure stronghold and his uncle was a powerful man who employed more than one hundred men-at-arms. The horses' hooves clattered across the wooden bridge, eleven men in all—and every one a good fighting soldier.

Zander hoped that soon he would recover his strength. He had taken two measures of the cure brewed from the herbs Elaine had given him and was feeling a little less exhausted. The dizziness that had plagued him for weeks seemed to have gone. He smiled as he bent forwards over his horse. He would not faint and fall again and they must hurry—if they delayed, it might be too late.

Elaine's heart caught with apprehension as they saw a band of men galloping down the road towards them. It looked a larger party this time and she feared that the Earl of Newark had sent more men to look for them. Here there were no woods to hide them and to flee back the way they had come would be useless.

'If they wish to take me, you must allow it,' she said to Janvier. 'I do not wish you to sacrifice your life for me. The Earl's men will not harm me; he needs me alive so that he can claim my lands without fear of reprimand or retribution.'

Janvier smiled as the horsemen came closer. 'Fear not, lady. 'Tis but my lord and the men who serve him.'

'Oh…' For some reason Elaine's heart beat even faster and her stomach twisted with nerves. There was something about the knight she could not place and yet instinctively she had trusted him. 'I must thank God for his arrival.'

The party of some ten men or more came to a halt. The knight lifted his hand in greeting. 'Well met, lady,' he said. 'Where are your companions?'

Was she wise to trust this unknown knight? She might be going from the heat of the cooking pot to the fire.

The knight dismounted and came to help her down. His men were also dismounting, to rest and eat, for they had ridden hard. He came to Elaine and held out his arms to assist her to dismount. She slid down into them and for a moment he held her. It was strange how comfortable and right it seemed, but she did not know this man and after a moment to catch her breath she moved away from him.

'We must talk, lady,' he said and took off his cloak, spreading it beneath the branches of a sturdy oak for her to sit. She declined and remained standing. 'You should know that I mean you no harm and will help you in whatever way I can—but you must tell me where you go and who pursues you.'

'I told your servant when he found me this morning,' Elaine said. 'A man who wishes to force me into marriage is pursuing me. He invaded my uncle's castle and killed him, before sending my aunt penniless from her home. Marion and Bertrand drew the earl's men off earlier this morning. Bertrand told me to hide in the woods—but then your servant came. The earl's men must have split, because some came after us, but Janvier led me to safety. I am grateful for your service, sir, and would reward you.' She took a deep breath, then, 'I am Lady Elaine Howarth and my only hope is to reach my dower lands.'

'Yes, it is much as I thought,' the knight said. 'Let us not speak of reward, lady. I am a true knight and it is my duty to protect any in need—particularly a lady of gentle birth.'

'Then I can only thank you—and offer my help if ever I can assist you.'

'Will you tell me the name of the rogue that plans such evil?'

'He is the Earl of Newark and ruthless,' she said, her eyes suddenly blazing with anger. 'I will never marry him. I would rather die.'

'Then he would merely take your lands for himself,' the knight said and something made her look into his eyes. They were grey and as cold as ice, and his mouth had become thin and hard.

'What do you know of him?' she asked, her pulses racing. Her heart was thudding now and she was certain that she should know this man. Her instincts could not be wrong. She'd met this man before, though she knew not when or how. 'Who are you, Sir Knight?'

'Newark tricked and murdered my father,' he said harshly. For a moment he turned away from her. His shoulders straightened and then he reached up to pull back the hood of chainmail, turning to face her. 'Do you not know me,

Elaine? I knew you at once, though you have hidden your hair and stained your face.'

She stared at him, her eyes drawn to the livid scar that ran the length of his face, from the corner of his left eye to his chin. It had puckered and the whole side of his face was red and inflamed. For a moment she did not recognise this man with black hair that was streaked with grey, but then, all at once, she knew. It was he, though the years and the hot sun of the Holy Land had wreaked havoc with his looks.

'Zander...?' She moved towards him hesitantly. He looked so different, sterner and older—much older than his years—and the scar was ugly, making her heart contract with pain. The beautiful youth who had declared his love before he left her had gone and in his place was a man she did not know. 'Is it truly you?'

'Yes, Elaine,' he said. 'It is I—older and battle-scarred, as you see—but I am Zander, lord of the lands my father bequeathed to me and I bear his name. I am Sir Zander de Bricasse and lord of Penbury.'

'Oh, my love, you have been sorely hurt,' Elaine said. Her instinct was to go to him and kiss him, but something held her back. He was Zander, the man she loved, and yet he was not the same. There was a distance about him, as if he had placed a barrier between them and she was not sure what to do. 'I am so sorry…'

'Save your tears for those who need them,' he said in a harsh tone. 'I do not wish for pity, Elaine. I should not have revealed myself had it not been that you must trust me if I am to deliver you safely to your home.'

'Zander…' Her lips trembled. 'It was not pity, but love that made me speak thus. I have always loved you.'

'You loved the man I was—not the man I am now,' he said, voice gruff with emotion. 'Give me no promises, lady. I do not ask them of you. I release you from the vow you made those many years gone.'

'I do not wish to be released,' Elaine said, but her voice was little more than a whisper, and in truth she was not sure what she felt. The scar was terrible and disfigured one half of his face, but she knew of unguents and cures that would help it, easing the pain and infection so that it would no longer be so inflamed. Nothing could make his beloved face as it had once been, but, if he would let her, she could ease the pain he must be feeling and heal the wound so the scar would not be so livid. It was not so much his appearance, but his manner, the distance between them, that made her hesitant. 'If you wish me for your wife, I should be honoured, sir.'

A nerve twitched in his throat, his eyes narrowing as they dwelt on her face. 'It is too soon to speak of these things, lady. For the moment I must see you safe to your home—and then I must avenge my father. I am not sure whether you knew that Newark was his enemy. My father slighted him once in some way, defied him and would not bend the knee to such an evil man. Newark never forgot or forgave him. He had him set upon by knaves and beaten to death, as if he were less than the lowest churl. I shall seek him out as soon as I am ready and avenge my father's death like a knight.'

'He is so rich and powerful,' Elaine said fearfully. 'You will need more men before you can challenge the earl.'

'This I know. These men are loyal to my uncle and will be loyal to me for as long as I need them, but I shall gather a powerful army and I will bring Newark to his knees somehow.'

Elaine's heart ached for his pain, physical and mental, but she could not take him in her arms for she felt he would reject her.

'Then I wish you luck, sir,' she said.

He nodded and replaced the hood of mail, hiding most of his face. Now she saw why it had been so difficult to recognise him, though her mind had sensed something. He looked so much older, hardened by battle and suffering. Elaine longed to reach him, to tell him that her love was strong enough to survive all that had happened, but what right did she have to claim his love? The Zander who had gone to fight in the Holy wars had loved her, but how could she know what was in this man's heart? In the years between he might have loved another. She might be merely a distant memory. How could she claim his love and loyalty if he did not wish to give them?

'We should leave if we are to reach your dower lands before Newark finds us,' Zander said. 'I can protect you from much—but not if we are too heavily outnumbered, so we shall move swiftly and travel through the night.' He held out his hand to her. 'Are you able to ride on alone, or shall I take you up with me?'

'I can ride alone, but you...' Her words were banished, for to speak of his weakness the previous day might anger or humiliate him.

'Your herbs have helped me, Elaine. Perhaps you would brew more for me this night?'

'Yes, my lord. I shall be happy to do anything I can to repay you. I could also help the pain in your cheek—if you would let me?'

'How do you know it pains me?'

'Because I can see that the poison has gathered beneath the skin. It needs to be opened and cleansed, the pus removed and then unguents applied to heal the flesh beneath.'

'Had you seen the wound Janvier tended you would not have thought this so terrible,' he said and smiled slightly. 'The pain I bear now is nothing to that I have suffered.'

'Yet it could be eased, sir.' Elaine looked at him proudly. She raised her head, gazing into his eyes. If he thought her still a child, he was wrong. 'I have spent the years you were away learning the skills a chatelaine needs to keep her people well and happy. I have learned much of herbs and healing.'

'Your mother was a healer, though she died too young—what happened to your father, Elaine?'

'My father died but a few months since. He had a wasting sickness that none could heal. My cures eased his suffering, but I could not save him—only God could have done that.'

'Is there a God?' Zander asked, a twist of bitterness about his mouth. 'Once I took up the Cross for His sake—but now I question He exists. Only a cruel god would allow the suffering

that I have seen, not just on the field of battle—
but innocents…children…'

Elaine stared at him. Her faith was strong
and it hurt her to hear such words on his lips.
'It is not God who makes us suffer, but the evil
that is in the world and in us. God forgives us
no matter what we do.'

'Such blind faith,' Zander said. 'I wish that
I could believe as you do, but I cannot—my
faith died with an innocent boy and so many
others. So much blood stained the earth of the
land we call Holy.'

'I cannot understand what makes you say
these words,' Elaine told him, 'but I know that
you have seen and felt too much. God will forgive you and take you back into His love, Zander. One day He will give you his peace.'

'When I am dead, perhaps?' Something
flickered in his eyes. 'Now you see why I am
not fit to be your husband, Elaine. Yet I vow
to protect you with my life, unworthy as it is.'

Her throat was tight with tears. She did not
know what to say to this man. He was bitter
and angry, disillusioned with all that had made
him the man of ideals and faith she had loved.
In truth, she was not sure that she would wish
to wed him now.

Keeping her emotions hid as best she could,

Elaine allowed him to help her mount her horse. His words had hurt her, but she would not let him see her weep. He was a stranger to her and only time would tell if there was anything left inside him of the man she'd loved.

They rode far and hard. Elaine was weary long before they stopped. When at last they came to a house that it seemed was known to Zander, she almost collapsed into his arms dismounting. He saw it at once and carried her into the house, the door of which opened, as if they expected him.

'Zander, my friend,' a tall blond knight said as he came to greet them. 'Welcome to my home. When I learned that you still lived my heart was gladdened. Come in, friends. My house is yours while you need it.'

'My lady needs a bed,' Zander said. 'She is in danger, Philip, and I have vowed to protect her—for that I may need your help. When she reaches her dower lands it may be that Newark's men are before us. I do not have the force to make him yield, but he would yield to you.'

'He will yield or I'll have him arrested and thrown in gaol. I am the King's Marshal in these parts and I have forbidden the barons to quarrel amongst themselves. Any that defy my decree shall be outlawed, forced to seek their bread in another land.'

'Then I can rely on you to protect her,' Zander said. 'But where may she rest this night?'

'Anne will take her to her own chamber,' Lord Philip Henry of Stornway said. 'My sister remains unwed, for she cannot find a man that pleases her and, fool that I am, I shall not force her.'

A tall woman came forwards. She was thin, but not uncomely, her long dark hair plaited and hanging down her back. Around her brow she wore a thin band of silver, to which a fine veil was attached. They were not alike—they had been born of different mothers, both of whom had died soon after giving birth.

'Come this way, sir,' she invited. 'I shall care of her this night.'

'She is but exhausted,' Zander said. 'I pushed her too hard, but I feared Newark still hunted for her.'

'He is not a good man,' Anne Stornway said, a thin smile on her lips. 'He asked for my hand when I was but thirteen, but my uncle and brother sent him away. I am five and twenty now and past the age of marriage, but if the earl asked me a thousand times I would not take him.'

Zander nodded grimly, carrying Elaine into the comfortable chamber that Anne led them to. The tester bed was hung with silk damask and the covers were fine Frankish velvet, woven in Rheims. Her pillows were of linen cases stuffed with goose feathers; it was the finest linen to be found in all Christendom, as were the sheets she pulled back so that he could place his precious burden down. For a moment he stood looking at Elaine as her eyelids fluttered and she cried out his name.

'You are betrothed?' Anne asked and Elaine heard their voices as from a distance.

'We were once betrothed,' Zander said and threw back his hood. 'How can I ask a gentle lady to look at this every day of her life?'

'If she loved you, she would seek only to ease your pain. I have unguents that would ease you. I shall give you some. Your servant may treat you, for the wound is healing, but needs something to ease it. I should be glad to offer you my cure, Sir Knight.'

'You are kind, lady,' Zander said. 'I have lived with the pain for months. I can bear it—at least until I have time to rest.'

Anne bowed her head and turned away. Unlike Elaine, she knew better than to argue with a man of his ilk; she had learned as a young girl that it was better to appease than quarrel, though he hadn't noticed there was a tiny flame of anger in her eyes.

Elaine moved her head on the pillows and her eyelids flickered. Zander looked at her and moved away from the bed.

'I shall leave you to tend her,' he said to Anne, walked away and left, closing the door behind him.

Anne gazed after him a moment and then shook her head. Men were such fools. There was no understanding them. And this one roused such feelings in her that she had difficulty maintaining her air of calm, but she must—she must for otherwise she would betray herself.

She moved back to the bed just as Elaine started up in fear. Again she called Zander's name and looked about her, tears on her cheeks.

'I dreamed he came to me...' she said. 'I dreamed he came back—but he was not the same.'

Anne sat on the edge of the bed. She reached out to touch the younger girl's face. Anne could feel only pity for this young woman.

'Hush, lady. Lord Zander is not far away. He is anxious for your safety—but he is a man.

They do not understand us or our needs. No man is worth a woman's tears, believe me.'

Elaine blinked the tears away. She pushed herself up against the pillows, looking at her curiously, for there had been bitterness in her voice. 'Who are you, lady? I have not seen you before.'

'I am sister to Philip, Lord of Stornway. In King Richard's absence he is Marshal here and tries to keep the peace between the warring barons, but 'tis a thankless task. Most are too stubborn and too proud. My brother is sorely troubled by their lawless behaviour. I wish that the King would return and bring some order to this land.'

'You speak truly,' Elaine said and this time the tears would not be stopped. 'The Earl of Newark gained my uncle's trust and then tricked him. He took all that was my uncle's— and would have had me, too, had I not run away.'

Anne listened to her tale to the end and then nodded. 'So Lord Zander came to your rescue, but it hurts you because he is not as he was?' Elaine nodded, noticing the odd look in Anne's eyes. 'He has suffered things you could not even imagine, lady. My brother has spoken to returning knights before this. He has told me some of what he heard, but some he hid from me—though I guessed what he would not say. Lord Zander needs time to recover, to heal inside as well as out. One day he will be himself again. He should allow me to help him cure the wound to his cheek, but he is too proud.'

'I fear that you are right and I hope that he will find peace one day.'

'Only God can heal what ails him. My brother finds comfort in the Good Lord and so must we all.' Anne crossed herself piously, but her eyes avoided Elaine's, as though she would hide her innermost thoughts.

'Amen to that,' Elaine said. 'My faith never wavered. I always believed that God would bring him back to me—but now…'

'Now your love must be stronger,' Anne said. 'You must fight not only for his love, but for his soul. Restore him to his faith and he will be the man you love again. His physical scars may remain, but they will fade and are as nothing to the loss of his soul.'

'How wise you are,' Elaine said and smiled at her. 'I must wait and see what time will do.'

'As we all must. Now I must go, for my brother needs me to order his house when we have guests. A servant will come to bring food and drink.'

'I am simply tired,' Elaine said. 'I shall sleep well this night, for I know we are safe. Even the Earl of Newark dare not attack the King's Marshal.'

'Not here in this stronghold for we are too well protected, but he might if he found us un-protected—that man is more evil than you know. I think there is little he would not dare.'

'I know well of his misdeeds,' Elaine said. 'My serving woman had a sister and she was sent to serve the Earl of Newark's first wife. When that gentle lady died at her vile husband's hands, because she gave him a daughter and not the son he craved, she ran away. I found a place for her with my aunt so that she could be close to her sister—but I do not know what happened to her when my uncle was tricked into surren-dering the keep.'

'Then you must take great care—Newark is a vengeful man. Sleep now, lady, and I shall wake you in the morning to break your fast in good time, though your journey should be safer now, for my brother will send an escort with you. If Newark defies them, he will bring the King's wrath on himself.'

'Thank you.' Elaine sighed as Anne went out and lay down, closing her eyes.

'Zander,' she whispered, tears upon her cheeks as she drifted into sleep. 'Zander, please come back to me…'

Chapter Five

Zander stood in the shadows of the room. The slitted window allowed little light into the lady's chamber, but his eyes were accustomed to the gloom and what light there was fell across her pale face. He had risen before cockcrow to prepare for the next day of their journey and Anne Stornway was already about her business, ordering her servants. She'd told him that Elaine was sleeping and advised leaving her to rest until the last moment.

'She has suffered a terrible shock and it is as much grief as the strain of riding so far that made her give way last night, sir. You should be gentle with her.'

'I am but a rough knight, not a courtier,' Zander said. 'You do not need to tell me that I am unworthy of her.'

'What do court manners matter where love is?' Anne asked, her head up. 'I do not boast when I say that more nobles than you may imagine have courted me. Only one hath touched my heart, but he died. If I had found another man I counted as true and honourable, I would have wed him, but I have not.'

'I am sorry for your loss, lady. You would make any man a fine wife, but I dare say your brother could not spare you.'

'He would be pleased to see me happy,' she said. 'I've hoped that he would fall in love and bring his bride here to bear me company, but he is as hard to please as his sister.'

Zander laughed. 'I think Philip hath too much comfort for his own good, lady. Why should he wed when he has you?'

'I have my uses,' she said. 'Once again I offer my cure. It would ease your pain and the redness.' There was something almost urgent in her tone, as if she wished to force acceptance from him.

'I thank you, but I prefer to leave such things to my servant.'

'Very well. Leave your lady to sleep a little longer.' Anne turned aside, but he caught the flicker of resentment in her eyes and wondered at it.

Zander inclined his head as she went about her work, but he had not been able to resist coming to Elaine's chamber to look at her. Now that her lovely hair was spread upon the pillows she looked more like the girl he'd loved, though her skin still bore traces of the stain she'd used to disguise herself. She was so beautiful that his heart caught and he longed to sweep her into his arms and kiss her, to feel her soft skin against his and to make her his own—but that could never happen now.

It would be unfair to her. He was not the man she'd loved. War had hardened him, made him bitter. He would hurt her and she might be left a widow before she was hardly a wife. Zander could never break the vow he'd made to avenge his father. In his heart he knew that the enemy he faced was treacherous and so powerful that even he might not survive the fierce fight that must ensue.

Zander was determined to challenge his enemy to single-handed combat, but first he must regain his strength. Janvier had made him more of the cure with the herbs Elaine had given them and, again, Zander felt an improvement. He was not so easily tired and yet still he could not swing his great broadsword with the strength he would need for battle. Much as he wanted to destroy his enemy, he was not yet ready.

Elaine was stirring. He was torn between leaving her and yet he stayed, wanting to see her wake. Her eyelids flickered and he noticed how dark her lashes were despite the fairness of her hair, then her eyes opened and she looked at him. The smile of wonder and joy that spread from her eyes over her face cut Zander to the heart; it was the smile he recalled so well, the smile that had helped him through the pain-racked nights, drawing him back from the very mouth of hell. It was her smile that had kept him hanging on by a thread, his spirit almost done, the pain so terrible that his body craved the peace of death—and yet he had lived. He had lived because she lived, and now he would live to serve her if he could.

'Zander...' The note of wonder in her voice made him frown. 'I dreamed of you...but you are here...'

'I am real, but not as you knew me.'

Elaine sighed and his heart caught with pain as he saw the joy and the wonder drain from her, leaving only sadness and uncertainty.

'I am sorry to wake you, lady,' he said. 'But

we should be leaving soon. I have sent scouts on ahead to see if Newark hath taken your manor and lies in wait, hoping to draw you into a trap.'

'And if he has?' Elaine was fully awake now, modestly drawing the sheet to her chest as she sat up. 'I do not know where else to go.'

'I have little to offer you. I think my father's manor may be almost a ruin—but Anne would take you back here until I could find somewhere suitable for you to live.'

'My lands are all I have.'

'I brought a fortune home, as I promised you, Elaine. If my father's manor lies in ruin, I shall buy a house worthy of you. One that hath stout walls, a moat and a gate that can be drawn up.'

'But...' Elaine blushed. 'I should not wish to be a burden to you if...'

'You could never be that,' he said. 'I shall leave you to dress, but I pray you come down to the courtyard swiftly, for I would be away.'

He turned and left her, his mind in turmoil. If Newark had stolen all Elaine had, it might be that his only course was to wed her. He knew her pride would forbid her to live on his charity. In that eventuality, she might be left penniless and vulnerable, forced to work as a servant for her bread. Marriage to Zander would then be the better alternative. He would honour and protect her while he lived—and if he died his fortune would be hers. To protect her he would appoint Philip of Stornway as her guardian.

Zander's heart thudded against his ribs as he went down the twisted stair to the great hall, which was a scene of activity as men prepared to leave with him. Armour and supplies had been loaded onto the packhorses, and knights were already wearing their coats of chainmail beneath their tabards.

Zander saw his squire talking with Lady Anne. She was laughing and talking animatedly, her face alight with interest as she listened to Janvier's words. Janvier turned his head and saw him; he bowed to the lady and walked towards Zander.

Zander caught the look of annoyance on the lady's face before it was swiftly hidden and once again he wondered. Why should Anne be angry and yet try to hide it?

He knew that the Saracen's family was noble, but he was penniless, stripped of his land and much he'd had by marauding knights. What little was left he had given to his mother and sister—all that was left of a once-proud family. He'd refused Zander's offer of gold for saving his life in favour of becoming his servant, but he was a proud and clever man. By birth and intellect he was the equal of Anne of Storn-way, but the colour of his skin and his lack of wealth made him a pauper in a strange land—and not a man her brother would consider fit to be her husband.

What nonsense was he at now? He must have a touch of fever to even think of such things. If the lady could guess at what was in his mind, she would no doubt think herself insulted. Zander smiled sadly. How unfair was life? Would that respect and love were all, but in the world Zander knew pride and prejudice ruled the heart and marriages were made for land, not love.

'Are you ready to leave, my lord?'

'We but await my lady,' Zander said and then something warned him and he turned to look at the stone steps that led to the solar. Elaine had taken him at his word and she was dressed, seemingly ready to continue.

'You feel able to continue?' Zander asked as she came towards him.

'Yes, my lord. I am fully rested. I think we have not so far to go now.'

'It is but a few hours' ride from here,' he said and offered her his hand. Even as she took it, Anne came up with them.

'If you wished, Lady Elaine could stay until you are sure that rogue has not taken her lands.

I should be glad of her company.' Anne said, smiling at them, no trace now of the resentment he'd glimpsed earlier. 'You know that you may trust my brother to guard her for you.'

'I must go with Zander,' Elaine said, an odd little shiver at her nape. Something told her not to stay here, though these people were clearly Zander's friends. 'My people will not be certain they can trust him unless I am there. If they have barred the gates against Newark, they will only open to me.'

'The offer remains if you need it,' Anne said. She smiled, but Zander noticed that her eyes were cold.

'We thank you for the offer,' Zander said and kissed the hand she offered. 'Should my lady need sanctuary, I shall bring her to you until I can find somewhere for her to live.'

'So you will marry her,' Anne said, taking his vow for proof of his intention. 'She will need a strong man to protect her, sir. She is the rightful heir not only to her mother's dower lands, but also those of Howarth Manor. My brother will petition the king as soon as he returns to England and then Newark must make reparation or suffer the consequences of treason.'

'Does his Majesty return?' Zander asked. 'I

had not heard he was released from his imprisonment.'

'Though most do not know it the ransom has been paid,' Anne replied. 'You will keep this to yourself, sir, for there are those who might seek to prevent Richard from returning to take back what is his by right.'

'No word of this shall pass my lips,' he said and bowed his head. 'We thank you for your hospitality, lady.'

'Return and you will be welcome. If you are settled at Sweetbriars, I shall hope to visit with you and you will visit with me sometimes.'

'I shall be glad to have a friend,' Elaine said. 'Mayhap once Newark's wings have been clipped I shall be able to ride out without fear of abduction.'

'You need a husband to protect you,' Anne said, smiled strangely and then turned away to her steward.

As they went out into the courtyard, Zander saw Philip standing with the escort he had offered. They carried his standard and a warrant demanding that the manor be handed over to Elaine, should the earl have sent men to occupy it. Lord Philip smiled and came up to them, bowing over the hand Elaine offered as she thanked him for his kindness.

'It was an honour and a pleasure, Lady Elaine. If ever you are in need of my services, you need only send word. I shall make it known in the area that your manor is under my protection. The greedy barons may still try to make war on you, but draw up your bridge and send a servant to me and we shall relieve you within hours.'

'You are very kind,' she said and her cheeks flushed, perhaps because his look was so obviously admiring.

For a moment Zander frowned, then he offered his mailed fist to his friend. 'You have my gratitude. You know I am committed to avenge my father, but if I live and you have need of my service in the future...'

'I need only ask.'

The two men clasped hands. Zander brought forwards a beautiful white palfrey, which Elaine would ride side-saddle. The saddle itself was wrought of leather chased with silver and padded with red velvet, and the reins had fine silver tassles. The horse and tackle were expensive, much more so than those Elaine had left behind at Howarth. She imagined they belonged to the Lord of Stornway and thanked him.

'Would that they were mine to give,' Philip told her. 'Zander had these things sent here some days ago, I presume as a gift for you. It is he you should thank.'

'A gift...' Elaine's throat caught and her eyes opened in wonder. Her startled gaze went to Zander. Surely such a gift was meant as a wedding present? 'I do not know how to thank you, for such a lovely gift. By what name is this beautiful creature called?'

'Moonstone Lady,' he said and laughed. 'I see she pleases you, Elaine, and so is worth the king's ransom I paid to a greedy Caliph who knew how much I wanted her. She came to England with us from the land of the Turks and is pure Arab.'

'She must be worth a great deal.' Her voice was breathy and something in his look at that moment made her heart race.

'Some would say she is beyond price.' Zander's eyes made her wonder whether he spoke of the mare or her.

Elaine had thought he no longer loved her, that love had been burned away by bitterness and sorrow, but the look he gave her made her heart race. No man would give a gift like this if he were truly indifferent—would he?

'It is the most precious thing anyone has ever given me,' she said huskily. Gazing into his eyes, which looked dark and bottomless this morning, she felt a spasm of desire. Her mouth felt dry, her tongue moving over her lips as she tried to control the sudden leap of excitement. For one precious moment she had seen something in his eyes—something that reminded her of the youth that had left her to fight for his ideals.

She felt light-headed and almost swayed towards him. It seemed to her that his mouth softened and she longed to kiss him, to be held in those strong arms, as she'd been held so many years ago—but she had been a child then and now the woman she had become longed for more. His courtship had been gentle, never sullying her innocence, but she was a woman and ready for marriage now.

'We must go,' he said and gave her his hand. A feeling of intense pleasure shot through her at his touch, but she managed to control her emotions and not give herself away as he helped her up to the saddle, though her knees felt weak and her stomach clenched. He turned to his friend. 'Farewell, Philip. You will hear from me—and if the lady needs you, I shall return her to you with your escort.'

They rode together over the drawbridge, the horses' hooves clattering on the wood-and-iron bridge. Stornway was a stout fortress, one unlikely to be breached by anything less than a large army. It was a symbol of power held by the King's Marshal, Lord Stornway, enforcer of the King's justice in this area.

Elaine glanced at Zander as she accustomed herself to the palfrey's ways. Although spirited and perhaps a little skittish in her excitement at being ridden for the first time in days, she was well trained to a lady's touch.

'You are pleased with her?' he asked. 'She was meant for an Eastern princess, but I thought she would be perfect for you, Elaine.'

'Nothing could have pleased me better.'

'I have other gifts. They are stored in chests and left with Lord Stornway until the time is right. Once you are settled at your home I shall have them sent to you.'

Elaine smiled, but made no answer. How could she accept such gifts unless he meant to wed her? She could not ask. The time for questions was not now, but so many buzzed in her head that she hardly knew how to shut them out.

'I pray that we shall find all well with my people,' she said. 'I do not think they would easily yield to the earl and may have suffered for it.'

'Your mother's house is not as stout as Stornway, yet it would withstand a short siege. We must pray that we are in time.'

So saying, he increased his speed. Elaine touched her heels lightly to the palfrey's flanks and felt her leap forwards. Excitement raced through her and as, for a while, they raced side by side over the flat terrain, her heart lightened. It was almost as if she were a girl again and Zander had never gone away.

When they approached the Manor of Sweetbriars, the gates stood open and Elaine's mother's standard still flew over the stone walls that guarded the house. They were hewn of mellow yellow stone and seemed to dream peacefully in the evening sun. Even so, Zander held up his hand to bring his men to a halt.

'It may be a trap,' he warned. 'Newark imagined you alone, Elaine. He may have left the gates open so that you walk into his web like the cunning devil he is.'

'What shall we do?' she asked. 'If I go forward alone—'

'No! I shall not risk your safety. You remain here under guard while I send an advance party to see how the land lies.'

As they deliberated, a woman suddenly darted forwards from the side of the road and flung herself at Elaine's horse. She had appeared to be picking herbs and no one had looked at her, but Elaine saw at once that she was her serving woman Marion.

'Marion,' she cried gladly. 'I am so glad to see you. I feared that something might have happened to you. Where is Bertrand?'

Marion looked distressed. 'The earl's men took Bertrand. He told me to run and hide while he rode off. They gave chase and I was unnoticed in the bushes as they followed. Later, I saw them return and he was their prisoner. He had been bound, his hands behind his back, and lay over the back of a horse.' A little sob came from her lips. 'They brought him here and I followed. I dared not go into the courtyard, though the bridge is always left up. I do not know if he lives…or even if he is still here, for they say some prisoners were taken away to the earl's stronghold.'

'I am so sorry,' Elaine said. 'Forgive me. I should never have let you sacrifice yourselves for me.'

'Bertrand would die for you, as should I, lady.'

'How many men?' Zander barked suddenly. 'Is the earl there himself? How many men does he have here?'

'How can Marion know these things?'

'I have not wasted my time, sir,' Marion told him proudly. 'The opinion of those who go in and out regularly with provisions is that there is no more than twenty men-at-arms at the most.'

'Thank you, lady.' Zander nodded to her. He looked thoughtfully at one of his men. 'Sir Robert. Will you ride ahead with the King's Marshal's flag, please? Demand the surrender of the manor in the king's name. If they throw down their weapons and surrender, we shall follow with the women.'

'Yes, my lord. You will wait here with the others?'

Zander shook his head. He looked at a man driving a cart loaded with fruit and vegetables. 'Have the driver come here to me. He looks much my size. I shall buy his cloak, hood and boots. It will be as well to have someone on the inside in case they try some kind of treachery.'

'What if they refuse and bring down the gate?'

'Exactly.' Zander smiled. 'It is for that reason that we need someone on the inside.'

'Let me go in your place, lord,' Janvier said. 'You are not strong enough to fight your way out.'

Zander hesitated, then, 'You may come with me, hidden in the cart.'

'I pray you, do not leave me,' Elaine cried. 'If you were caught or killed…'

'Then my men will escort you to Stornway.' The flicker of a smile was on his lips. 'I am not that easy to kill, Elaine. Wait here if you care for me. I should be more at risk if the earl took you.'

'We'll go into the village and hide,' Elaine said. 'Even if Newark's men are in the house, my people will not betray me.'

'Go with her and guard her well,' Zander instructed his men.

The driver of the cart had proved only too willing to exchange his clothes for the lord's gold, but when he saw Elaine he would have given them for nothing.

'Let me come with you for my lady's sake,' he cried. 'Alone we could do nothing for the earl came under guise of friendship and tricked us into thinking our lady was his wife.'

'At Howarth, he also played a trick to take the castle,' Marion said. 'He is an evil coward.'

'Yes, come with us,' Zander said to the villager, 'but your money will be paid—to your family if need be.'

The man nodded, remounting his cart and

telling Janvier to hide beneath the sacks of food, which were piled high. Zander rode beside him in borrowed clothes, a villager's hood over his head.

'Come to the village, my lady,' a woman urged. 'Come quickly and we shall hide you should the earl's men come looking. We have a place to hide food that Prince John's taxmen would otherwise take from us. Always, they take everything we have, though they are entitled to no more than three-tenths.'

'Such iniquitous taxes shall cease when I am your lady here,' Elaine promised. She gave her precious palfrey to one of the soldiers, choosing to walk with Marion and the others into the village. 'Wait here for your lord—but go to him if he needs you. I shall be safe enough in the village.'

Zander's second-in-command looked at her uneasily. 'My lord bid us guard you, lady.'

'I am with my people now,' Elaine said. 'My lord may need your services and I shall be safe in the village.'

'None shall find her until her lord comes,' the woman said, clutching Elaine's arm. 'Come now before the earl returns. He took a hunting party out early this morning and has not yet returned, but may do so at any time.'

Elaine hurried away with the woman. Zander's men looked uneasily at each other, knowing that he would be displeased if his orders were disobeyed, but even as they debated whether to go after her they heard shouts from the manor and the sound of steel against steel.

'We should join them...'

'My lord said to wait here and protect the lady...'

'She hath gone to the village. We protect Zander...'

As they argued, one of them turned and saw a party of some eight or nine men approaching. They wore Newark's colours of black and yellow, and the runners and dogs clustered about the horses told them it was the earl's hunting party returned.

'We stay here and prevent them reaching the manor,' Sir Robert said. 'If they come up on his back, Zander will be vulnerable. They do not pass us.'

A murmur of agreement issued from every throat. Their duty was now clear and as one they turned to face the earl's men. It was obvious that the oncoming party had sensed something was wrong; they were few in number, for there were only six mounted knights. The others were servants and armed for hunting rather than fighting. They had the carcasses of a deer and also a wild boar strapped to a packhorse at the rear.

It was easy to pick out the earl. His men were looking to him for judgement. He deliberated for a while, then sent a man forwards.

'The Earl of Newark demands to know who you are and why you dare to block his way?'

'We are here in the name of the King's Marshal, Lord Stornway,' Sir Robert said. 'We bear his standard and a warrant for the surrender of the lands you have unlawfully taken from the Lady Elaine.'

His voice had carried the short distance to the earl's men. Some shouted their defiance and would have drawn their swords, but their master gave the order to wait. He looked towards the manor house and saw that a new pennant had been raised—it was the King's Marshal's standard, placing Sweetbriars under his protection. Now any man that lifted a hand against the manor would be guilty of treason and outlawed on the king's return to his kingdom.

Some of the earl's men were still arguing for attack, but the earl ordered them to stop. Then he turned his own horse and raced off, his mounted men following after, though one or two looked back in anguish as though they retreated against their will.

The packhorse, most of the dogs and the huntsmen had been left behind. They debated for a moment, then walked towards Stornway's mounted men-at-arms, and one of the huntsmen looked up at Sir Robert.

'We served the earl because he forced us, lord—but we are the Lady Elaine's men and would serve her if she will have us.'

'Take the meat into the manor,' Sir Robert said. 'If the earl returns and lays siege, we shall need all the food we can store.'

'Yes, lord.' The huntsman signalled to the others and they began to run or walk towards the manor house, the dogs barking wildly as they followed.

Sir Robert decided to lead his men into the manor, but as he approached Zander came riding towards him. He rode up to them, looking pleased, for there had been but token resistance and the Earl of Newark's men had soon surrendered once they saw the King's Marshal's standard. Ten of them, led by a man called Stronmar, had asked for permission to leave and been given it under a white flag, but fifteen had fallen to their knees, begged pardon and asked to be given service by Zander. It seemed

they hated the earl, but had been forced to serve
him. Now they were free they had chosen to
remain at Sweetbriars to serve a new master.
The outcome had pleased Zander very much,
but now, when he saw that Elaine was not with
his men, his smile vanished.

'Where is my lady?'

'The villagers took her and her woman into
the village to hide her.'

'And you allowed it?' Zander's face darkened. 'If she is harmed or has fallen into
Newark's hands…by God, you'll wish you'd
followed my orders.'

Sir Robert did not answer. He had allowed
the lady to have her way. Had they not held true,
the earl might have attacked from the rear. The
men in the castle would not then have surrendered so tamely and more blood would have
been shed. Yet he made no attempt to defend
himself, for the order to protect the lady had
been given.

Unaware of the injustice of his harsh words,
Zander galloped on towards the village, his
horse bursting upon the startled villagers in a
cloud of dust as he skidded to a halt. He leaped
down from its back, sword in hand, bristling
with rage as he demanded to know where
Elaine was. His anger succeeded in convinc-

ing the men of the village, who thought him a stranger bent on evil and formed ranks, their stout cudgels at the ready to defend their lady. Sir Robert and some of the men came upon a scene fraught with tension. Had Elaine not rushed into the small circle of men, murder might have been done at any moment.

'Put down your weapons,' she cried. 'This is Sir Zander de Bricasse. He comes to defend me, but I need no defence here.' Turning to Zander, she smiled and held out her hand. 'My lord, come and meet my people. You have no need of your sword here.'

Zander stared at her for a moment, then inclined his head and sheathed his sword. 'My men should have been here to protect you.'

'I needed none—and they guarded you, Zander. The earl's hunting party returned, but the way was barred against them and they were forced to turn back. Had they come up on you from behind, you might not have taken the manor so easily. I thank them for saving the shedding of blood. I would have as little blood spilled in my cause as possible.'

'I feared you might have been led into a trap.' Zander's eyes were hard, dark with anger. 'I am accustomed to being obeyed—if men disobey their captain it leads to disorder in the ranks and disobedience must be punished.' There was something dark in his eyes then, something that made her feel icy cold.

'It was I who disobeyed you, not your men,' Elaine said, her eyes sparking as she looked at him defiantly. 'Will you punish me, my lord?'

Zander glared at her a moment longer and then gave a reluctant laugh. 'I see I need to teach you to obey your lord, my lady,' he said, but there was a smile on his lips. 'Methinks you need Lady Anne to set an example. 'Tis a pity that you did not invite her to stay.'

Elaine smiled, relieved that his white-hot anger had suddenly evaporated. 'I think even Anne would have acted as I did, my lord—but correct me if I am wrong.'

'You are wrong,' he said and threw his reins to one of the villagers; the man caught them and led the horse to a drinking trough. Zander walked to greet Elaine, offering her his hand. 'Lady Anne is far too careful to confront any man; she would bow her head, agree with everything—and then do exactly as she pleased. She hides her emotions well, but sometimes they show through despite her.'

Elaine's eyes sparkled with merriment for she sensed that he was teasing her, as he'd so often teased her in the past. In that moment she saw the young squire she'd loved before he left to become a knight. He was still there somewhere, though changed by the years.

'I see you know her well,' she said and smiled.

'I knew her as a child—and we met again before I left to join the king. At that time she was much admired at court and it was thought that she would marry well.'

Elaine nodded. She wondered if he had admired the young woman then, but thought her far above him, then she quashed the maggot of jealousy before it could become embedded in her flesh. Zander had truly loved Elaine when he had left to join the crusade. It was not another love she had to fight—but the pain of disillusionment and the loss of faith. When he'd gone to join the cause he'd spent night after night in vigil, praying for his soul…praying to become worthy enough to fight for the Cross. He had been honourable, earnest and devout. What had happened to this man? What terrible deeds haunted him? She could see the scars on his face, but she believed other scars ran deep and it was those not visible to the eye that festered and corrupted inside him.

'Anne of Stornway is a lovely lady, sir.'

'Indeed she is, but…' Elaine thought he meant to say more, perhaps to compliment her, but instead he shook his head. 'Come, lady. Thank your people for their care of you. Tell them there will be a feast in the hall tomorrow night and all those who are loyal will be welcome to join us. We must go to the house, for there is much to do before I can think of leaving.'

'Leaving?' Elaine's heart caught. 'I thought… hoped…'

'I shall not go before I am certain that you are well protected here,' Zander said, eyes dwelling on her face. 'You know that my feud with Newark does not end here. He had my father foully slain and I have sworn to avenge him. I shall not rest easy in my bed until that is done. Fear not, lady. Newark will have too much on his hands to think of defying the King's Marshal by attacking your home.'

The pain caught at her heart. He had been so anxious for her that she'd been misled into believing that he still cared—that he would stay and wed her—but it seemed that she was wrong. He would protect her, as he would any lady he considered in need, but he did not need or want her.

Chapter Six

Raising her head proudly, Elaine allowed one of the knights to help her mount her palfrey. Marion was put up to ride pillion behind her and they said their goodbyes to the people who had been prepared to give their lives to protect them.

Elaine had earlier told the headman to come to her at the house. She wanted to know what her people needed from her. Much of her life would be here now and she would spend it serving her people. If Zander did not wish to wed her, then she would not marry. She knew she would be more vulnerable, for some unscrupulous knights would see her as prey and do their best to entice or trap her into marriage. However, she was under the protection of Lord

Stornway and would make sure that her home was always well guarded. Even though he was determined to leave her, Zander would make sure that she was adequately protected before he went.

She deliberately kept from looking at him. Sometimes his smile was her undoing and she feared he had already seen the love and need in her. She had done her best to subdue it, for her pride would not let her beg for his love. At times she was not sure who this knight was— he could be as sweet as honey with a smile to charm the birds at one moment and the next he was like stone, impenetrable.

A part of her wanted to rage at him, to rake him with her nails and beat him with her fists. How dare he come into her life and break her heart again? How many times had she wept for him in the dark of night? Too many! He did not deserve her love—and yet she cared. She cared too much.

When they rode into the inner bailey of her home, she slipped from the saddle without help and began to walk towards the house. Her mother's steward Elgin came running to her. He fell down on his knees before her and, wringing his hands, begged her pardon for allowing the earl to take the manor.

'We did not know what to believe, my lady. He claimed he was your lord and that you had ordered us to give him service.'

'He lied to you, old friend,' she said and smiled, tapping his shoulder. 'Get up, Elgin. I would not have you or any of my people kneel to me. Had my uncle allowed it I should have been here months ago. The earl would not have gained entry so easily then. Our walls are stout and can be defended with a handful of strong knights.'

'You are the image of your sainted mother,' Elgin said as he rose to his feet. 'We have prospered well here, my lady—but the earl took much of what he could find and our stores are depleted. Fortunately, we have our secrets and the gold and silver, pewter and your mother's jewels are still hid where she bade us place them in times of trouble.'

Tears sprang to Elaine's eyes. Her mother had been on a visit to her dower lands when she herself was but seven years of age. Taken by a fever that laid her on her bed, she'd sent for her husband and daughter, but they had arrived too late to do more than kiss her pale face before she was laid in her coffin in the crypt at the church, her stillborn son with her.

The sudden death of Eleanor Howarth had destroyed her husband. He had never been the same again, his health failing year by year until he died a shadow of his former self—and left his only child to the care of his brother, whom he had trusted to care for and protect her.

'We shall prosper again,' Elaine promised. 'Newark stole my uncle's castle and lands. They were my heritage, to pass to my husband when I wed. I shall petition the King to have my lands restored, but until then we must work to make sure that our people do not starve this coming winter.'

'We shall not starve—if Prince John's taxmen leave us enough to live on. We need a strong lord to protect us, my lady. Lord Zander is one such man. If he were master here, the prince's tax collectors would not dare to ask for more than their fair tithe.'

Elaine's throat stung. She smiled and turned her head to watch as Zander gave orders in the courtyard. Men sprang to attention, running to do his bidding, eager to serve. If he would but wed her before he left her, his reputation would keep her safe. He was a knight that others respected, a man of zeal who had faced death a hundred times on the battlegrounds of the Holy Land and yet survived. The scars he feared might cause her revulsion brought him instant respect from men who understood what pain he had endured and yet survived. They looked at him as if he were holy, almost a living god amongst lesser mortals.

Her chest tightened and for a moment the pain was intense. He was too proud to ask her to wed him now, but he was too honourable to break his vow to her if she demanded that he keep it.

Elaine knew what she must do for the sake of her people—to keep them safe she must sacrifice her own feelings.

For the moment Zander was too busy to talk to her. She saw Marion speaking with other ladies and knew they were waiting to take her to her chambers so that she could change and refresh herself.

Elaine had borrowed some of Anne's clothing, but she knew that her mother's clothes were still here, packed in chests of camphor and cedarwood. They would fit her and their scent would bring her mother closer.

'Lord Zander asks that you join him and his men to sup in the Great Hall,' one of the young handmaidens said, curtsying to her. 'All is ready, my lady—if you would care to come down now?'

'Yes, I shall come now,' Elaine said. Marion gave her a mirror of beaten silver and she glanced at the rather misty image of herself. Her hair was a golden cloud about her pale face, for her ladies had at last managed to get rid of the walnut juice she'd used to stain her skin. Her gown was blue silk embroidered with silver thread and beads and covered by a filmy over-gown of pale gauze. Her headdress was a coiled band of velvet twined with silver wires and caught with pearls. Fastened to her ears were large pearl drops held by silver wires and about her throat was a long string of creamy pearls, at the end of which was fastened a silver cross. These were her mother's jewels, which had been kept safely for her by her steward these many years. 'Thank you, ladies—you have done well.'

Her ladies smiled and cooed about her, assuring her that she was so beautiful that it was easy to dress her. Elaine shook her head. She left her chamber and went down the stairs to the huge hall below. Even though her mother's dower was a moated manor house rather than a castle, the hall was long and the ceiling high and vaulted with ladder beams. Pennants hung from the beams and on the walls hung shields and swords, axes and pikes. The heavy oak furniture was set with gleaming pewter, silver ewers and plates, and a few gold pieces here and there. The people of Sweetbriars had brought out all the precious plate to celebrate their lady's return.

Fresh rushes had been strewn on the stone flags and sweet herbs had been scattered to scent them, sweeping out the dirt and stench left by the earl's men, who, she'd been told, threw discarded food on the floor and let the dogs fight over it. They'd taken their dogs with them on the hunting trip and Zander had given orders that they were to be penned outside. Only his own lurcher was permitted within the house, a great grey beast that lurked at his feet and viewed all comers with suspicious eyes.

Despite that it was a mild day, a fire had been lit in the huge fireplace and a log that must have been half the trunk of a tree was crackling and spitting, giving off the scent of fresh pine. Above that Elaine caught the scent of suckling pig, roast capons, cinnamon and spices. It seemed they were to have a feast this night, as well as the following day.

Zander was standing at the far end of the

hall, where the high table stood. Two rows of trestle tables had been set up at right angles to the board where she and her principal guests would sit and men were already lined up behind the benches waiting for her arrival. As they saw her a cheer went up and they began to stamp their feet in appreciation.

Zander turned to look at her. His eyes seemed intent on her as she walked towards him, but he did not smile, nor did he give any indication that he was impressed by her appearance, though he must have noticed the difference.

'My lord,' she said and made a slight curtsy. 'I hope I have not kept you waiting?'

'No, you have not,' he said and still he did not smile, though his gaze was so hot that it seemed to devour her. 'I dare say we are all hungry and the feast shall begin as soon as you are seated.'

'Then let it begin,' she said and took her place at the centre. Her chair had arms and a thick wooden back and seat, but for her comfort soft cushions had been placed to ease her. To either side of her was a chair with a straight back, but without arms; neither of these chairs had a cushion to make them more comfortable. Everyone else sat either on stools or backless benches.

Elaine smiled and waved her arm as the sig-

nal that the food should be brought in immediately. The men cheered her again and then
sat, reaching for bread and the wine that was
already in their cups. Pageboys dressed in blue
and silver, and house churls wearing grey home-
spun, began to bring in a succession of dishes.
Some were served to the lower benches, others were brought to the high table and a taster
stood between Elaine and Zander. He tasted a
small portion from each platter and it was then
served to Elaine, Zander and the other men who
formed the guests honoured with a place at her
board.

Dishes of suckling pig were followed by roast
capons, pigeons in rich sauces, sweetbreads,
roasted chitterlings and caramelised onions
with nuts, tarts of quince and plums with cus-
tards and syllabubs of honey and wine. There
was a pig's head stuffed with apples, plates of
dates and almonds and figs, many of these del-
icacies brought back to England for the first
time by the crusading knights who had seen a
market for them here. A mess of mutton with
turnips and leeks from the land of the Welsh-
men, neats' tongues and carp from the stew-
pond in the inner bailey formed the main course
of the meal.

Elaine ate sparingly from the dishes she favoured, tasting the suckling pig, capons and some stewed apple flavoured with cinnamon, followed by a syllabub of honey and wine, then declared herself satisfied. She would eat no more, though she nibbled a stuffed date when Zander insisted, and sipped from her cup of sweetened wine.

A minstrel was strolling about the room, strumming on his lyre and singing songs for any that would offer him a coin. At times Elaine caught a few words of a ribald song from a far corner of the room, which was followed by raucous laughter. Mostly the lyrics were sung in French and she simply ignored the lines she knew were outrageously *risqué* and not fit for a lady's ears. She watched a tumbler perform-ing his tricks and then the minstrel was sum-moned to the high table. Zander gave him gold and told him to sing a gentle love song, which he did, smiling and bowing to Elaine. Although still in French, the language of love, she under-stood perfectly and smiled, because she knew this song was not so outrageous as those the minstrel had sung to entertain the men.

Zander signalled to his men and one of them rose and began, with a young woman of the camp followers, to dance a very stately, but strangely sensuous dance, their bodies making snakelike movements that were very erotic and made Elaine blush. However, she kept her smile in place, wondering where a rough soldier had learned to dance in such a way.

'Ranulf learned to dance from Arab slave girls we liberated from a slaver on the way to the Holy Land,' Zander told her as she turned to him with the question on her lips. 'The girls danced to thank us for their lives and freedom, and the men imitated them; some of the women chose to become camp followers—and these two have somehow perfected their own routine. Did it please you, Elaine? It was meant to amuse.'

'Yes…' She felt her cheeks heat as she gazed into his eyes and her mouth tingled with the need to be kissed. The dance had been oddly arousing, making her aware of feelings deep within her. Her flesh was melting in the heat of his eyes and she wanted to be held, to melt into him and… Her immodest thoughts made her look away. 'It was interesting…'

'Interesting?' Zander sounded amused. 'Yes, I dare say you could call it that.'

Elaine did not dare to look at him. Her body felt as if it were on fire, as if little hot coals were touching her skin, causing her a sweet agony that made her break out in beads of sweat. The dance had been so sensual, so arousing that it had made her long to be in the arms of the man she loved, to be kissed as he had kissed her long ago. What did Zander want of her? Her throat was so tight with longing that she could hardly breathe, but she was afraid to let him see lest he despise her for her immodesty.

'I believe I should retire to my chamber,' she said at last when the silence between them seemed almost unbearable. 'The men grow merry and I think my ladies and I should leave them to their fun.'

'They have half an hour before the drinking stops,' Zander said and now his eyes were cold once more. 'I do not tolerate all-night drinking sessions. My men must be ready to fight if need be at all times—and those who have feasted must relieve those who are on duty.'

Elaine rose and walked away. A faint cheer echoed round the room, but the laughter and jesting went on as she left. Her ladies followed her to her chamber, chattering amongst themselves.

'What did you think of the dancing?' she asked her ladies as they undressed her, bringing her fine silk garments for the night.

'It was immodest,' Marion said disapprovingly, but some of the younger ones giggled and whispered behind their hands.

'Yes, Gelda?' Elaine said. 'Will you not tell us all what you thought?'

Gelda blushed and bowed her head. 'It was sensual, my lady—a dance for lovers. I've seen gypsies dance like that in their firelight. One of the villagers called it erotic—but I did not know the word.'

'And when did you see this dance before?' Marion demanded.

'When they came to our village. They were travelling people from the east, perhaps Egypt. They wore gold rings in their ears and on their fingers—and they danced the dance of love.'

'Yes...' Elaine nodded. 'I have heard of this...but is it not immodest for a man and a woman to dance together thus?'

'Yes...' Gelda hung her head and mumbled something.

'What did you say?'

'It is for lovers...whether they are betrothed or not.'

'Wash your mouth out, woman!' Marion cautioned.

'She speaks only what she has heard,' Elaine said. 'Thank you for telling me. I wondered...'

As her ladies left her to seek her bed alone,

Elaine wondered why Zander had ordered his soldier and the slave girl to dance for her. Had he wanted to see how she would react to something so sensual? Why should he—unless he wanted to evoke a mood…a mood of love and sensuality that would prepare her…

Elaine's cheeks were on fire as she ran to her cold bed and scrambled inside. Such immodest thoughts! Zander was far too honourable a knight to think of such things. She was not yet his wife—might never be. How could he ever think of coming to her bed, if the church had not first blessed them?

Zander stared out into the night from the battlements. His heated thoughts had brought him here, as if with the cold night air he would drive out the hot need and longing that had built inside him in the hall.

Had Elaine realised what her beauty did to him? The scent of her, of her hair, was more intoxicating than any wine, but she seemed unaware of her power.

She'd been but an innocent child when he had left for the Holy Land and he an untried youth. Since then he'd known his share of women, though in his heart he'd remained true to the woman he loved. The rigours of war were such that men sought relief in many things—wine, dance and song were some, but a warm body to cling to in the deep of night when the nightmares came was something they all needed and found in the willing camp followers. He'd known his share, though not as many as he might have had he chosen, for he was popular with the women, especially the slave dancers they'd rescued from cruel masters.

One of the dancers had been very beautiful. Esmerala had taught him to dance as she danced and the hot insistent beat of the drums and pipes had brought him to fever point. Grieved by the death of friends, his heart and body in need of comfort, he had claimed her as his own and she'd given him much pleasure, though when she left to return to her own land, he had forgotten her, for she had meant little to him but the comfort of a soft body. He was not her first lover and knew that she would find another as pleasing to her as him. Zander knew that despite his disfigurement there would always be a woman available to him if he chose to look for comfort. In the dark of night they could not see his face and he could pleasure them enough to make them forget his scars—but Elaine was different.

From Elaine he wanted so much more. The

sensual dancing had aroused his needs. He was haunted by the scent of her, by his need to hold her and touch her, feel her soft skin beneath his as he loved her. Had he escorted her to her chamber that night he could not have held back from her. She belonged to him. She was his and he wanted to claim her—but his pride forbade it. Even if she came to him with softness and talk of love he would doubt her. He would fear the day she realised that she was caught, trapped into marriage with a man who was not the man she'd loved. No, he must resist his needs...he was not worthy of her.

The Zander who had gone away might be there somewhere deep inside him, but that man of ideals and high values had changed, disappeared, replaced by someone who had been killed in battle. A man who was tainted by the death of innocents, though he'd spared those he could—but he'd been there as their blood was spilled, trodden into the sands of the land they called Holy. He had taken the life of a man he'd once called friend, and though in justice he could do no other, it haunted him still.

He'd heard dying men call out to their god as they lay bleeding, heathen and Christian side by side, unanswered by their various gods until someone took pity and drove a sword into their throat to end their pain.

What kind of a god could be so pitiless? Zander asked himself. What kind of men were they who carried the Cross of Jesus and claimed victory in his name? What kind of man was Zander de Bricasse?

The answer could not please him, because he knew that whatever he was he was not worthy of the woman he wanted with such a burning need—a need that made his groins ache and kept him wakeful.

Her chamber was next to his, in so much as it could be reached by a long walkway that did not take him through the hall. It was not particularly convenient, but better than having to climb the stair to her solar via the hall, thus advertising his intentions to any that observed. Her servants had arranged it so because they thought he would be her husband and they would occupy the rooms when they were wed. He thought that one day he would purchase a house with a more comfortable arrangement so that he could simply walk from his chamber to hers…if he wed her.

He was uncertain of what he ought to do. She had made it clear at the start that she expected him to keep his word to her—but would he wrong her by taking what she offered?

Zander had seen her beauty that night as never before, seen the sensual lovely woman she'd become and desired her. As his men sang, drank and danced, he'd known a burning desire to go to her that night and make love to her— but if he did that they *must* marry. He could not dishonour and then leave her.

She would wed him willingly. He knew that, just as he knew it was what he wanted in his heart—but it was not right. She was too pure and lovely, like a goddess or a queen. His touch would sully her. He could only defile her.

He turned away, looking up at the moon, a howl of pain in his heart, though he was silent. How could he in honour go to her when he knew what it must mean for her?

She might think she still loved him now, but what of the years ahead—what if she began to see the blackness of his soul? He had lost his faith while she held hers fast. He no longer loved God, nor did he hate him—he simply did not believe.

Rising to the sound of swords clashing against shields and feet thudding below her in the courtyard, Elaine looked out. She'd heard such sounds all her life, for men-at-arms must train every day to retain their strength and skill. It was a fact of their age that no baron was safe within his castle unless he had strong men to keep out those that would try to steal what he had. England was a lawless land with its King gone to fight the heathen and a prince who cared only for his own pleasure on the throne. The barons made war on each other if they pleased and stole their neighbour's cattle, sheep—and sometimes his wife.

Zander's men trained hard. They fought as if it were for real, knocking their opponent off his feet and forcing a surrender, if they could. Sometimes a man was slightly hurt—a fact of life, though not intended by his brothers-in-arms, but preparation for the real thing. It was a moment or two before she realised that one of the men training was Zander. He was fighting hard, though she could see he was sweating more than was usual and, even as she watched, he stumbled. His opponent stepped back and lowered his sword. Had the fight been for real Zander would probably have died before her eyes.

As she watched in horror, he got back to his feet and began to press forwards, forcing his opponent to fight harder. Elaine feared that he would collapse and could hardly bear to watch, yet she could not draw away. Not until he was exhausted did Zander call time and lean on his sword. His opponent slapped him on the back and praised him and, at last, he smiled and shook his hand.

Elaine stepped back from the window, afraid that he would think she was spying on him. She turned as her ladies entered, bringing her a gown of silk in one of her favourite shades of green.

'No,' she said, shaking her head. 'Not this morning, Hilda. I need a working gown. I mean to begin as my mother would. The house has been too long without a mistress. We must check the stores so that we can begin to prepare for the winter. I would know what linen we have and what preparations are on the shelves of my stillroom—and whether we have stores to feast again this night as we did last.'

'Lord Stornway sent a load of preserves and food, which Lord Zander had ordered for us, lady. The steward says we are well stocked with all we need.'

'Indeed?' Elaine was slightly annoyed to hear it, for it seemed that Zander was taking over her tasks as chatelaine. He was acting as if he

were her lord and yet he had not asked her to
be his wife.

Just precisely what did he think he was
about? What did he want of her? He gave so
much, he must want something in return.

Remembering a look in his eyes the previous night, Elaine thought she knew what Zander
wanted. He felt desire for her, if nothing more.
Had he kept a distance between them because
he thought her still a child?

No man had kissed her lips since he'd left—
or none that she'd allowed, though one or two
youths had tried it in their cups, to their sorrow after she'd kicked them. Yet Elaine was not
innocent. She had understood the meaning of
those gyrations the dancers made, and the sensual music of drums and the lyre had not left
her untouched.

She tossed her head, determined to have her
way. 'I shall start as I mean to go on—summon
my ladies and I shall assign you all duties. I
want to know everything there is in the house:
silver, pewter, pots and chattels. You and I will
make a start with the linen…'

Hearing the woman's sigh of resignation,
Elaine smiled. Her people had grown lax and
must mend their ways, for she intended to be
mistress in her own home.

Chapter Seven

Zander noticed the bustle and stir as he entered the house. He could smell lavender and beeswax and every maid or serf in the house seemed to be busy.

'What is going on here?' he asked of a passing housecarl.

'Lady Elaine has set us all working. She wants an inventory of everything—and those not put to that are either scrubbing or polishing, my lord.'

'Ah, I see.'

A little smile touched his lips. It seemed that Elaine had decided to show her authority and take the reins into her own hands— or perhaps she had been as restless as he had after the previous night. Perhaps her blood had heated watching the dancers, as his had, which was one of the reasons he'd pushed himself so hard in the training yard. He'd slept but fitfully the previous night, for the dancing had aroused such need in him that his mind was filled with pictures of what might have been.

Zander had found it difficult to sleep with Elaine lying in such close proximity. He'd wanted to walk through the door and passage that connected them and claim her for his own, but he'd resisted valiantly. She was a gentle lady and would have been shocked had he taken her from her bed, kissing her awake and then making love to her. Besides, he could not afford to let himself become seduced by her beauty and the softness of her skin.

Once he felt strong enough, he must go in search of their mutual enemy and force Newark to meet him in single combat. It was the only way to settle what was between them, for otherwise many lives could be lost and too much blood spilled.

Going to his chamber, Zander stripped off his clothing and began to wash the sweat and dirt from his body with cold water from a silver ewer. He used a washing cloth and a scented soap to smooth over his skin before applying some of the oil that he'd purchased on his travels. It smelled of musk and ambergris and, if rubbed into the skin, kept his muscles from aching and helped to heal the wounds he'd received when the renegade Saracens had found him burying Tom. He would have died that day, left to bleed out his life alone beneath a burning sun, had not Janvier and his servants found him in time. He dismissed the thoughts, for those pain-filled nights were behind him.

After it had been oiled, his skin gleamed. He eased his shoulder back and forth, feeling the way the stiffness was gradually easing. Zander had learned long ago that only exercise would ease the aching caused by stiffness after a wound healed. If he continued to practise hard, he would soon be back to two-thirds of his old skill, though he was not sure he would ever regain his full fitness or dexterity. Elaine's mixture had certainly made a difference, but the process of healing was slow and tedious to a man in a hurry. The scar on his cheek was still painful sometimes and he wondered if he should submit to Elaine's healing, but some stubbornness within him made him hold back.

Hearing a sound behind him, he turned and saw Elaine staring at him. The slight noise was her indrawn breath as she saw him standing, naked to the waist, a drying cloth slung casually about his lower body.

'Your back…those scars…' she said and then blushed. 'Forgive me…I did not know you were here, my lord. I came to bring these.' She placed a pile of clean linen on the bed and made to withdraw. Zander caught her arm, preventing her from leaving.

'The scars you mention are long healed,' he said, his eyes burning into her. Suddenly, he remembered the way the sensual dancing had made him feel; the need to hold her and kiss her that had been aroused in him the previous night was so strong that he felt it sweep over him, destroying his good intentions to keep a barrier between them. She was here, in his chamber, the scent of her so sweet and enticing that he moved closer, letting it fill his senses and driven by a hunger he could not control. She looked so cool, fresh and lovely, so desirable that he forgot all his good intentions as a surging need took hold. Zander knew that this was wrong; she was too far above him, but he could not control the fire blazing through his body. He wanted her, more than he'd ever wanted any woman, and the need tore at his resolve to remain aloof. Before he knew what he did, he had reached out and brought her close to him, holding her as he bent his head to kiss her on the lips. She gave a little start, but his kiss was soft and after a moment he felt her relax, her body moving closer of its own volition. Zander smiled a little and released her, gazing down at her. 'I have wanted to do that since the first moment we met again. It has been a long time since we kissed, Elaine.'

'Yes, my lord.' She smiled at him and then reached up to touch the livid scar on his face. Even the softness of her fingers hurt him and he flinched. 'Will you not let me try to heal this for you—or allow Janvier to use my poultice?'

'I thought it was healing slowly?'

'Yes, but I can make it feel so much easier, take away the tightness that causes puckering and pain.'

'Then send me the balm and I will apply it myself.'

'As my lord wishes. You shall have it this night,' she murmured and turned to leave. Once again he caught her, this time by the wrist.

'You do not feel revulsion at the sight of my scars?'

'Revulsion? How could I feel anything other than sympathy for your pain and the wish to help you?'

'I have seen other women look at my face and flinch away.'

'Then they are fools, my lord.'

'Or perhaps you are more compassionate than some.'

'Anne Stornway would have healed you had you let her.'

'Yes, she is a remarkable woman.' Zander felt her pull away, but held her still. 'You are more beautiful, Elaine, and younger. Do you wonder that I feel it wrong to take advantage of your promise?'

She stilled then and looked up at him. 'I thought you had forgot it?'

'How could I ever forget you or the vows we made before I left?'

'Then why…?' Her cheeks flushed. 'I have not changed, Zander.'

'You think not?' He smiled, arching his right eyebrow. 'I see many changes. The girl has become a woman, I think. I believed you still as innocent as you were, but I was wrong.'

'Of course I have grown up, but in all else I am unchanged. My love is as strong now as it ever was…' Now her cheeks flamed, but this time she did not run away. Instead, she waited for him to speak. When he did not, he saw her hand tremble. 'Do you wish me to release you from your promise?' she whispered. 'Is there another you love?'

Zander swore beneath his breath. 'No! In the name of heaven, if there be one, I say it is not so. Do not look at me that way, lady. I would not desert you—but if we were wed you might be a widow before the month is out. And if by some good chance I live and Newark dies...' He shook his head. 'My lady, you do not know what I have done...what I have been since we last met. I tell you truly that I am not worthy of you. I could not help myself when I kissed you, for I have thought of it so many times through the years—but I should defile you.'

'Why do you not tell me what haunts you so?' she asked, holding herself proudly.

'I am shamed by things...' He shook his head. 'If I told you, you would hate me. I cannot see hatred in your eyes, for it would kill me.'

'What can you have done that is so terrible?' she asked. Still she looked at him, but he saw the uncertainty and knew the doubts were close. 'I pray you tell me, my lord.'

'I have killed too many, seen too many slaughtered...some were soldiers, but others were innocents, Elaine.' She flinched and her eyes darkened, but she did not turn away. 'A child...I saw a child killed as it clung to its father's knee and he begged for mercy. I should have done something…acted sooner. Too much innocent blood was spilled that day.'

Now he saw a flicker of fear and revulsion in her eyes. He wanted to stop, to leave it there, but was forced to continue by an unstoppable tide from within.

'We were told the renegades lived in the village and we were ordered to clear them out, to spare no one—but we were not told they would be hiding amongst women and children…innocent women and children. Just as we were due to leave the camp, I was called to attend the King and I sent…a friend I trusted with the men who served me. I gave orders that they should take prisoners and bring them back to our camp for trial, but I had forgot how much my friends had suffered. We had seen too many of our number cut down and killed without mercy.

'In their blood lust and zeal my men swept into the village on their destriers. They called for the renegades to come out and fight, but they hid and sent out women, children and old men…' Zander shuddered, for the sight burned in his head and the screams echoed in his ears.

'When my interview with the King was done, I rode to meet them, but the sight that met my eyes…men, women and children dead or dying. My men were lost to reason and continued to kill and burn though I ordered them to stop and the village burned around us. God forgive me that I could not stop them...' he cried. He had forgot that Elaine was there, did not see her as he relived the awful pain and smelled the stench of burning—and the tears trickled down his cheeks unheeded. 'In the end I had to punish them for their senseless destruction...I had to order my friend hanged for disobeying my orders. He looked at me as they took him away and I saw the disbelief and hurt in his eyes... but I had to show them that I would not allow them to behave like savages...it was my duty.'

'Oh, my love, my love...' Zander sensed rather than knew that soft arms held him as his body was racked with shudders. 'You did not know what would happen...it was a terrible mistake, but it was not your fault.'

For a moment he allowed himself the comfort of her arms, but then he pushed her away and turned his back. When he faced her again he had himself under control.

'Now you know the beast that lives inside me, Elaine. You know what I have done. I am forever tainted, shamed by that day. It is for that reason and that alone I say I am not worthy of your love.'

'I do not pretend that I am not shocked and hurt by what you have told me,' she answered calmly, though tears stained her cheeks also. 'Yet I do not hold you to blame for what you did. In war these terrible mistakes can happen. You followed your orders, as a knight must, that is all.'

'You can still bear to look at me?'

'Yes.' Elaine did not smile, but she reached out to touch his hand. 'I do not turn from the scars you bear—inside or out, my lord.'

'And you would still wed me?'

'Yes.' She stood straight and proud, her eyes meeting his. He did not know whether she spoke from pride or love. 'I am ready to wed you.'

Zander knew that he could not refuse her now. If she would take him, knowing him for what he was, then he must honour his promise. To do anything less would be to dishonour both her and himself. He was not worthy of her, but he would strive to be a better man. Perhaps God had not turned His face from him, perhaps there was yet hope that he could be redeemed.

'You speak of a child killed and blame yourself,' she said, 'but I remember the child you saved when we were younger. Have you forgot what happened that day?'

He frowned, not understanding her. 'I am not certain of what you speak, Elaine?'

'I was a child of eleven and you but a youth. Do you not recall the child that played by the river and fell in? You had been practising with your bow when we heard his screams.'

He frowned, for other memories had pushed out the earlier time. 'I remember the river was swollen after much rain and the banks slippery. Yes, I do recall something now.'

'You threw off your boots and jerkin and dived in after him. I think it took all your strength to pull him from that raging torrent to the banks. You could not lift him out, but several others had seen what was happening and they came to haul him out.'

Zander nodded as the memory returned, 'I remember they stood looking at him. He was not breathing at first, but I breathed into his mouth and then turned him on his side and he vomited water.'

'He spluttered and choked, but you saved him, Zander—you saved that boy's life. He would have died had you not gone in after him at some risk to your own life.'

'I did not consider it...'

'You were a hero to the village people that

day. I think such a man would never stand by and see a child killed if he could prevent it.'

'You are determined to see only the good in me,' he said, a faint smile on his lips.

'Whatever happened that day in the Holy Land—whatever you were forced to do in the name of justice—you are still the man I loved. I could never think evil of you, Zander.'

He looked at her in silence for a moment. She had not seen what he'd seen. If she had witnessed the carnage, smelled the stink of death and blood, she would not so easily dismiss his guilt, but he found that he did not have the strength to deny her. He wanted her more than his life and if she would have him, he would take the gift she offered...though one day he might see that shining belief turn to horror.

'Then we shall marry,' he said. 'Yet I would ask you to wait until I have dealt with Newark. I must give all the strength and purpose I have to becoming the warrior I once was—and to the challenge I must issue to our mutual enemy. If I allowed myself to be distracted...'

'Of course.' Elaine almost smiled, but not quite. 'It will give us both time to become adjusted to our...thoughts.'

She turned and walked from the chamber, leaving behind the scent of her hair and her skin to haunt him. For a moment he stood unmoving, then he dropped his loincloth and walked to the bed, picking up a tunic and pulling it over his head. Even here the scent of her clung, making him acutely aware of a need that had been growing embarrassingly beneath his loincloth. Despite everything that had passed between them, Zander had been conscious of his burning desire to have her naked in his bed.

So, she would be his wife, even knowing it all—but had she spoken out of pride or impulse? Would she begin to regret once she had time to think and would she feel revulsion when the realisation of what he'd done began to sink in?

Elaine was still shaking when she closed the door of her chamber and leaned against it. She did not know how she'd managed to conceal her trembling from him. What he'd told her was so terrible that it brought vivid pictures to her mind, making it whirl in horror. She could almost hear the screams Zander must hear in his dreams and smell the awful stink of blood.

How could he bear such torture? How could he live while such a sin lay on his soul and not seek God's forgiveness? Only then would he find peace again. He needed the cleansing of the Lord's mercy, but he refused to seek it and claimed there was no true god.

Yet in her heart she carried the picture of a young man who thought nothing of his own safety when a small boy was in danger of drowning. It was true that he had seen and done things that had changed him, but surely deep down inside he was the same man?

That man would never allow a child to be slaughtered intentionally. Whatever had happened that terrible day, he had not been to blame. She could see that he felt a terrible guilt because he had caused his friend to be punished for allowing the slaughter of innocents against his orders—but there were times when a man had no choice but to uphold justice.

His sin could be forgiven. God would give him peace—but could he ever forgive himself?

Elaine felt her doubts ease. She wanted to return and tell him she understood…to tell him that she truly loved him…but she held back.

Zander would not want her to cling to him. He had to be strong. He needed to regain all his strength to fight their mutual enemy—but then he would return to her and claim her as his bride.

* * *

They held a feast for the village people that night. Several more rows of trestle tables filled the hall so that everyone might sit and eat. The servants took it in turns to serve the tables and then took their places to join in the celebrations. Halfway through the evening, the guards on the stout battlements were changed and the men came in from the cold to eat their fill and enjoy their ease.

Once again there was music from the fiddler and dancing, but this time it was the country reels and carols that Elaine knew and understood. She joined in some of the dances, laughing to see her people so happy and looking to Zander for approval. He nodded and smiled, but then turned away to talk to Sir Robert.

Elaine felt a foolish prick of pain. She had hoped that now they had spoken so frankly he would smile more and look at her with love, but still she saw only the proud cold face he showed to the world. He wanted her and he had told her they would be married, but where was the love and tenderness that had meant so much to her?

Why must he shut her out? Did he need the barrier that he had built about himself to remain strong? If she tried to break it down, would she weaken him? She turned away, joining in the fun of the dance once more. She would not let herself be hurt. Elaine would hold fast to her love, even if she saw no sign of it being returned.

Alone in her bed that night she had wept a little, but in the morning her tears were gone. Once again she rose filled with zeal. There were tasks that needed to be done to make the house a home, but it was mostly needlework and genteel occupations. She dressed in a gown of blue wool and bound her waist with a wide belt of woven silver that ended in tassels of the same thread bound with glass beads. The counting of linen had resulted in the discovery of torn sheets and hangings, some of which ought to be discarded while others could be repaired.

Setting her ladies to work on some of the linen, Elaine chose a hanging that needed some repair before it could be used again. She selected her silks, sorting the colours into shades of light and dark, and then began the work.

It was almost half an hour later when her steward came to announce the arrival of a guest.

'Lord Stornway, Marshal to the King, my lady.'

'Lord Stornway is here now?' Elaine laid her

needlework to one side and rose to her feet. 'Where is Lord Zander?'

'He rode out with some of his men not thirty minutes since, lady.'

'Then I must welcome the King's Marshal in his stead,' Elaine said. She glanced at her ladies. 'You have worked long enough. Tidy these things away and then you may seek some refreshment yourselves.' To the steward she said, 'Bring wine and comfits to us in the hall, Elgin.'

'Yes, my lady.'

Elaine went down the twisting stone steps that led to the hall below her solar. She had half expected Lady Anne would have accompanied her brother, but Philip was alone. He turned as she came up to him, a smile of welcome on his lips.

'I have not called at an inconvenient moment?'

'No, my lord—how could you?' She held out her hands to him with a smile. 'You know that you must always be welcome here. Zander sent you word of what took place here?'

'Yes. I am glad that my standard was instrumental in the surrender of your manor with little or no bloodshed.'

'I was thankful for it. Had we been forced to

hold them to siege, my people might have suffered. That would have caused me some distress.'

'I should never wish to see you in distress, lady.' He had her hands in his and leaned forwards to lightly touch his lips to her cheek. 'I admire you very much, Elaine.'

Elaine did not flinch away, though her cheeks burned. The look in his eyes was almost intimate and she wondered if she had been wise to greet him alone. He was Zander's friend, but he was also a man—an unmarried man. She liked him and was grateful for his kindness, but the look he gave her was too warm for friendship.

She moved away from him towards the fire and pulled the rope hanging there, which set a bell pealing. Servants appeared with wine and trays of almond comfits and pastries. They set their trays on trestles and withdrew, but the moment of awkwardness had passed. Lord Stornway had remembered that she was the chatelaine of her own manor—and promised to his friend.

'How do you settle here, Lady Elaine? Is there aught you need that we might supply?'

'We have most of what we need—I have investigated our stores. We shall need more preserves for the winter, but my ladies and I will supply that lack—though we must send to Shrewsbury for supplies of sugar. I dare say it will be costly, more than six silver pennies a cone, but I prefer its use to honey. I have not yet enquired how the hives do here. In my mother's time they produced enough honey for all our needs, but I am not sure how they do now.'

'Anne's hives thrive. If you need fresh blood in yours, I am certain she could find you a healthy queen. It is the queen that makes or breaks the hive, do you not agree?'

'Yes, I am sure of it,' Elaine said. 'I think Lady Anne keeps your house well, my lord.'

'She is an excellent housekeeper and would make a wonderful wife, but she is too particular and will not settle for any knight I have brought before her, though...' Philip looked thoughtful. 'Just this morning she told me she might one day decide to seek her own life and that I should think of taking a wife.'

Elaine did not dare to meet his eyes. Was he testing her? Surely Zander had made her position clear? He must know that she was promised to his friend?

Her breathing was shallow, for she did not know how to answer him. Even as she framed the words in her mind, Zander strode into the hall and came towards them.

'Did you send word of your coming?' he asked. 'I was not told or I should have been here to greet you. Forgive me for my discourtesy, Philip.'

'Your lady hath made me welcome,' Philip said and smiled at her in a way she found too intimate. 'I rode this way and decided to call by chance. Is all well here?'

'Yes,' Zander said. 'I had meant to send word, but we were short of meat and I went hunting this morning. We were lucky and took a boar and a hind within a short distance of the house and so returned with our supper. Will you stay and dine with us? I had intended to invite you and Lady Anne to share my betrothal feast two days hence.'

'So it is settled, then?'

Elaine saw a shadow of disappointment on the lord's face. He'd known they were to marry, but had hoped her plans might change—had he sensed the distance between her and Zander while they stayed at Stornway?

There was no sign of his disappointment as he smiled at Elaine. 'Anne and I will be delighted to join you for your feast, but, no, I shall not stay now as I am expected home and would not cause my sister anxiety. I came only to enquire if there was anything you needed.'

'Nothing—unless you have news of Newark?'

'I have heard nothing of him at all,' Philip said. 'I am told his Majesty may soon be released. The ransom has been paid—or it was arranged so, though as yet no further news has come.'

'Richard will need all his knights about him when he returns to England,' Zander said. 'I think Prince John would prevent it if he could.'

'Hush, you speak treason, my friend,' Philip said. 'It is true, but we must tread carefully. John is ruler here until Richard sets foot on English soil.'

'Come, let me see you out,' Zander said and the two men walked to the door. 'You will let me know if you hear anything—of Newark or his Majesty's return…'

Elaine stood stiff and stunned as they walked away. Zander had hardly glanced at her and yet he'd invited Lord Stornway and Lady Anne to join them at their betrothal feast. He had said nothing of the feast or a betrothal to her privately and his lack of courtesy made her angry. How dare he treat her in so casual a fashion? Their marriage was something she would expect to discuss, but he treated it as if it were merely a matter of business.

True, she had told him that she would wed him and that her love held fast, but he'd made no attempt to court or consult her and she was hurt that he should behave in such a high-handed way.

Did he imagine that she had no feelings?

Leaving the hall, she held her head high, but inside she was seething. The least he might have done was to tell her of his plans.

Chapter Eight

'Lord Zander asks why you do not come to table, my lady,' Marion said, looking puzzled. 'Are you ill? Would you have me serve you here in your chamber?'

'I am not hungry,' Elaine said. 'Tell my lord that I have been waiting to hear from him what he requires of me.'

'Surely—' Marion was silenced by a flash of Elaine's eyes and went away without another word.

Elaine stood at her slitted window and stared out at a sky that was bright with stars. She had begun to count them when she heard the step she had been waiting for, yet still she did not turn.

'Why do you not come to supper, Elaine?'

'I was not sure what you required of me,' she answered, but did not turn.

'What nonsense is this?' he asked gruffly and took her shoulders, swinging her round to face him. 'You are mistress here—you do not need me to tell you what is required of you. The men are hungry and waiting for their supper—but unless you send to say you will not dine with us they must wait.'

Elaine gazed up at him. 'I thought you made the decisions concerning such things,' she said defiantly. 'You invited Lord Stornway to our betrothal feast.'

'Good grief, Elaine—is that what this is all about?' Zander frowned at her. 'You said you were prepared to wed me so I thought we would hold a betrothal feast before I left.'

Her heart caught instantly, her irritation at his high-handed behaviour dissolving in sudden fear for him. 'You are leaving soon?'

'In a few days, soon after the feast. We are trying to locate Newark.'

'But you are not yet strong enough,' she cried, forgetting her annoyance. 'If you challenge him too soon, he will destroy you.'

'I cannot hide here for ever. I am growing stronger every day. Besides, the challenge must be lodged in the proper manner—and if I do not issue it before Richard returns it may be too late. He will forbid his knights to quarrel amongst themselves.'

'Is that why you announced our betrothal without consulting me first?'

'Yes, in part…' Zander frowned. 'I saw the way Philip Stornway looked at you. I thought I could not have made myself clear to him, so I asked Philip and Anne to our betrothal feast.' His gaze narrowed, becoming intent on her face. 'Did I do wrong—have you changed your mind? I know that Philip was struck by your beauty when we stayed at his home. I think he hoped he had misunderstood my intentions.'

Elaine nodded. 'Yes, he did look at me… but I made it clear…' Her cheeks flamed. 'You could not think that I would change my mind?'

'Why not? He bears no scars, physical or mental. He is a gentler, more fitting knight. I could not blame you if you preferred to wed him, Elaine.'

'Do you think me so shallow?' Her throat caught with tears.

'Then why will you not come to table?' His mouth thinned. 'I had not thought you so sulky, Elaine.'

'I am not sulking.'

'Are you not?' Zander laughed softly. 'You

want proof of your worth to me?' He moved closer, drawing her in with one hand placed in the middle of her back. Lowering his head, he began to kiss her, softly at first, but then with an increasing passion. His tongue flicked at her lips and she parted them, allowing him entry. The sensation of their tongues touching and meeting was pleasant and aroused stirrings of a strange but exciting feeling in the pit of her stomach. Heat pooled inside her and she moved closer to him, wanting something more. 'Enough, Elaine, or our poor men will not eat this night. It is long since I have lain with a woman and my respect for your modesty may not withstand the need you arouse in me. Come now, take my hand and we shall go down.'

Torn between pique at his manner, which seemed to vacillate between that of a lover and a stern guardian, she refused his hand but turned and preceded him down the stairs to the hall below. She could hear the men murmuring amongst themselves and was suddenly shamed. These men worked and trained hard and they were hungry. She must find another way to bring Zander to his senses in future.

She took her seat at the high board and nodded at the servants. Food was brought hurriedly forwards—the first dish, soup, which had been cooling in the pot. Elaine allowed the house-carl to serve her, waving aside the services of a taster to save time. Only when she had been served would the men have their food.

She was about to taste her soup when she noticed something odd in the servant's manner as he began to ladle the soup into Zander's bowl. She made a signal to her steward, who hurried to her side.

'That man is new,' she said. 'Tell him to taste the soup he would serve my lord.'

'My lady?' Elgin looked puzzled. 'He is the nephew of—'

'Tell him to taste it himself.'

'Do as your lady bids you,' Zander said, reaching out to bar the servant's way as he tried to move away. 'Drink it, damn you.'

'No...' the servant's eyes rolled in fear. 'You can't make me...' He tried to make a bolt for it, but was brought down by one of the knights further down the table. 'He made me do it.'

'Drink...drink...drink...' the men demanded that the traitor drink the soup, which was so obviously poisoned.

'No,' Zander said. 'Take him away and detain him. He shall be questioned later.' He summoned another servant. 'Take this soup away and bring something else. No one will drink the soup lest it has been contaminated.'

A flurry of servants hurried to take away the contaminated soup and a new dish was served, which the cook volunteered to taste himself. As nothing untoward occurred, the mess of rabbit and onions was distributed to the hungry men.

Zander took his place beside Elaine and signalled for the roast meat to be served. 'What made you suspect him?'

Elaine shook her head. 'It was just a look in his eyes as he passed his hand across your dish. I do not think the poison was intended for any but you, Zander. He was new at table and was sweating badly.'

'Then I thank you for my life, Elaine. Had you not been so vigilant he might have succeeded in his aim.'

'Why would anyone try to poison you?' Elaine asked, feeling shocked and puzzled. 'I thought you in danger if you fought Newark in single combat—but here in this house...' She was angered that any of their servants should behave so ill.

'The servant will be questioned,' Zander promised and laughed softly. 'It seems I have an enemy—mayhap one I did not reckon with.'

Elaine shivered as a cool breeze touched her. Suddenly, her behaviour earlier seemed childish.

'Forgive me for making you come to ask me.'

'I think your little scheme may have worked in our favour. The delay made our would-be assassin nervous and that in turn caused him to be careless. Had all been as usual, you might not have noticed anything amiss.'

'Yet I am sorry.'

Zander touched her hand. 'You felt I was arrogant and mayhap I was. I am used to command, Elaine. Once I knew how to smile and court the girl I loved, but now...' He shook his head. 'I shall try to remember that you are a lady and not a soldier waiting to do my bidding.'

Elaine saw the wicked light in his eyes and laughed. The tension had evaporated between them and she knew he was teasing her.

'You mock me, sir. I shall have to think of a suitable punishment for you.'

'And I for you,' Zander murmured huskily, leaning close so that only she could hear. 'Methinks my lady could do with a spanking.'

'You would not dare...' She sent daggers of fire at him with her eyes, but saw him smile all the more. 'Or perhaps you would.'

'Oh, you can be sure of it,' he promised in such a way that tremors ran up and down her spine and she thought that what he promised was perhaps less a punishment than a pleasure.

* * *

'You tread on dangerous ground, my lord. I am no milk-and-water maiden.'

'I never thought you were.'

Zander stood up and clapped his hands. 'Music and dancing to delight my lady. Forget the foolishness earlier. None was harmed save the knave who would have poisoned me. Enjoy yourselves, for in a few days we leave to seek my true enemy—but not before we have celebrated the betrothal of your lord and lady in two nights hence.'

Cheers greeted his announcement. Men got up and began to dance a jig as a fiddler played and a minstrel sang. Wine and ale was flowing freely, though Elaine noticed that Zander drank sparingly, as she did.

When the night was well advanced and the men were a little rowdy, she took her leave. Zander walked her to the bottom stair that led to her solar and kissed her hand before returning to his men.

Had Elaine looked back she would have seen that Zander left the hall almost immediately with half a dozen of his men, but she was smiling and happy as she went to her room and did not notice as the sound of men's voices became muted and then died away.

* * *

'Why did you try to poison your lord?' Elgin demanded. The knave had been bound and was on his knees, his head falling forwards when Zander walked in. A bucket of water was thrown over him, making him lift his head. 'Speak or you will suffer a beating and worse.'

'No, stay your hand,' Zander said. 'I did not order torture.'

'This man must speak. He tried to murder you.'

'We know what he did, but not why.' Zander approached the man. He took a ladle, filled it with water and offered it to the offender. 'Drink. It is not poisoned. You will not be tortured. I simply want the truth. Who paid you to murder me—and why?'

The man hesitated, then drank the water. 'I was not paid, lord,' he said and looked up proudly. 'When the men came to our village they took my wife and son hostage. I was told to poison you and they would be spared.'

'You knew you would die for it?'

'Yes, lord.'

'So you were willing to die for your family?'

'Yes, lord.'

'Who sent the men to take your wife and child hostage?'

'I do not know for sure, lord—but they spoke of the earl.'

'Newark,' Sir Robert said grimly. 'I never thought him a coward—to send a churl to do his work.'

'Nor I…' Zander frowned down at their prisoner. 'You can tell me nothing further?'

'No, lord.'

'Very well, let him go. You are free to leave, sirrah, and you may return to your home and farm your strip without hindrance, but if you enter the castle again, you will be arrested on sight and next time I shall not be so lenient.'

'You will let him go free?' His men stared in amazement, for the usual punishment for such an offence was death and his forbearance might be seen as weakness.

'He is but a pawn in a wider game,' Zander said. 'Send him on his way.' He turned to leave, but the man caught at his robe. Zander turned. 'Yes?'

'My wife and child? He will kill them.'

'I doubt it,' Zander said. 'When word gets out that I set you free, even though you tried to kill me, the earl will see that holding your family hostage does no good. I dare say your wife and son will be returned to you. Had you come to me for help rather than try to kill me I would have done what I could for you. Give me the name of the man who sent you and I will try to have your family released.'

'He would kill them rather than release them to you,' the man said. 'You give me my life, but it has little use to me without my wife and my son.'

'If you will not confide in me, I cannot help you,' Zander said.

He turned and walked from the chamber, leaving the men to stare at their prisoner uneasily, for they did not understand their lord's leniency in sparing his life.

'We should teach the scum a lesson,' one of them said.

'No,' Sir Robert said. 'Follow my lord's orders. He has his reasons. Throw this piece of filth from the manor. If he crosses our bounds again, kill him.'

'I did not wish harm to Lord Zander, but my wife and son are lost to me…' The man wept.

'Thank God for your life,' the steward said. 'Most lords would have you hung, drawn and quartered for what you did. Lord Zander has shown mercy. Go now before he changes his mind.'

The man was dragged from the castle weep-

ing and his cries could be heard for some time,
until he was beyond the moat.

Sir Robert followed Zander from the chamber and caught up with him before he entered
the hall.

'Why did you not have him punished? He
would have seen you die horribly.'

'I have an enemy I do not know,' Zander said.
'If I killed the knave, my enemy would think he
was safe, but since I spared him my enemy must
wonder if the rogue confessed his name. In his
anxiety he may become careless. I would know
who my enemy is, sir. And I would have my
lady's people know that I shall treat them fair.'

It was not all his reason in showing mercy.
The man's plight had touched him, for he had
been willing to give his own life to save his
family and was therefore more to be pitied than
reviled. Zander knew that by being so lenient
with a knave who had tried to kill him, some
might think him weak, but he had had enough
of death and slaughter. Zander could not return
his family to him, but he had given him his
freedom. The rest was in God's hands.

Sir Robert inclined his head, but looked
thoughtful. 'Surely it must be Newark? Who
else would want you dead?'

'I do not know and yet I have thought there must be someone in the shadows for a while, even in the Holy Land. When I went to bury Tom only a few men knew where I was going. The assassins that struck me down may have come upon me by chance, but I have always wondered if someone wanted me dead—if those Saracens were sent to murder me.'

'Yet Newark is your enemy. You believe him guilty of your father's murder—why look elsewhere?'

'Mayhap you are right,' Zander said, 'but Newark is more likely to try a frontal attack to take the manor than poison. Somehow this seems more personal—as though this man wants me dead, but does not wish to harm anyone else. And for some reason he would keep his identity secret.'

'Yes...' Sir Robert frowned. 'I can hardly believe any of your uncle's men would try to murder you.'

'No, not my uncle's men, though I suppose he stands to inherit my wealth since I have no son or yet a wife. Even so, I do not think it.'

'What do you intend to do about it? Someone should guard your back.'

'Someone does guard my back at all times,'

Zander said, a slight smile on his lips as he looked at the great grey shadow that followed at his heels. 'Both Vulcan and Janvier are always in the shadows waiting. I think that is why poison was chosen as the weapon. Anyone who tried to plant a knife in my back would be stopped in his tracks before he could get near. Poison is a deadly weapon, but silent and unnoticed—unless one has a quick-eyed wife.' He smiled. 'My lady saved my life, Sir Robert. I must reward her. Please send word to Lord Stornway that I would have the trunks I stored with him sent on to me here.'

'Shall I send the men Lord Stornway sent as escort back to him, my lord?'

'Yes, I think we cannot keep them here any longer. I have recruited men from the surrounding villages. They are raw and untried, but I trust them.'

'Surely you trust Lord Stornway's men?'

'Yes, of course. Philip has always been my friend,' Zander said. 'He is above suspicion. It was he who told me what Newark had done to my father. When I had nothing left, he gave me money to buy the sword and armour I needed to follow the Cross.'

'As I thought. So where do we look for your enemy?'

'We do not waste our time in searching for him. He will come to us because he will be curious as to why I let his assassin live.'

Sir Robert nodded and smiled. 'I knew you had a good reason for letting the rogue live. The men were for slitting his throat, but I told them to obey your orders. It will be interesting to see what now transpires, my lord.'

Zander's eyes narrowed to slits of ice. 'Newark I can deal with, but I can't fight an enemy who comes in guise of friendship, for it could be anyone.'

'You must be vigilant, my lord.'

'I have learned to live that way. I dare say I made enemies in the Holy Land when I protected innocent Muslims from my fellow knights.'

'I heard that at one time the King summoned you to explain your actions?'

'Richard thought the sun had turned my brain, until I told him that some of his knights were killing indiscriminately for no reason other than the colour of a man's skin. Some of the men and women they murdered were Jews, not Saracens, and some of those they killed were converted Christians, but because they looked like their Muslim brothers they met the same fate.'

Sir Robert nodded. 'I have heard of men killing indiscriminately in their blood lust, but to kill simply for…' He shook his head and made the sign of the cross over his breast.

'Simply because they could,' Zander said. 'Richard decreed that I must meet the knight I accused of being their leader in single combat to prove who was right since both accused the other. I won and, though I would have spared his life, Richard commanded that I kill him. His name was Jonquil—Sir Jonquil of Knaresborough.'

'Perhaps this Jonquil had friends who seek revenge?'

'Yes, perhaps—though I won by fair combat.'

'That might not appease someone who felt that you should have spared him.'

'I had no choice but to obey the king.'

'As you say.' Sir Robert inclined his head. 'I shall bid you goodnight, my lord. Someone will guard your door this night.'

'It is not necessary,' Zander said and smiled. 'I am always well protected.'

He turned and walked up the twisted stair to his chamber, which was in the opposite tower to Elaine's solar, though he could enter her chamber without returning to the hall. As he entered the room a dark shadow came towards him.

'Has the traitor confessed the name of his enemy, lord?'

'No, Janvier. He says the men that took his family came from the earl but that is not proof.'

'There is more than one earl, lord.'

'Yes, exactly.' Zander smiled. 'All we can do is wait until he grows frustrated enough to strike at me himself.'

'Poison is more often a woman's weapon, but I would swear all Lady Elaine's people are true to her. We must simply watch and wait—and be ready when the attack comes,' Janvier said. 'Sleep well, my lord. None shall strike you while we guard you.'

Janvier touched the head of the great dog that had followed from the dark shadows of the hall below.

'I know I am safe with you and Vulcan to keep me so.'

'If I slept and neglected my duty, Vulcan would not,' Janvier said and smiled. 'He well remembers the hand that fed him when you found him and he was near to starving.'

'Yes, at least there are two that love me.'

'And your lady. Do not discount her, lord. Her quick eye saved you this night.'

'Yes.' A smile touched Zander's lips as he threw off his outer robe and sought his bed. 'Had she not been observant, they would have buried me this night.'

Elaine lay restless after she had dismissed her ladies. Who wanted Zander dead so badly that he would stoop to poison? It was a coward's way to send a knave to do a man's work.

A little shudder went through her—had she not seen the sheen of sweat beading on the servant's brow and wondered at it, Zander would have eaten the tainted food. The tiniest drop of some poisons was enough to cause almost instant and violent death and she would not have had time to discover the antidote.

She felt cold all over. Who desired Zander's death and why? Was it so that he could take possession of all that Zander owned? Did this unknown person want her and her inheritance? Or was there some other reason…perhaps revenge?

Elaine knew that somewhere the Earl of Newark was plotting his revenge for being cheated—as he would see it—of Elaine's hand in marriage and her fortune. He'd taken Howarth by force, but if the king returned and decreed it, he could be made to give it back—and if Elaine were wed to Zander he would lose all he'd hoped to gain.

He had reason enough to murder Zander, but would he choose poison? She could not be certain.

For a long time she tossed and turned on her pillow, seeking some elusive fact, something that would solve the puzzle. At last her eyelids grew heavy and she slept.

In the morning Elaine rose feeling drained and listless, but when she had washed the sleep from her eyes and eaten a breakfast of bread, honey and milk, which she preferred to the watered ale the knights drank in the mornings, she was feeling much better. She went down to the hall and enquired for Zander. She was told that he and a handful of his knights had gone to Zander's own lands, which lay some ten leagues to the west. It meant that he would be gone for most of the day and she felt at a loss, knowing that she would miss the sound of his voice in the house.

How much worse would it be when he went in search of Newark? Supposing he were killed and did not return? She felt cold all over and, try as she might, could not settle to her sewing.

It was a bright but cool day. Elaine would have liked to go foraging for herbs, roots and berries to make cures, but she'd given her word that until the quarrel with Newark was settled she would not leave the manor grounds.

It was past noon when Marion came to her and told her that she had a visitor. 'Lady Anne is downstairs, mistress. Will you come to her or shall I bring her here?'

'I shall come down,' Elaine said, feeling pleased. She was glad of a visitor and had liked the King's Marshal's sister when they first met, though there had been an odd look in her eyes once or twice that made her wonder what lay behind the smiling face. 'I wonder what made her decide to visit.'

Anne was waiting in the hall downstairs when Elaine joined her. She turned, looking serious, and held out her hands.

'Lady Elaine, my brother bid me come to see you. He would have come himself, but had urgent business elsewhere. What is this we hear—an attempt to murder Lord Zander with poisoned soup?'

'Yes, there was such an attempt last night,'

Elaine confirmed. 'I...was delayed in coming to table and the wait had disturbed the knave. He was shaking and sweating when he served me and then I saw him pass a hand over my lord's bowl. When challenged he refused to taste the soup and later confessed that he was forced to do it because the earl had taken his wife and child prisoner.'

'Is there no infamy to which Newark will not sink?' Lady Anne cried, looking shocked. Her cheeks were pale and her eyes wide with horror. 'Thank God that you were vigilant, Elaine. My brother was concerned when he heard the rumour. Newark should hang for this.'

'Zander is determined to meet him in hand-to-hand combat,' Elaine said. 'He will issue the challenge soon, because once King Richard returns to England he may call a halt to all feuding and force sworn enemies to put aside their quarrel.'

'Yes, his Majesty would do that,' Anne agreed, an odd look in her eyes. 'Yet sometimes he does allow a quarrel to be settled by combat.'

'My lord brought forwards our betrothal because he wished to make me safe before he challenged Newark. Once our vows are exchanged 'tis almost as sacred as the wedding and must prevent others from trying to snatch me.'

'Perhaps…' Anne looked at her from narrowed eyes. 'Is your heart given to Lord Zander? I had thought that perhaps you were unsure of your feelings?'

'I was for a short time, but now I am certain,' Elaine told her. 'Now I know that he is the same man I loved before he left for the crusades. He has suffered much and is changed both physically and mentally, but I understand him now.'

'In war many terrible things are done,' Anne said. 'You should not judge him because of what was done when the bloodlust was on him. I am sure he never meant to kill women and children.'

'He and his men were deceived. They believed the village to be inhabited by renegades, but the rogues sent out innocent women and children and Zander could not prevent what happened.'

'No, I dare say he could not,' Anne said, her eyes not quite meeting Elaine's. 'I did not wish to put doubt in your mind.'

'I might have doubted, but he has told me it all,' she said and smiled.

'Indeed?' Anne inclined her head. 'Then I

shall not concern myself for your happiness. If you are content with what you know, I shall say no more.'

Elaine frowned, for she did not quite understand the other woman's manner. Anne seemed to say one thing and mean another. Was she hiding something? Was there something Elaine still did not know?

'I must return to the castle, for my brother will be anxious if I am not there when he comes back from his business.'

'It was good of you both to concern yourself for me.'

Anne moved towards her, taking her hand. 'You must know that my brother is devoted to you, Lady Elaine. If ever you should have cause to doubt…or need of our help, you have only to send word.' Her manner was intent, almost insistent, and something in Elaine drew back; it was almost as if the lady were trying to warn her of something…to plant a seed of unease in her mind.

'Yes, thank you. I am glad to have such good friends so close at hand.'

'I shall never marry now,' Anne said suddenly, surprising Elaine by the change of subject. 'I had hopes once, but they died long since... I hope that you fare better than I.'

She smiled at Elaine and then walked from the hall, leaving Elaine to stare after her and wonder.

Why had Anne come all this way to enquire after Zander's health and then seem to imply...? Elaine shook her head. She was puzzled for she did not quite know what the lady Anne had been hinting at. Something in her manner warned Elaine that things were not just as they seemed.

Perhaps she had merely appeared to imply more than she meant, because she was concerned for Elaine? It must be so, for she could not have come to make mischief.

Elaine frowned, remembering Anne's manner at her home, which had seemed more natural and friendly. She'd seemed to like Zander very well, then...had something occurred to change her opinion? Elaine felt that the lady had been hiding something or pretending to an emotion she did not feel.

Or was there another reason why she'd seemed to be warning Elaine? Did she perhaps want Zander for herself?

No, she was wrong to doubt her friend. The

slight hesitation in Anne's voice could mean nothing. Elaine had imagined it…

She returned to her solar determined to put her uncertainty from her mind and settle to her work.

Chapter Nine

Zander looked about him and felt the heaviness of despair seep over him as he saw what remained of his father's hall. The stone keep still stood despite the marks of fire, which had robbed it of its wooden roof. The wooden hall was gone completely and the peasants had carried away much of the stone that had formed the outer walls of the compound, to be used for their own cottages.

Some of the land was still farmed and in good heart and Zander would seek payment of his tithes from the tenants when he was ready, but all that had been parkland or part of the manor gardens was overgrown and neglected.

His uncle had warned him what he would find, but still it hurt him to see the wanton destruction of his old home. He frowned, because everything would have to be pulled down and built anew, which meant it might be years before he could bring his wife here. It seemed that they would have to live at Elaine's house until he could find something decent to house her. Mayhap he could find a sweet manor nearby that he could purchase while he restored his father's lands to their former prosperity.

'Is this all Newark's work?' Sir Robert asked him as they surveyed the destruction. 'Or merely the neglect of time?'

'I dare say it may be some of each,' Zander replied. 'What Newark hoped to gain by destroying the house I know not. My father's death was not enough, it seems.'

'Or someone else hates you...' Sir Robert frowned. 'The neglect of years is one thing—but the fire is more recent. I spoke to a yeoman farmer a moment ago and he said the hall still stood until just a few months ago, when a fire was set. He says the people would have tried to fight it, but your steward died of a fever two years ago and they thought you had abandoned both the hall and them, so none tried to put it out.'

'I suppose I did abandon them when I took the Cross—yet my steward had orders to do

what he could for them. I demanded no tithes
from them, which, if they worked their strips
diligently, should have meant they had sufficient for their needs—and God knows, I had
nothing left to give them. Philip told me that
he would protect the village in times of trouble; they had only to send word,' Zander said
and frowned, because as soon as he had begun
to amass wealth he had sent a chest of silver to
Lord Stornway, which should have been passed
on to his steward for the upkeep of the estate
and to provide work for his people. 'Mayhap
the building was struck by lightning. That will
often fire an empty shell.'

'What will you do now?'

'I must look for a new home for myself and
my bride. We have her dower lands, but they
are not enough to support us. I shall appoint a
new steward and set work in hand here, which
will bring prosperity to those that have suffered, but I must also purchase more land and
a stout manor house.'

'The Castle at Howarth belongs to your lady.'

'And shall be restored to her when I can force
Newark to give it up. No matter how many
manors my lady might own, I would have my
own. The gold I won and traded for is stored

with trusted goldsmiths. I shall find something that will suit.'

'Until then?'

'We must leave my lady at her manor, but I shall have it reinforced and hire more men to protect her when I leave.'

'It is not the easiest manor to protect.'

'She will be safe enough while the King's Marshal's standard flies over her towers.' Zander looked once more to the blackened ruins of the keep. He had an enemy closer to home than he had thought. A new suspicion was gathering in his mind, one that he did not care to examine.

Elaine went to greet her lord with a smile when he returned. She saw at once that he was disturbed and decided not to mention Anne's visit or her own silly doubts.

'Something troubles you, my lord?'

'My uncle warned me I should find nothing but destruction at my father's lands and I fear he was right. It will take two or three years before the house is rebuilt and the land in good heart.'

'We can live here, my lord. My mother's land was always productive and sweet. I know you must want to restore your father's manor, but there is no hurry.'

'We can live here for a part of the year,' Zander agreed. 'But you know we must move from manor to manor if we are to support a large household. It is always the way and gives the house time to be cleansed and sweetened again, and the land and husbandry a chance to recover.'

Elaine nodded. It was the custom of the nobles and barons to move their large households from one manor to the other, otherwise the middens would overflow and the land could not support them.

'Do not frown so, my lady,' he said. 'I shall find us another manor and my father's house will be rebuilt. I have already given orders for the lands to be put into use again and the house will be started when I have the leisure for it.'

Elaine nodded. She would be content to stay on her dower lands, but Zander's following was too large to make that viable.

'Some carts came from the King's Marshal this afternoon,' she said. 'I ordered that the locked chests were to be carried to your chambers, my lord. Some of the carts carried trunks of armour and chattels and these remain loaded until you are ready to deal with them.'

'You did well, Elaine. I shall need to take the armour with me when I go and so it is as well on the carts.'

She bit her lip, because the day when he

would leave was growing closer and she did not want him to leave her.

'I have been thinking…' She placed a tentative hand on his arm.

Zander arched his brow. 'There is something you wish to ask of me?'

'If we are to be betrothed tomorrow, would it not…would it not be better to marry? I shall be alone here and at the mercy of those who would snatch me or my lands. If I was your wife, it would not happen, for my lands would become yours and I would no longer be a prize worth the taking.'

Zander's gaze narrowed, surprised and yet thoughtful. 'What has brought this on, Elaine?'

'I do not know,' she confessed. 'Perhaps it was what happened last night. I feel that it would be best to show everyone that the deed was done. A betrothal is sacred, but it can be broken. If I am your wife, then while you live my lands are yours.'

'You believe that the motive for the attempt on my life was to secure your hand and dower lands?'

'Perhaps. I am not sure…' She frowned. 'Once we are wed you can claim the castle in my name—and all the manors that belong with it.'

'Mayhap you are right.' Zander looked into her eyes. 'Is that what you truly want, Elaine?'

'Yes.' She moved to take his hands, looking at him earnestly. 'I think it might make us both safer—though I do not know why I feel it.'

Zander hesitated. 'It was for your sake that I thought to wait until my return, but if you would have it so… Yes, perhaps, you might be safer.' He lowered his head to kiss her on the lips, his tongue lightly tracing hers until she opened to him. He held her close and she felt the shudder of desire that ripped through him. Yet there was still darkness in him, a secret shadow that lay between them. 'I wish only to please you, my lady.'

He seemed distant, as if something worried him, as if he were angry—or hurt by something. She wanted to ask, but felt that he would not have told her.

'Thank you for your consideration.' Elaine did not understand where the feeling that they should wed before he left had come from, but something had been making her uneasy all day…since Anne's visit. 'I know it is short notice, but…'

'The priest was ready to betroth us, a marriage will be little more trouble to him. We have invited our good friends to feast with us.

I might have invited my uncle to join us, but he will understand—and he can visit us when we are settled in our new home, for I may ask for his assistance in finding a suitable manor close by his own.'

Elaine's heart surged as she looked at him. She scarcely saw his scars now and sometimes it seemed to her that her young knight had come home to claim her. Yet at other times the shadows descended and he seemed to withdraw from her, his eyes dark with remembered grief—and was there more? A new source of disquiet or doubt that plagued him, perhaps?

No, surely not. She knew of no reason why they should not be happy. The shadow of Zander's challenge to the Earl of Newark remained, but when that was over he would return to her.

If he still lived.

A cold chill had settled at the nape of her neck. Something was wrong. Elaine was unable to say what or where the menace lay, but she felt it waiting in the shadows, to claim them and ruin all her plans.

'I must go and change for the evening,' Zander told her and held her hand briefly to his lips. His slate-dark eyes looked into hers and her insides turned somersaults. 'I vow that you shall not suffer for this trust you show in me, Elaine.

I shall honour and protect you all my life. I pray that God will forgive and guide me.'

'If you could but trust in Him…'

'I have thought He had turned His face from the wretch I am become but…' Zander shook his head. 'If I could but forgive myself.'

Elaine let him go, the chill creeping down her spine, and she looked over her shoulder as she went to her own chamber to change her tunic for the evening. She ought to be happy. Zander had returned to her and if he was not quite as he had been, she was content to have him with his scars and hoped to ease away the bitter memories with her love.

Why did she feel that there was a dark shadow at her shoulder? What did she not know that had caused Anne to make such odd comments and look at her as if…? Elaine was not sure what her expression had conveyed. Pity, anger or was it hatred—or even sympathy?

The feeling that Anne had been trying to warn her would not leave her, but she dismissed it from her mind. The next day would be her wedding day and she must find a gown to wear that would not disgrace her.

Her clothes had been left behind in the flight from Howarth. All she had were the gowns left in her mother's chests. They were well enough for everyday wear, but her wedding was special. Somehow she must find something that befitted the occasion.

The morning was fine and sunny. Elaine rose and was about to dress when Marion entered bearing a gown that she had never seen before. It was a tunic of white silk embroidered about the hem with silver and beads. The hanging sleeves were of some filmy stuff that would let the contours of her arm show through and there was a jewelled band of silver set with rubies to wear about her waist. Another lady followed with a headdress of rolled silver and white velvet and a long veil of the same material as the hanging sleeves.

'That is beautiful,' Elaine cried, touching the tunic reverently. 'Where did you find it? I did not see it in my mother's chests.'

'Lord Zander sent it for your wedding gown,' Marion said. 'He has sent a casket of jewels for you to choose from, my lady. There is a whole chest of beautiful silks and velvets and furs for you.'

'For me?' Elaine was surprised but delighted with her gift. 'I had wondered what to wear...'

'The silks and jewels are your wedding gifts

from Lord Zander,' Marion said. 'He must be very rich to give you such gifts, my lady.'

'He promised to bring a fortune back with him,' Elaine said, overwhelmed by such treasures. She opened the lid of a casket made of gold and saw the rings, strings of lapis lazuli, pearls and rubies nestling against a bed of white silk. 'I think I shall wear the pearls about my neck, but I shall not wear a ring until my lord puts a wedding band on my finger.'

She allowed Marion and her ladies to dress her. A string of long pearls was slipped over her head; they hung to her waist and she fastened the silver cross her father had given her to them. The headdress was placed around her forehead and her long tresses allowed to flow freely on to her shoulders.

Marion handed her a silver mirror to look at herself. It reflected a hazy image, but her ladies told her that she looked beautiful and Elaine felt beautiful. She had applied a little rose-scented oil to her wrists and her neck, and her hair had been rubbed with dried lavender to give it a faint fragrance.

Just as she was finishing her *toilette* a knock came at the door and her steward was admitted. He bowed to her and then smiled.

'May I be permitted to say that Lord Zander is a fortunate man,' he said. 'I am sent to tell you that the priest is prepared, my lady. The ceremony will take place in the chapel as soon as you are ready.'

'I shall come now,' Elaine said and looked at her ladies. Each of them was wearing a tunic she had not previously seen and she guessed that Zander had brought gifts for her ladies, as well as her. 'Wish me happy, Marion...Ellen... Mary...Hilda...'

One by one they wished her happiness and kissed her cheek. They had brought strings of rosemary to lead her to her bridegroom and flower petals to shower over the happy couple once the knot was tied.

Elaine's heart was racing as she went down to the chapel, her ladies fluttering about her and laughing, teasing her and chattering like a flock of birds.

The chapel had been decked with greenery and all the household had assembled to see her wed. Sir Robert stood as Zander's witness and her steward was to give her away, her ladies to stand witness to her consent.

Zander was dressed in black, as he habitually was, but his long tunic was embroidered with gold and sewn with beads. About his waist he wore a wide gold belt with a short jewelled scabbard, which housed a dagger with a gold handle. He wore no other jewellery, but his hair had been oiled and was brushed back and curled under in the manner of the day rather than hanging wildly about his face. He turned and smiled at her as her ladies led her towards him and a sweet boy's voice sang a melody of joy.

Elaine took her place beside him. Zander reached for her hand and held it, as it trembled slightly, and then the priest began the service that would bind them for the rest of their lives.

A ray of sun had pierced the high windows of the chapel, sending a myriad of colours on to the ancient stone flags. The silver cross gleamed in the light and Elaine felt its warmth on her face. They were asked and gave their vows. She smiled at Zander and her fears melted as he lifted her veil and kissed her lips.

'We are now man and wife,' he said. From the back of the chapel a gasp was heard and an odd scuffling sound. Elaine resisted the urge to look round until the bells started to ring and, taking her husband's hand, she began to walk from the chapel.

She saw that Lord Stornway and his sister had joined the congregation, a little late it seemed for what was supposed to have been their betrothal. The earl stared at her so strangely, almost as if he could not believe what he had heard and seen. Anne's face was frozen in an expression of disbelief—and was that anger she was trying to hide?

Elaine's hand trembled on Zander's arm as they left the chapel and everyone formed a line behind them. Her ladies and Zander's men were cheering and laughing, and they were sprinkled with dried flower petals, which smelled of lavender and roses.

'May God bless your union, lady.'

'May the Good Lord send you sons, my lord…'

There were jokes and good wishes, and round after round of cheering as they all trooped into the Great Hall, where the feast had been prepared.

Dishes of dates stuffed with nuts and marchpane, sugared plums and other fruits were piled high on silver dishes. All kinds of little tarts and cakes were set out for the guests to indulge their appetites as they would. Wine, ale and sack were being served to everyone by those chosen to wait on the tables at the wedding feast, but every member of the household would at some time share in the delicious food that Zander had provided.

Anne came up to Elaine as she paused in her progress to the high board. 'I brought but a small token, for I thought today merely a betrothal,' she said, an odd tone in her voice. 'Had I known it was to be your wedding I would have selected something more worthy.'

She presented Elaine with a small gift wrapped in silk. It turned out to be a small box of silver and horn, which might be used to keep a token in. Elaine thought it pretty and thanked her, but Anne did not smile, merely gave her what she could only think of as a pitying smile.

Lord Stornway was congratulating Zander. The two men shook hands and seemed perfectly at ease with one another.

'Lady Elaine,' Philip said easily, smiling at her. 'I must offer my congratulations—or should it be commiseration? You have married a man dedicated to his cause and will, I fear, be left too often alone while he is away fighting.' He spoke in jest, but there was something that made Elaine's spine tingle.

'My lord must do as he thinks fit,' she said. 'I shall not be the first wife to wait for her husband's return.'

'No, indeed,' Philip said and laughed. 'I thought I should never see this fellow smile again, but you seemed to have banished his nightmares, lady. I am heartily glad to see you both so happy.'

Elaine thanked him for his good wishes. Glancing at Anne, she saw her frown, quickly hidden, and wondered.

'My gift to you is a silver chalice and for Zander a sword I think he will value,' Philip went on. 'They were meant to be betrothal gifts, but a wedding is even better.'

'My bride and I are happy to welcome you as our principal guests,' Zander said. 'I thought for a moment you might miss the ceremony altogether.'

'We were late, were we not?' Philip apologised and looked at his sister. 'Anne was not quite herself this morning and I told her she should stay in her chamber and rest, but she insisted upon coming. I fear it made us a little tardy.'

'It matters not. You are here for the feasting,' Zander said and smiled. He clapped his hands. 'Let the celebrations begin…'

Zander led Elaine to the high table. After she had taken her seat next to him, Anne and Philip were seated, and then the others gradually found their places. At a signal from Zander, food was brought to table. Tasters had been appointed to sample each dish before the guests were served, but nothing untoward happened and everyone ate and drank heartily. The minstrel sang songs that all the company could enjoy and the tumblers performed their tricks, followed by a fire eater and dancers.

Elaine ate sparingly. The feasting would go on all afternoon and into the evening, and fresh dishes would be served continually. She drank wine sweetened with honey and diluted with water, but only sipped it, just as she merely tasted some of the dishes offered her.

It was some time later that she glanced down the table at Anne and saw her staring at Zander with such a look that she shivered. What could that expression mean? In that moment Anne seemed almost to hate Elaine's husband, yet the next moment she was smiling and laughing at something Sir Robert said to her. Was it merely Elaine's imagination—or was Anne pretending to feelings that were far from those she truly felt?

'Lady, will you dance?'

The question took Elaine by surprise. She looked up at Lord Stornway and smiled, then glanced at Zander, who nodded his approval.

'Thank you, my lord,' she said and offered her hand. He helped her to rise and they went down the steps of the dais to the floor of the hall. The musicians began to play a slow, stately dance and Elaine laughed with pleasure as Philip pointed his shoe elegantly, then bowed to her. She curtsied. 'You dance like a courtier, sir.'

'Alas, I had a misspent youth,' he said and smiled at her in a way she thought a little too intimate. 'While Zander was away fighting the heathen, I fear I was dancing at court.'

'Do you go often to court, my lord?' Elaine was puzzled for he was the King's Marshal. She wondered that he would attend Prince John's court more often than necessary.

'I thought it right to present my sister with opportunities for marriage, but, alas, she found no suitors that pleased her.'

'Did she not once think of marriage?'

'Did Anne tell you that?' Lord Stornway looked surprised. 'She seldom speaks of her disappointment to anyone. She must truly value you, Elaine. Her childhood sweetheart took the Cross at the same time as Zander, though they came from different parts of the country. He promised to return and wed her when his fortune was made—but he was killed in the Holy Land. I had hoped she might forget him and take another husband, but I fear she will never marry now.'

'She told me as much,' Elaine said. 'I am sorry for her loss. I have been luckier.'

'Yes. Zander returned to you, did he not?' Philip said and for a moment his eyes were oddly distant. 'I pray that you shall not have cause to regret.'

'What mean you, sir?' Elaine shivered, though she tried to control it. The ice was at her nape once more.

'Why, only that he is a man obsessed by his need to avenge his father,' Philip replied. 'I could wish he would settle here with you and forget his quarrel with Newark, but I fear he will press it to the limit.'

'Yes, I know that nothing will sway my lord from his vow to be avenged on the man who murdered his father.'

'If Richard were to return in time, he would forbid it. For all his faults, Newark is the King's man. Richard will need all his loyal knights, for if the common man does not flock to his standard he may find that Prince John has too strong a hold on the throne.'

'The prince would not deny his brother's rights?' Elaine was horrified. She knew that Prince John had ruled harshly in his brother's absence, ill treating the poor and the nobles who remained loyal to Richard and committing many injustices. Yet surely he would not defy his rightful king?

'I only say it could happen.' Philip shook his head. 'But I should not speak of such things on your wedding day, my lady.'

Elaine frowned. 'I know Zander craves revenge for the wrong done his father—but he is loyal to Richard. If the king returned before it was settled between them, he would accept his judgement.'

'Perhaps...' Philip's expression was thoughtful. 'I would not see you a widow too soon, Elaine—but if it should happen, remember I am your friend. If ever you should need me...'

Elaine nodded, but did not smile. Why did she feel his words were almost a threat rather than an act of kindness?

'No more of this—it is your wedding day, a celebration,' he said as the music died. For a moment his fingers closed possessively over hers and then released her.

Elaine returned to her seat beside Zander. He had been talking to Anne and was smiling. Anne had been laughing and Elaine could only think she had mistaken her expression earlier.

These people were Zander's closest friends.

She was foolish to suspect them of not being honest in their good wishes. She was letting her own fears cloud her mind. It was ridiculous to see something malicious or menacing in the warnings of both brother and sister.

No, she must forget these foolish imaginings and think only of the coming night, when she would at last be Zander's wife in truth. Her heart beat wildly and she was suffused with warmth when she thought of the pleasure to come.

Chapter Ten

The evening was well advanced when Elaine left her place at the high board to return to her chamber. Zander had whispered to her that it was time.

'Go now, my love, before it becomes too rowdy. The men have drunk well and their tongues grow loose. I shall follow in a while—and do not worry, I shall come alone.'

Elaine nodded. She had wondered about the bedding ceremony, which some men insisted on. It was humiliating for the bride, for in some cases the groom's guests and friends insisted on being shown proof of the bride's virginity and the groom would toss out the sheet with her blood on it to those who waited near the door. Zander would spare her such heavy jesting and she went happily to her own chamber. His friends might come as far as the door, but then he would send them away.

She allowed her ladies to help her disrobe, and dress her in a fine, silken night-chemise. Her hair was brushed and allowed to flow freely down her back and then her ladies departed. Elaine walked over to the bed and sat down on the edge. She was nervous now and did not want to lie in her bed too soon lest she fall asleep.

She waited, listening for sounds from below in the hall. They were growing less and less and now it was quiet. She sat up straighter, expecting Zander would come, but the time passed and still he did not come to her. Her eyes were growing heavy. She crawled up the bed and lay against the pillows, determined not to give in to the urge to sleep.

Why did he not come to her? Her eyes would hardly keep open now. It must be almost morning? Where was he? Was it his intention to leave her waiting all night in vain?

Exhausted by the events of the day, Elaine's eyes closed and soon she was sleeping. She did not wake when Zander entered the room just before dawn sent fingers of rose through the sky. He bent over her sleeping figure, pulled a coverlet over her and smiled, then bent to kiss her cheek. Then he placed a beautiful, late-blooming rose and a note by her pillow before turning to leave the room.

Elaine woke later than usual. She frowned as she sat up and stretched. Why had her ladies not woken her?

Of course, they imagined that she had spent the night making love. As she moved from the bed, the small piece of parchment and the rose fell to the ground. She bent to pick them up and saw the letter was in Zander's hand, recognising it because of the document he had given her containing her wedding settlement. Elaine had not bothered to read it for she knew he would have provided for her if something should happen.

God forbid! She felt coldness at the nape of her neck as she broke the seal. Zander had written:

Forgive me, my dear wife, I could not come to you last night, as I planned, for there was a fire in the village and we thought the people were being attacked. When my men and I reached them, we discovered that it was merely the hay that had been set alight. However, when I returned to the manor, I was given a letter from the Earl of Newark. He has challenged me to meet him and that means I shall leave at first light to make the appointed time.

You were sleeping so sweetly and I did not wish to wake you. I am sorry that our wedding night was not as I planned, but I shall return to you as soon as I am able.

Your servant and devoted husband, Zander de Bricasse

Elaine sighed as she held the rose to her nose. It had a wonderful perfume and she knew that it grew in a sheltered spot by a south-facing wall, which was why it was always the first and last to flower each year. Her mother had loved the rose, because Elaine's father had planted it for his wife.

She would press the rose between the pages of her bible. It was a huge book of handwritten scripts in Latin, bound in leather and decorated with bright colours and gold leaf at the beginning of each page. It must have taken the monks who produced it many years to complete and was very precious. Lady Howarth had written Elaine's birth on the first blank page and then her husband had added the name of her still-born son. Elaine's mother had passed it down to her and she would pass it on to her daughter if she had one.

Elaine frowned, for her marriage had not been consummated before Zander left. She felt a little uneasy, because she knew that some would not consider her truly married—and it was possible to overturn a marriage that had not been properly consummated by means of an annulment.

Who would want to overturn her marriage? Certainly not Zander or Elaine herself—besides, how could anyone but she know that he had not come to her in the early hours?

'You are awake, my lady?' Marion looked in at the door. 'My lord left orders that you were not to be disturbed, even though he left at first light.'

'I am not ready to rise for a few minutes. Bring me food and drink and I will be ready when you return—until then I am not to be disturbed.'

'Yes, my lady. I shall tell the others.' Marion smiled as she closed the door behind her.

As soon as she had gone, Elaine jumped out of bed. She found a little knife that she used for cutting herbs and pricked her finger, pressing it so that the blood flowed. She then sprinkled a few drops on her linen sheets and smeared the remainder on her night-chemise. Her ladies would see the stains and take it as proof that her virginity had been lost. She was not sure why she'd done it, but something had made her feel it was necessary to practise the deceit.

She returned to the bed and rose, stretching and yawning when her ladies brought food, ale and fresh water for her to wash. Getting out of bed, she left the covers thrown back. She saw their secret smiles and heard them whisper and laugh when they saw the bloodstains. At least her ladies were convinced that she was truly wed to Zander. Elaine did not know why that was important, but she had felt instinctively that it might be best to have proof if proof were needed.

'I think I shall spend the day sitting quietly,' she told them. 'We shall embroider a new hanging for my husband's bedchamber. We must think of a suitable theme.'

'Lord Zander is a truly honourable knight,' one of the ladies said. 'We should picture him riding his horse on the way to the crusades, with the Cross before him.'

'Yes, that is a good idea for a part of the hanging,' Elaine agreed. 'But I would show him being a good overlord, tilling the land and husbanding the soil of his fields.'

The ladies joined in with ideas of their own and a length of silk was fetched from the chests. Threads of all hues were matched and cut to lengths with a tiny knife from the chatelaine Elaine wore. Each lady chose her colour and they took a corner of the cloth, each to begin working out the emblems they would depict and matching the shades they would use.

Elaine asked Marion to read to them from the scriptures. Her mother's bible was the only book she owned, though she knew that there were transcriptions of fables and love poems from France. Such volumes were rare and neither Elaine nor her mother had ever owned such a book, though she'd heard stories and poems told by minstrels or storytellers. Now and then one such man would come to the manor and be invited to tell them a story for his supper.

The day passed quietly. Sometimes, Elaine left the sewing to her ladies and went to the narrow windows of her solar to look out. As each hour passed she hoped for news of her husband, but none came. She had no idea where the meeting was to take place or what would happen, and, as the night fell softly around them, she began to worry.

'Tell the men that I shall dine here while my lord is away,' she instructed. 'They may sup when they are ready. Marion, you will sup with me, but those who wish to eat in the hall may leave us once we have been served.'

The other ladies got up and left to bring food and wine. Elaine sighed heavily, going to stand at the window once more.

'Looking for Lord Zander will not bring him home, my lady.'

'I know, but I cannot help it. I wish we'd had longer together.'

'He will return to you.'

'Yes, of course.' Elaine turned to look at her. 'You have heard nothing from Bertrand since the earl's men took him.'

Marion flinched and shook her head. 'I know he would send me word if he could. Sometimes, I fear the worst...'

'You think he is dead? How can you bear it?'

'I cry every night,' Marion confessed. 'He did not even know that I loved him, for I thought it immodest to tell him until he had asked for me.'

'I am so sorry,' Elaine said and looked at her

with sympathy. 'Yet perhaps he still lives. If he is a prisoner...'

'He may be suffering at the hands of the earl,' Marion said. 'I am not sure whether I should wish him alive or be glad that he can suffer no more.'

'I would always wish Zander to live,' Elaine said. 'I know he would bear whatever they did to him in the hope that he might escape and return to me.'

'At least you had one night with him.'

'Yes...' Elaine turned away, because she did not wish her serving woman to know the truth. Her heart ached, because she did not have even that memory to keep and cherish. Zander had kissed her a few times, making her body melt and her longing to be in his arms become a living flame—but she was still untouched. 'I have my memory...but he will return to me. I know he will.'

'Yes, my lady. I am certain of it...' Marion looked at her uncertainly. 'If he should not... will you take another husband?'

'No!' Elaine shuddered. 'I would rather die than marry the Earl of Newark.'

'I know. That is why I asked, my lady. If you are to defend yourself against men of his ilk, you need a husband. Lord Stornway loves you. I think you would be happier wed to him than the Earl of Newark.'

'What makes you say such things?' Elaine frowned at her. 'How could I think of marriage to any other man when I am just wed to Zander?'

'Forgive me if I offend you, my lady. I saw the way Lord Stornway looked at you—and he told me to send for him if ever you should be in trouble.'

'When did he say that to you?' Elaine was a little annoyed with her companion. 'I think he must have forgot himself.'

'You are angry, but I believe he meant it for the best, lady. Without your lord's protection you are vulnerable here. We have enough men to defend the walls, but we could not withstand a long siege. You need to salt meat and make preserves that would last for several weeks.'

'Yes, I dare say you are right,' Elaine agreed. 'While my lord was here there seemed no need, for we had fresh meat all the time—but I should ask the steward how our stores stand and begin to build them. We have feasted often since we came here and I dare say much needs to be replenished. Tomorrow we shall make a start on salting meat—and we should buy more sheep and cattle so that we can prepare for the winter.'

'I think you may need to prepare a great deal of food, should we be forced to winter here rather than move on to a new manor.'

Elaine nodded. Zander had made other plans, but he had gone to meet and fight with his enemy. She could not be certain that he would return to her again.

Her steward confirmed that their stores were running low on various goods, including flour, sugar and salt, which was so important for preserving meat for the winter.

'You must send to market and buy enough stores to last us for several weeks,' she told him. 'And buy in sheep and cattle so that we can salt meat for the winter—or to withstand a siege.'

'My lord told me he would see to the stores when he returned, my lady.'

'These are my dower lands. I am your lady and you will do as I bid you,' Elaine said, feeling annoyed because Elgin seemed to imagine she was not fit to have charge of her own manor. 'My lord will order these things when he is here, but for the moment he is gone. I would be prepared should we have to draw up our bridge because of an attack.'

The steward looked surprised at her order, but did not question her again.

Over the next few days, Elaine continued to watch for Zander's return, but received no word from him.

A week passed and then another. She and her ladies began to preserve plums, apples and berries and to pickle walnuts—and then to salt meat into large barrels. When after a month, she considered that they were provisioned sufficiently to go through the winter or withstand a siege, Elaine found herself at a loss. She spent hours standing at her window, just looking out into the distance and sighing.

Where was Zander and why did he not either send word or return?

'You will be ill if you continue to fret for your lord,' Marion said to her one afternoon. 'Sit with us, my lady. We have half finished the hanging for my lord's chamber. Come and see how fine it is.'

Elaine went to sit in her chair, looking round at her ladies. They regarded her with anxious eyes and she knew they were concerned for her. Marion was right; she was foolish to let her thoughts of Zander occupy her every waking moment. She had not been thus all the years he'd been away fighting, but somehow this time she was shadowed by constant fear.

Getting up once more, she went to the window of her solar and looked out. 'I cannot help worrying for him,' she said. 'To send word from the Holy Land was much harder, but he is in England—and we are married. He must know that I am anxious. I fear that he cannot send word to me.'

'You should send to the King's Marshal,' Marion said. 'Mayhap he can find out what has happened to your husband.'

Elaine shook her head. She was reluctant to send to Zander's friends for help, though she knew it would be the sensible thing to do. Lord Stornway could make enquiries and discover what had happened between Zander and the Earl of Newark.

'I shall wait another week,' she said. 'If by the end of that time I have still heard nothing, I shall ask Lord Stornway for help.'

Elaine woke startled from her sleep. She sat up in bed, shivering and feeling afraid. Her dream had been so terrible that it frightened her even now that she was awake. Zander had been imprisoned in a bleak place. It was a castle surrounded by mist that rose from a deep lake. He'd called to her to help him and she had tears on her cheeks.

Zander was in trouble and he needed her help. She'd waited another ten days and it was more than five weeks since her husband had slipped away at dawn without waking her. In all that time she'd heard nothing from him. He must be in trouble. Either he was dead or his enemy had defeated him and held him captive.

Elaine must help him. She could wait no longer. A part of her shrank from asking help from Lord Stornway, but the sensible part of her mind told her that she had no choice.

She rose from her bed and went to her coffer. It was a handsome chest on a stand and heavily carved, which had been her mother's. Opening it, she took out a quill, parchment and ink in a closed pot. The ink was still moist, for it had been prepared just the previous day for making a list of linens. Dipping her sharpened quill into the pot, she began to write very carefully.

My Lord Stornway,
I have heard nothing from my husband,
Lord Zander de Bricasse, for more than

*five weeks. I am concerned that something
terrible has happened to him and I am
writing to beg you for news. Could you
enquire what has happened to him? I cannot rest while he is away and I hear nothing of his welfare.*
Yours in hope, Elaine de Bricasse.

Elaine rang a bell to summon her ladies.
Marion was the first to respond. She looked at
her anxiously.

'Are you ill, my lady?'

'I could not sleep,' Elaine told her. 'My lord
has been gone more than five weeks with no
word. I am certain that if he could he would
have sent a message—either to tell me that he
had beaten his enemy in fair fight or that he
was in hiding...or taken prisoner.'

Marion nodded. 'You wish to send for help
to Lord Stornway?'

'Yes, I think I must,' Elaine said. 'I have
waited too long already, but I would not ask for
help too soon, because...' She shook her head,
for it was impossible to explain her fears; they
were too vague, too foolish to mention even to
the faithful Marion.

'Give me your letter, my lady. I shall give instructions that it is to be sent at once.'

Elaine looked at the parchment she'd sealed. Even now she was reluctant to pass it over, but she did not know what else to do. Zander had not disclosed his plans to her. She had no idea where he'd gone or what he planned. He might have told his friend Philip Stornway more and her only hope lay in him. If Zander was languishing in some awful prison—as her dream had told her—then his friend might be the only one to help him.

'Yes, take it, before I change my mind,' she said, thrusting it at Marion. 'I have no choice.'

'Lord Stornway may know something—and he can find out things that you could not, my lady.'

'Yes, I know.' Elaine turned away. She was shivering and cold all over though the day was mild.

Where was Zander and why had he not returned to her?

Elaine's letter brought Lord Stornway that same day. He came late in the afternoon, bowing over her hand to kiss it and apologising for visiting so late in the day.

'Forgive me, lady,' he said when she greeted him in the hall. 'I was out visiting a sick tenant when your letter came, but as soon as I had it, I rode straight here.'

'You are very kind. I did not wish to trouble you, sir, but I have heard nothing from Zander.'

Philip looked concerned. 'Nothing in all these weeks?'

'Not one word.' Elaine's throat tightened with fear. 'I had thought he would send word to tell me what was happening.'

'I am certain that he would if he were able...' Philip frowned and reached out to touch her hand. 'Why did you not send to me sooner? Something must have happened.'

'Do you know where he went? He said nothing of his plans to me—only that he had received some message from the Earl of Newark...'

'I believe the Earl had summoned him to Howarth to settle their quarrel. I understood it was to be by single combat.'

Elaine closed her eyes as the pain swept over her. If Zander was lost to her, she would be a widow before ever she had been a wife.

'Could you discover what happened?' she asked. 'It is but three or four days' ride from here. Surely Zander would have sent word if...' The horror of what might have happened made her throat close and she could not go on. She sat down and bent her head, the tears so close that she could hardly bear to look at him.

'Sweet lady,' Philip said and reached out to touch her shaking shoulders. 'Fear not, I shall protect you. Whatever has happened…but we shall not assume the worst yet. I will send couriers to Howarth and demand to know what happened there.'

Elaine looked up at him. 'I want to know the truth—whether he lives or…' She shook her head. 'No, he cannot be dead or I should know in here.' Her hand went to her breast. She stood up, lifting her head bravely to meet his pitying glance. 'You think the worst. I can see it in your face.'

'I know he loves you dearly,' Philip said. He took a step towards her, but then stopped. 'If he has not sent word somehow…he would not distress you so…and yet he may still live. He may be a prisoner.'

Elaine gasped, her chest feeling as if a giant hand squeezed it. 'You will discover the truth— and if he should be a prisoner…'

'I shall do all in my power to release him,' Philip promised. 'He is my friend, but even if he were not…I would do anything for you, Elaine. You must know how much I admire you…but of course you do not wish to hear this now.'

Elaine forced herself to smile. 'I thank you, sir. Find my lord for me and I shall be eternally grateful.'

'Leave it to me, my lady. No stone shall remain unturned in my efforts to discover Zander's whereabouts. I shall come to you as soon as I know anything at all.' He turned to leave the hall.

'You are leaving at once?'

Philip hesitated, glancing back at her. 'The hour is late, lady, and I have some leagues to travel.'

Elaine hardly knew how to answer and yet Zander would never have let his friend go without refreshments—or a bed for the night.

'If...you wished, you could stay the night and journey home tomorrow.'

Philip smiled. 'How gracious of you to offer, but I think the tongues might wag if I took advantage of your hospitality at such a time. My men and I will return to the castle and tomorrow I shall begin the search for Zander.'

Elaine inclined her head, but said no more. Did he think she wanted his company? She had offered from politeness, but would have found it hard to entertain him without Zander at her side. There was something about him that made her uncomfortable, even though she needed his help.

'Where are you, Zander?' she asked in a whisper none could hear. 'Why do you not return to me?'

Holding her head high and fighting her tears, she mounted the stairs to her solar. Lord Stornway believed that Zander was either dead or a prisoner. He had looked at her with sympathy and assured her of his protection.

What would she care what became of her if Zander were lost to her?

Entering her room and finding herself alone, Elaine let the tears fall. Why had Zander left her like that…without even saying goodbye?

She loved him so much and her heart was breaking.

Lord Stornway had sent a message the next day to say that he was riding to Howarth Castle himself to enquire what had happened between the two men. He had assured Elaine of his regard and vowed to let her know as soon as he knew anything.

She had spent the next few days pacing about the house and gardens, her heart aching as she tried to maintain hope of Zander's eventual return, but with each day that passed her fear that he must be dead or a prisoner grew inside her.

It was almost a week before Lord Stornway came and requested an interview with her. Her heart was in her mouth as she hurried down to the hall and went to meet him. He was still covered with the dust of the journey, and, as she looked into his face, she saw the news was not good.

'You saw the Earl of Newark?'

'He denies all knowledge of Zander,' Philip said. 'He denies sending a challenge to him.'

'But the letter came!' Elaine's heart stood still. 'He must be lying.'

'I accused him of it and I demanded that he return your property to you, but he refused. I told him that I should complain of his behaviour to Prince John—and to King Richard, when he returns from his imprisonment...and he said he would consider his situation.'

'I care little for the castle,' Elaine cried. 'Where is Zander? What has happened to him?'

'I do not know, Elaine,' Philip said and hesitated. She sensed at once that he was hiding something.

'What do you know?' she asked, her hand going to her mouth. 'There is something you are not telling me...I know it. Please, you must not hide anything from me.'

'I do not know if Newark lies...but someone attacked Zander and his men as they rode towards Howarth. They were outnumbered and, although they fought hard, were overwhelmed.'

Elaine gave a little scream. 'He is dead...'

'We do not know what happened to Zander—but one of his men has been found. He was badly wounded and lay close to death for some weeks. When we found him he was still ill, but attempting to return here and tell you the terrible news.'

'Where is he?' Elaine asked. 'Is he here? I must speak with him...I must know the truth.'

'He is lying in bed at my home,' Philip said. 'Anne is tending the poor fellow, for he is still weak. I could not bring him, for he might not have stood the journey.'

'Then I shall come to him,' Elaine said. 'I will summon Marion and she may accompany me. I must speak to this man and hear his story for myself.'

'I thought it was what you would want,' Philip said and smiled; he turned his head aside and she missed the sudden gleam in his eyes. 'Tell your women to pack enough things for the night, because you must stay with us until the morning. Anne will be there to chaperon you.'

'Yes, yes, I shall come,' Elaine said. 'My women can send whatever I need on after me. I shall call for Marion. We must go at once. I shall not rest until I hear what has happened to my lord.'

Chapter Eleven

Elaine hardly knew what she did as she followed in Lord Stornway's train. Her face was pale, but she lifted her head proudly and tried not to show that her heart was breaking. Zander had been attacked without warning and was either dead or a prisoner. Newark denied having sent him a letter to ask for a meeting—and would deny all knowledge of Zander if asked. He might languish in the dungeons at Newark or Howarth for years until he died and she would never know.

Her throat ached with the effort to hold back her tears. She did not wish to break down and let everyone see her grief, but she found it difficult to breathe. Everything was unreal, as if she were moving in a dream—as if a wall of mist imprisoned her. How could Zander be dead and she not know it? She ached as if she had been beaten all over and yet within her some spark of hope clung to the belief that her husband still lived.

'I love you so,' the words echoed over and over in her head. 'Zander, do not leave me. What is life to me without you?'

Tears burned behind her lids, but she would not shed them. If she wept, it would mean that she had given up all hope and she could not give up hope. Zander must still be alive, even if he were imprisoned and unable to write to her.

When they arrived in the inner bailey at the castle, Philip dismounted and came to help her down. His hands lingered on her waist too long, but she was too numb to push them away. She gave him a brave, pitiful smile and his hands fell away.

'I pray that the fellow still lives,' he said. 'Come, Elaine, I shall show you the way.'

She followed him into the castle. They turned towards the north tower and Philip led the way up to a small room at the top of the turret. He knocked and Anne's voice called out that they might enter. Philip stood aside and allowed Elaine to go in. Anne turned, smiled, put a finger to her lips and beckoned her to the sick man's bedside.

'He is very ill, but he wishes to speak with you.'

As Elaine reached the bed, the soldier opened his eyes. She knew him as one of Zander's men and her heart lurched.

'My lady, forgive me,' he cried out and his face twisted with pain. 'My lord sent me to tell you we were betrayed and attacked.'

'You tried to bring me this message?'

'I was only slightly wounded in the attack, but as I rode towards Sweetbriars, I was shot down by an arrow in the shoulder. I fell from my horse and would have died had not a cottager taken me in. I lay for weeks between life and death—and then, as I was beginning to recover, Lord Stornway came and brought me here. Forgive me…'

Elaine put a hand to his fevered brow. 'You need no forgiveness, sir. You did your best and it was the hand of an assassin that brought you down.'

'Aye, my lady. We were set upon without warning. My Lord Zander cried that we had been lured into a trap. We fought hard, but when he saw that the numbers were too great, he sent me to tell you…' The soldier broke down, tears streaming down his cheek. 'As I rode away, I saw…I saw…'

'What did you see?' Elaine's heart felt as if it was being crushed.

'I saw my lord dragged from his horse and…' He shook his head. 'I do not know…but he is either taken or dead.'

Elaine turned away as the pain swept through her. It was more than she could bear. In her mind she could see Zander being hacked to pieces by the assassins' swords.

'No…' she whispered and then the chamber began to whirl about her. Her head was spinning and the darkness started to close in around her.

'Catch her, Philip,' Anne cried and that was the last thing Elaine heard before the blackness took over.

The blackness gave way to flashes of light and pain. She suffered terrible dreams in which she wandered in thick mists searching for her love. Lost and alone, she traversed thick forests, dark mountainsides and then saw again the lake with the island shrouded in mist in the centre of the deep water. The water looked black and she could see no way across until a small boat came towards her. An old man dressed in black, a hood covering his face and head, rowed the shallow boat.

'Give me a coin and I will row you to the Isle of the Forgotten,' he said and held out a hand. His fingers were bones and had no flesh. 'You shall join he whom you seek in death...'

Elaine screamed and sat upright. Her eyes were open but she was still caught fast in her dream. 'No...not dead...not dead...' she cried out. 'I pray you, sir...take me to him...not dead...'

'Hush, sweet lady,' a voice said close to her ear. 'You must not grieve so. I am here to care for you. I shall always love and care for you.'

'She is caught in her fever. She cannot hear you,' another voice said. 'I warned you what might happen...'

'You can make her better. Do this for me, Anne. I beg you, as your brother. You had your revenge. Now give me my heart's desire.'

Elaine did not hear what the woman's reply was, for she had sunk back into her fever. Now she was dreaming of another time and another place. She saw Zander walking towards her and he was as he had been before he went to the wars. He was smiling, happy and free of care.

'Do not fear, my love,' he told her and held out his hands to her. 'I am waiting for you. I shall be here when you cross over. Come to me, my darling. I am waiting for you.'

'I am coming, Zander. Wait for me…show me the way…'

'No! Elaine, you cannot die. I shall not let you. I love you. I command you to live for me.'

'Zander…I must go to Zander…he is waiting for me…'

'No, he would not want you to die,' the voice said. 'He would think you a coward. Zander would say live. I say live for me. I love you, Elaine. I live only to serve you. Live and I shall protect you all my life.'

'Philip…' Elaine's voice was barely a whisper as she looked at him. 'Zander is dead?'

'I fear it is so,' he said and grasped her hands. 'You must let him go, my darling. Soon you will feel better. Live for me and I promise I shall make you happy again.'

She struggled to remember. 'The soldier…'

'I fear he died the same night you saw him.'

'God rest his soul,' she said and tears trickled down her cheek. 'I know he did his best to reach me.'

'Rest now, my darling. You must grow strong and well, and then I shall teach you to be happy again.'

Elaine's eyes closed. She slipped away into

sleep. As she slept Zander's name was on her lips and she whimpered sometimes, calling for him, but the nightmares had ceased. Her fever was done and now she slept the sleep of the exhausted.

Several days passed before Elaine woke to see Anne bending over her. She had been bathing her face with cool water and Elaine had been conscious of the kindness before she woke.

'Thank you,' she said weakly. 'You have been so kind to me. I think you saved my life.'

'Perhaps,' Anne said. 'Philip watched you constantly. He has been called to a meeting, but will come to see you as soon as he returns.'

'I fear I have been a deal of trouble to you?'

'You are as a sister to me. My brother loves you. You must know that he wants only to devote his life to making you happy.'

'Yes…so kind…'

Elaine lay back and closed her eyes. She felt so weak and it was as if she had no will or strength of her own. Something at the back of her mind told her that things were not as they should be, but she could not recall what had worried her before…she was ill.

She knew that Zander was dead. The soldier had seen him fall and in her dreams Elaine had seen him as a youth; he'd told her to come to him in death. She would have died if it had not been for Philip's devotion and determination that she should live.

Elaine did not care whether she lived or died. All emotion had drained out of her and she no longer had the will to do anything but as she was told.

'You must eat some of this soup.' Anne's voice seemed to come from a long way off. Elaine tried to recall what her voice had said when she was ill, but she could not. 'You must get better, Elaine. Philip loves you. You owe him your life. You must live for him.'

Elaine was too weary to resist. Why did she want to live without Zander? Yet these people had been so good to her, fought so hard to save her. Perhaps she did owe them something.

She sat up and swallowed some of the soup. Her throat hurt as she felt it go down, but it gave her a little strength.

'Good, you are awake,' a voice said from the doorway. Philip walked in. He presented her with a sprig of some winter flower with the dew still on it. 'I picked this for you, Elaine, as I have very day since you were taken ill, but this is the first time you've known us.'

'You are so kind...'

'We care for you,' Philip said and sat on the edge of her bed, reaching for her hand. 'I love you, Elaine. When you are better I shall show you how much I love you…'

Elaine smiled, but made no reply. How could she tell him that she did not want his love when he had saved her life?

'So, you are almost better,' Marion said as she entered the bedchamber the next morning. 'You look rested, my lady. Lady Anne and Lord Stornway have saved your life.'

'Perhaps it might have been better had they let me die.'

'Do not say such a thing!' Marion scolded. 'You are loved by many and your people need you. Lord Stornway loves you. He wishes only to care for you.'

'I am Zander's wife.'

'His widow,' Marion said. 'You must face the truth, my lady. Lord Zander is dead. You must learn to live without him—for the sake of others, if not yourself.'

'Do not scold me, Marion.'

'Do you think I shall let you throw your life away? You are young and beautiful. Lord Zander should not have gone to fight a superior enemy. He should have put aside his desire for revenge and given his life to you and your people. If he loved you, he would have forgotten his need for revenge.'

'Do not speak to me like that!'

'I speak only the truth, my lady. You grieve for him, but when you are ready you will see the truth is as I say.'

Elaine turned her face aside. How could Marion be so cruel? She had loved Bertrand—would she so easily find another lover in his place?

'What of Bertrand?'

'He has come back to me,' Marion said. 'He was Newark's prisoner, but released after Lord Stornway demanded the release of all prisoners.'

'Has he heard anything of Zander?' Elaine asked eagerly.

'Nothing. Your lord was slain and buried where he lay,' Marion said. 'I know you grieve, but you must learn to put your grief behind you, my lady.'

'I am glad that Bertrand came back to you,' Elaine said wearily. 'You have my permission to wed him.'

'Lord Stornway hath given us a few acres and a cottage of our own. I shall stay until you are well again and then I shall marry and leave you, my lady. You have good friends and other ladies to serve you.'

'Yes, I knew you would leave me when you married.'

Elaine turned her face to the pillow. Once she would have protested that Marion and Bertrand should stay with her, but now it no longer seemed to matter. Everything was too much trouble...

'I am glad to see you so much better,' Philip said on the morning that she came down to the hall for the first time. 'At one time we feared we should lose you, but you are feeling more yourself now, I think—are you not?' He was so anxious that Elaine smiled.

'You have been very kind to me, sir.'

'It is not kindness. I loved you the moment I saw you, but you were Zander's. I knew you would not look at me, nor would I have tried to come between you. Now that you are alone and at the mercy of rogues, I know that Zander would want me to take care of you.'

'I shall be able to go home soon,' Elaine said, but she knew that without her husband she would be vulnerable and at the mercy of rogue barons, unless this man continued to offer her protection.

'Yes, if you wish it,' he said. 'Yet I would ask you to stay for your own sake—and for mine. Be my wife, Elaine. I know you grieve for Zander, but in time you may learn to love me a little...it is all I ask...'

Elaine caught her breath. 'I was his true wife,' she said. 'The marriage was consummated, the law would not let me marry until I have proof that Zander is dead.'

Something flickered in his eyes. 'But he was called away because the village was attacked...'

'Yet still he came to me,' Elaine said, an instinct she hardly understood making her lie. 'Ask my ladies, they will bear testament and tell you. I could not remarry without proof of my lord's death—the Church would not allow it.'

'Supposing his body cannot be found?' Philip asked, an odd expression in his eyes. 'Could you not claim that the marriage was not consummated and let me ask the Pope for an annulment?'

'My ladies would know that I lied—and I am not ready to take another husband in Zander's place.' Elaine sighed and put a hand to her eyes. She still felt weak and it was hard to resist his will. 'I am grateful for your kindness, sir. I shall never forget that you and Anne saved my life. Perhaps in a year or so...'

Philip looked at her, such an intense expression in his eyes that she trembled. 'If there were proof of Zander's death...if we could gain the Church's permission for our union, would you consider wedding me sooner?' He reached out for her hands and held them. 'I fear for you alone in your manor, Elaine. I think I must insist on your staying here as my ward until you feel able to marry.'

Elaine blinked back her tears. It was the same old story—the same fear of her being forced to marry a rogue baron. Her uncle had given her until Christ's Mass reluctantly. Now the feast was almost upon them and once again she was being pressed to marry.

'You must give me a few months to think and grieve,' she said. 'Ask me again in the New Year and I may be able to think more clearly.'

'You know I would love and honour you. I do not desire your lands, Elaine—though I shall force Newark to return them to you.'

Elaine sighed, bowing her head. She was not strong enough to fight him. If Zander was dead, there was nothing to hope for in life. She must take what she could from it.

'If there is proof and the Church will permit our wedding next spring, then I will wed you,' she said. 'There is no other I wish to marry, sir. If I must take a husband, I would as soon a friend than a stranger. I shall never cease to re-member and to love Zander, but...' She shook her head as the tears stung her eyes. 'I can say no more...'

'How can you provide proof of death without a body?' Anne said. 'It is not possible. I warned you that she would not be as easy to persuade as you thought.'

'They told me that he was fatally injured in the attack. He could not have lived,' Philip said and glared at her. 'You promised me that I should have my heart's desire if I gave you your revenge.'

'I wanted him my prisoner so that I could tell him why he was going to die,' she said and gave him a scornful look. 'I wanted him to suffer and die slowly. He ought to have known why he was being punished. He killed the man I loved—the only man I ever loved.'

'I gave you his gauntlet stained with blood. It has his crest embroidered upon it.'

'Present that to her and hope that she will take it as proof.'

'I was sure that he would not have time to consummate the marriage. Cardinal Woolston would have petitioned the Pope on my behalf and I might have secured an annulment by the spring. If she remains obstinate, it might be years before I can persuade both Elaine and the Church that she is free to marry again.'

'Can you not provide a grave and pay one of your underlings to swear to it that he lies in it?' Anne frowned. 'As yet I am not certain whether to believe he is truly dead. Your men botched the deed, Philip.' She looked scornful. 'Had they brought him to me, as I desired, I would have guaranteed his death—as I did his messenger.'

'I thought the messenger's tale would be enough to convince her,' Philip said. 'While she was ill and under the influence of your drugs she seemed docile, but now her will seems stronger.'

'Then drug her again,' Anne said. 'Arrange the marriage without her consent.'

'She would hate me.'

'Are you the King's Marshal or a weak knave with no power?' his sister demanded. 'Gather evidence whether it be false or no. Present it to your tame cardinal and get your dispensation, then, if she still resists, drug her. I will give her something to make her forget. When she recovers you may tell her that she consented to the marriage.'

Philip flinched from the scorn in his sister's face. It was Anne who had plotted her revenge from the moment Zander killed her promised husband in single combat. It was she who had caused his father's keep to be fired and she who had plotted to have Zander killed by poison. Zander had once been Philip's true friend, but then something had happened to change his feelings—and now he'd seen Elaine—and Anne had whispered in his ear that they might both have what they wanted.

Sometimes Philip wished he had not listened to her poison in his ear, but he wanted Elaine too much to resist his sister's pleas to give her revenge. He had sent men to fire the village haystack and a false letter from Newark, sending Zander on a wild goose chase. Before he could reach Howarth Castle, he and his men had been set upon and overwhelmed. The men Philip had employed to carry out the evil deed were renegades, thieves and murderers, men who should have died on the gallows. He'd spared their lives and promised them gold when they brought him poof of Zander's death.

He'd hoped for a body, but all he had to show for his scheming was a bloodstained glove with Zander's initials and his crest embroidered on the black velvet in gold thread. He'd given it to

Anne as her proof, but even she had not been satisfied. Would Elaine believe that Zander was dead if he showed it to her?

Supposing by some chance Zander had survived against the odds? The leader of the rogues he'd employed had told him that he saw Zander take a fatal blow and fall—but his men had immediately surrounded him and dragged him away into the forest.

'They simply disappeared, my lord. We searched for them for two days, but no trace could be found. On the third day we caught his messenger and he was wounded, but not fatally. He escaped into the woods and we could not find him.'

Philip had found the man lying near to death in a woodsman's cottage and taken him to his castle. He'd been allowed to live long enough to tell his story to Elaine, but not long enough to remember the details more closely. Philip had believed she would accept Zander's death and turn to him in her loneliness, but she was stubborn and would need more convincing.

Philip had believed that Zander's men had carried their lord's dead body away. He'd hoped they might take it back to Sweetbriars, but it had not happened and now Philip began to wonder why.

It was strange that Zander's men had not taken the news of the attack back to the manor. He'd ordered that that they should all be slaughtered so that only one witness survived, but they had fought too well. Though some lay dead and were left to be buried by village folk, at least seven or eight had survived to carry off their lord's body.

So why had they not taken the news back to Zander's wife?

Philip felt a chill at the nape of his neck. He had only that rogue Bartholomew's word that Zander was dead.

Supposing he lived and discovered who was his true enemy?

Zander could not be alive. He would have sent word to Elaine—but more importantly, he would have come after his one-time friend and demanded revenge...unless he lay close to death and had finally breathed his last.

Yet still the problem remained. Why had no one come to tell Elaine what had happened to her husband?

Chapter Twelve

The sick man opened his eyes and glanced up at the person who tended him. 'You should not do this for me, my lord,' he said. 'It should be I that tends you.'

'My wounds healed quickly,' Zander said and smiled. 'You were close to death and I wanted to care for you myself. You have saved my life twice, my friend. You covered me with your body when they would have hacked me to death—and once again I am in your debt.'

'You would have done as much for me.'

'Yes, because we are as brothers.' Zander frowned. 'You know we were betrayed? Those rogues lay in wait for us and we were outnumbered, for I thought Newark had given his word that we should come in peace.'

'Someone betrayed us.' Janvier tentatively moved his neck. The blow to his shoulder had cut deep and he'd lain in pain for weeks, not knowing what was happening about him. 'Who was it that laid the trap—Newark or…' his eyes widened in shock '…your friend Lord Stornway. The message came through him…he could have betrayed us, lured us to what should have been certain death had your men not fought so valiantly.'

'Exactly,' Zander said. 'Newark has made no move against Sweetbriars. My spies tell me that he recently allowed his prisoners to go free—and is making plans to leave Howarth. I do not know whom to trust, which is why I dare not send to Elaine again, though I do not know if she had my message. If she revealed that we were alive and where we were hiding, we should have no chance against a superior force. Our best plan is to stay hidden until we are ready to return to the manor.'

'But why would your friend betray you?'

'I have thought long and hard,' Zander said. 'I believed we were as brothers before I left for the Holy Land. Philip wanted to take the Cross, too, but Richard made him his King's Marshal and he was forced to stay in England. I sent him money and jewels…he could have robbed me of my fortune, but he did not…even the silver I sent for my steward was returned to me.'

'But now you have something of far more worth,' Janvier said. 'I think he envies you your wife.'

'Elaine…you think he wants Elaine?' Zander frowned. He cursed beneath his breath. 'I have been a fool dallying here. I wanted time to recover and plan before I sent word to my uncle. I need more men…and I must have proof of what Philip has done or we shall never be sure.'

'You should send your lady word that you are alive, but warn her to keep it secret,' Janvier said. 'You should have left me here and gone home, my lord. In your absence anything may have happened.'

'I could not leave you, my friend, but I should have sent word to her. Yet she would not leave the manor…'

'Unless she was tricked.'

'God forgive me!' Zander cried. 'If he has harmed her, I shall kill him.'

'You must leave me here and go home,' Janvier urged. 'I can manage alone. I pray that it is not already too late.'

'But if she had my message…' Zander frowned. 'Unless Eric was murdered before he reached her.'

'You must return to the manor and make certain she is safe,' Janvier urged. 'I do not trust Lady Anne. She asked me some strange questions concerning your time in the Holy Land— and about Sir Jonquil... I think he meant something to her, though she tried to hide her feelings. Forgive me, I should have told you... this is my fault...'

Zander shook his head, still hardly able to believe what his mind told him. 'It was not your fault. I trusted them both, thought them my true friends—but if they are behind this...'

'You should send word to your uncle at once and then ask the Earl of Newark to meet with you at Sweetbriars,' Janvier said. 'You cannot fight two enemies, my lord. You must make your peace with the earl if you can.'

'Newark had my father beaten to death...'

'Have you proof of this?' Janvier asked. 'Who told you of your father's death? You were not present when he died?'

'No, I was at Richard's court, planning my journey to the Holy Land.' Zander's gaze narrowed in thought. 'Philip told me what happened that day.'

'Then you have only his word.'

'Yet why should he hate me enough to lie... to cause my father's death...?'

'I cannot tell you, my lord.' Janvier made to rise, but could not manage it. 'I am weak now, but soon I shall be better. Let me go to Newark and ask if he will meet you at Lady Elaine's manor. You must send messengers to your uncle, asking for help, and return to the manor. Send one of the grooms to tell your lady to meet you in secret. If Lord Stornway has plotted mischief, she will know.'

'Your advice is sound as always,' Zander said and smiled. 'I have two men watching Newark, but until the last day or so I did not consider that Philip could be my enemy.'

'What made you begin to suspect him?'

'I could not think why Newark should ask for a meeting between us only to set a trap. If it were his intention to murder me, he would surely find it easy enough to dispose of me when I was at Howarth without sending men to waylay us?'

'Perhaps you have been mistaken in your enemy, my lord.'

'Yes, perhaps I have…' Zander's eyes narrowed. 'Yet why should Philip hate me?' he asked again.

'I cannot answer that,' Janvier's reply was the same. 'Perhaps it was merely a young man's jealousy—that you had taken the Cross while he was forced to stay at home.'

Zander shook his head. 'I would swear he was well satisfied with his lot, proud to be the King's Marshal in these parts.'

'Did he see you as a threat—or your father?'

'I do not know how a poor knight like my father could threaten Lord Stornway,' Zander said. 'My father was a truly honest man with no desire for advancement. I can see no reason why anyone should want him dead.'

'Only Lord Stornway can tell you the truth. Return to Sweetbriars and make sure your lady is safe, my lord. Then you can confront Lord Stornway and demand an explanation.'

'Yes, you are right—but I do not like to leave you here alone, my friend.'

'I shall do well enough now—and I will take your message to Earl Newark in a day or so.'

'Yes, I must go,' Zander said. 'Forgive me that I leave you—but I grow anxious. I shall set out at once for Sweetbriars.'

Zander was at fault, he knew it. Even after he had decided to wed Elaine, he had been haunted by his memories—and the suspicion that had been growing in his mind concerning Philip had been hovering like a dark cloud. If Philip was not the friend he had always thought him…

Elaine might be in danger even now. God forgive him, if his carelessness led to her death for he would never forgive himself.

'I do not trust Lord Stornway,' Bertrand said to Marion as they walked in the woods near the castle and picked herbs to make a tisane for Elaine. 'He and his sister have deceived you, Marion. His talk of giving us a cottage and land—why should he do so much for us? Methinks 'tis a bribe.'

'I thought him a good man.' Marion stared at him intently. 'What makes you distrust him?'

'He looks at Lady Elaine in a way I do not like. I think he seeks to marry her whether she will have him or no.'

'How could he? She is wed to Lord Zander and without proof of his death she must wait for some years before the Church will grant her permission to remarry.'

'Yet he is making arrangements for a wedding before Christ's Mass.'

Marion gasped. 'How can that be? It would not be lawful. Besides, she grieves for her lord. She would never agree.'

'I heard him speaking to the priest. I saw money change hands—and I think he means to force her.'

'I should never allow that,' Marion said fiercely and then bit her lip, looking at him with regret. 'I have been on his side...I told her he was a good man. Surely he would not do anything so wicked?'

'I heard something about one of Zander's men. He was ambushed and wounded, but brought here still alive and in his senses. He told someone that Lord Zander had sent orders that Lady Elaine was to remain at the manor.'

'She does not know that,' Marion said. 'The message she received was that her lord had been betrayed...we thought by Earl Newark.'

'Something is not right,' Bertrand said and frowned. 'Lady Elaine should be at home to grieve in peace. She should not be forced into another wedding so soon after her lord died... if he is dead. Where is the proof? Has anyone seen his body or even a grave? I am uneasy, Marion. I think Lord Stornway sought to get rid of you by giving us land, so that she would have no one to help her.'

'You must return to the manor,' Marion said. 'Find out if there is any news. I shall remain here to guard my lady.'

'What can you do alone?' Bertrand frowned. 'We should take our lady and return to the manor with her.'

'If you are right, he would not let her go.' Marion was thoughtful. 'Go back to the manor and then send word to Lord Zander's uncle. If our lady is a prisoner here, she will need to be rescued.'

'Very well,' Bertrand agreed. 'But be careful, Marion. If Lady Anne or her brother discovered that you suspect them, they would not hesitate to kill you.'

Marion shivered. 'You cannot think they are so evil? I am sure they will be proved innocent.'

'Take care, my love—and trust me. I know what I saw and heard and 'tis not right. Lady Elaine would never marry so soon...and I fear she does not realise how evil some men can be.'

Marion agreed. 'I shall watch over her like a hawk. Go now, Bertrand, and return to me as soon as you can.'

Elaine stood at the window of the tower in which she had been lodged. She was beginning to feel better and to think for herself. She should never have agreed to wed Lord Stornway in the spring if he brought her proof of Zander's death. She did not wish to marry again. She'd agreed in a weak moment, but now she thought she would prefer to enter a nunnery. The Abbess would accept her dower lands as her dowry and she would take her vows rather than be persuaded into a marriage she did not want. In a nunnery she would be safe from men who wished to wed her for reasons of their own.

Her heart belonged to Zander and she would never love anyone else.

'Where are you, my love?' she whispered. 'I love you so much. How could I ever marry again now that you are gone from me?'

She had been grateful to Lord Stornway for his help. He and Anne had saved her life, but she did not wish to remain here a moment longer. She would return to Sweetbriars and then she would decide what to do with the rest of her life.

The door of her chamber opened behind her and Anne entered bearing a silver tray with a pewter cup filled with a hot liquid that she knew would taste of wine and honey.

'I have brought you a drink to ease you,' Anne said, smiling at her.

'Thank you, I shall drink it later,' Elaine said. 'You and Lord Stornway have been so good to me—but I have decided that I shall return home tomorrow. Would you send word to let my people know, please?'

'Are you sure you wish to go? Have we not

made you welcome here?' There was a flicker of displeasure in Anne's eyes, but quickly hidden.

'Yes, most welcome,' Elaine said. 'I am grateful for your care of me—but I wish to be at home to grieve in peace. I think I may enter a nunnery. I thought I might marry your brother in time, but it is impossible. I could never be happy as the wife of any other man.'

'You must not break his heart…'

'It would hurt Philip more if I married him without love. He would grow tired of a wife who could feel nothing for him. I shall beg his pardon and hope that he will continue my friend.'

Anne frowned but said nothing. 'Drink your wine, Elaine. It will make you feel much easier in your mind.'

'Thank you…in a moment…'

'It will grow cold and not taste so good,' Anne warned and went out. As she left, Marion entered. She curtsied to her and then stood waiting until Elaine turned. For a moment she pressed her ear to the door, then opened it and looked out. Lady Anne had disappeared down the corridor.

'Why did you do that?' Elaine asked.

'I am not sure we can trust her—or Lord Stornway,' Marion said and frowned as Elaine reached for her drink. 'Let me taste that...' She took the cup and smelled it. 'Honey and lemon...I think there is nothing more, but it would be best if you did not drink it.'

'How can you doubt Lady Anne or her brother after they have been so kind to me? She cared for me when I was ill and you told me that he'd offered you a cottage and land.'

'Bertrand is suspicious of him. Why should he offer us so much? We are but servants and have done nothing that deserves such reward. Bertrand thinks he means to force you into wedding him before Christ's Mass.'

'But that is no more than a week away...' Elaine shook her head. 'How could that be possible? My husband...no one knows for certain that Zander is dead. The Church would not allow it.'

'Bertrand says that Lord Stornway claims it was no true marriage. He says it was not consummated and therefore he has asked the Church to set your marriage aside.'

'But I told him...my ladies will bear witness that my sheets bore evidence of my blood...'

'Only I and one other could swear to it,' Marion said. 'If I had left you, who would believe a serving woman? Lord Zander's men would say that he was with them most of the night and left for but a few minutes.' She paused, 'Besides, we saw only a smear of blood—no one saw him come to you.'

'He left me a letter and a rose. I pressed the rose in my Bible.'

'Do you have them?'

'I left them in my chamber at the manor.'

'If Lord Stornway swears you were not properly wed, the priest will believe him and grant the dispensation. You will be wed whether you choose or no, my lady.'

'But he cannot force me.'

'When you heard of Lord Zander being wounded you fainted—but then the Lady Anne tended you and you were ill. So ill that we feared you would die. She gave you her cures and for some days you did not know me when I bathed you. I know you grieved—but why were you so ill?'

'You are saying she might drug me…that they could make me believe I had consented to the marriage?'

'I think it is possible,' Marion said. 'I have heard of strange poisons that control minds and make people docile—for a while you hardly cared whether you lived or died…is that not so?'

'Yes, I wanted to die. I must leave here,'

Elaine said. 'I will not marry anyone else. I would rather die.'

'Bertrand has gone to Sweetbriars. He will send to Lord Zander's uncle and ask for his help. Somehow, we must slip away and reach the manor this night.'

'If Anne suspects…they would not let us go.'

'Give me the drink she prepared for you,' Marion said, 'then lie down on your bed and pretend to sleep. I will empty the cup and then I shall tell everyone you are resting, but I shall come back here and hide in your room. As soon as they are at table this night, we shall leave together.'

'My lord…' Elgin faltered, staring at Zander as if he'd seen a ghost. 'We thought you dead… my lady was near unto death for grief of you.'

'Then she did not get my message telling her we had been betrayed and to remain here and trust no one until I came?'

The steward turned pale. 'Lord Stornway came with news and my lady rode with him to the castle. It was there that she was taken ill and we heard you were slain by the Earl of Newark's treachery, my lord.'

Zander cursed. 'Methinks Newark had little

to do with any of this,' he said. 'I have been betrayed, but not by the man I thought my enemy.'

'My lady is still a guest at Lord Stornway's castle.'

'Or his prisoner,' Zander said. 'How many men are within the castle? How many can I count on to ride with me to rescue her?'

'There are thirty men-at-arms here, my lord, but there must be three times that many at the castle. You left sufficient force here to withstand a siege, but an attacking force would need to be much larger.'

'I took fifteen men with me when I left to meet, as I supposed, with Newark,' Zander said. 'Five were killed when we were ambushed, four badly injured and five returned with me, the other able man remains to guard the wounded. It would be impossible for a force like ours to lay siege to Stornway Castle.'

'Would your uncle send men to help you?'

'Perhaps—and yet he might not wish to offend the King's Marshal. I should need to convince him that Lord Stornway is a traitor to Richard.'

'My lord...' A servant had come up to them. 'Forgive me, but a person hath arrived.'

'Not now, sirrah,' Zander said. 'Can you not see that I am busy?'

'But my lord…he says he comes from your lady.'

'Elaine has sent…' Zander turned at once, all attention now. 'Pray, where is this man? Tell him to come forwards.'

'I am here, sir,' Bertrand said and stepped forwards. 'You may remember that I was escorting your lady when you helped her once before?'

'Yes, I recall you. I thought you Newark's prisoner?'

'And so I was—but Lord Stornway ordered the prisoners released.'

'Do you come from him or my lady?'

'I serve only my lady, sir.' Bertrand raised his head. 'I heard Lord Stornway speaking to the cardinal, my lord. He was arguing with him, persuading and threatening by turn.'

'And what were they arguing about?'

'The cardinal said he must have proof of your death before Lord Stornway could wed Lady Elaine—but the King's Marshal said that your marriage was not a true one, that it was never consummated and could be annulled by the Church. The cardinal was reluctant, but in the end he took gold from Lord Stornway and agreed the wedding would take place before Christ's Mass—as soon as he received word from the bishop that the marriage was annulled.'

'The devil!' Zander glared at him. 'For an annulment Elaine would need to consent.'

'She could be made to seem as if she consented,' Bertrand said. 'Lady Anne is clever with drugs, my lord. For a while after you were reported dead my lady did not care whether she lived or died…they controlled her mind then and might again.'

'What proof of this have you?'

'None but what I have seen and heard.'

'Yet I believe you.' Zander's hand clenched on his sword hilt. 'We must get her away from that devil…but how?'

'You could not take the castle by a frontal assault,' Bertrand said. 'The only way is if a few of us could enter the castle secretly and snatch her.'

'Could you get us in without raising the alarm?'

'If you were willing to accept a disguise,' Bertrand said. 'Every morning the side gates are opened to allow villagers to bring in food or come to their work. We could mingle with them, hiding our weapons, and make our way to Lady Elaine's chamber.'

'Your face is known.'

'Aye. I shall drive the cart in which you and two of your best men will hide. If we are to succeed, we cannot risk a larger force.'

'If we fail...you know it would mean certain death?' Zander glanced about him. 'Who will follow me?'

Every man present stepped forwards.

Zander smiled. 'I thank you all. Sir Robert, Sir Henry, you will accompany me. The rest of you must stay here to protect the manor and wait for us to return.'

'And if you do not, my lord?'

'Then you must ask my uncle to avenge us and to free my lady.'

'She drank the tisane you took her?' Philip looked at his sister through narrowed eyes. 'She almost died the last time—she will not be ill this time?'

'I have given her just a small measure of the cure. It will make her sleepy, but she will not be harmed. Tomorrow I will give her a little more and she will feel tired, hazy in her mind, just as when she lay ill before—but in a few days she will do everything you tell her without question. The priest will not notice that she seems odd—even if he cares.'

'I have paid him well enough, but there must

be witnesses to the marriage so that she cannot protest she was tricked.'

'You worry too much, Philip. I do not know why you want this woman so much. She is beautiful and she has some land—but you might take her lands anyway.'

'Yes, she is beautiful,' he agreed. 'I coveted her as soon as I saw that Zander wanted her.'

'You hate him as much as I, do you not?'

'More…' Philip's eyes went cold. 'His father threatened me…he threatened to have me disgraced and exiled by the king.'

Anne inclined her head. 'That is why you had him beaten to death,' she said. 'Because he threatened you?'

'Because he knew…' Philip's mouth was hard. 'He knew that I had murdered my uncle, as he lay sick in his bed. I did not know that he had witnessed my act until he accused me of murder.'

'You murdered our uncle to become Lord Stornway and the King's Marshal?'

Philip smiled queerly. 'He was old and weak. I wanted the power that was his—and I did not wish to go to the Crusades with Richard. Such adventures are for fools like Zander de Bricasse. He was so proud to take the Cross—and look where it got him.'

'He came back scarred but rich, richer than you,' Anne said. 'Why did you not keep his jewels while you had them? He trusted you with his fortune.'

'He is a favourite of the king,' Philip said. 'Richard's ransom has either been paid or will be paid soon. He will return to England and if Zander had lodged a complaint against me...'

'So you plotted to make him believe that Newark was his enemy.' Anne laughed. 'You are so clever, Philip. I admire your ruthlessness—but you promised me Zander's head. I still have nothing to prove he is dead.'

'You complain too much,' Philip said. 'I tell you he was slain. If he lives—where is he? Why did he not send word to Elaine or to me?'

'Perhaps he plays a deeper game than you think, Philip? Mayhap he no longer trusts you.'

'I tell you he is dead,' Philip replied. 'Go up and give Elaine another of your foul potions—but take care you do not make her ill.'

'What would you do to me if I did?' Anne asked and shivered as she saw the truth in his eyes, though he gave no verbal answer.

Turning, she walked away, her head bent and deep in thought.

She had always known her brother's devious nature—the streak of evil that he kept hidden behind a charming smile. As a girl she'd come across him torturing a puppy. When she'd tried to rescue it, he had slapped her and made her cry. Afterwards, he'd given her a fairing and begged her pardon, but she'd learned not to cross him again.

She'd been fond of her uncle, who had brought them up when their father had died in battle. Anne had not loved many people in her life, but she'd cared for Sir Jonquil and for her Uncle John. She had been careful not to reveal her shock at her brother's casual revelation. Because she had wanted Zander de Bricasse dead, and because she'd helped him subdue Elaine, he believed that she was completely on her side— but now she felt a strange revulsion. Her bitter disappointment that the only man she'd ever wanted to wed had been killed in combat with Lord Zander had made her strike a bargain with her brother—but she had not known then that he'd murdered their gentle uncle.

Anne was not sure how she felt, but one thing was certain. She must be very careful—once Philip had what he wanted, he would no longer need his sister.

'We must go now,' Marion urged. 'You need take nothing with you, but we must leave before Lady Anne comes to see if you are still sleeping.'

'Yes…we must go,' Elaine said, then stopped as she heard a noise outside their door. 'Someone comes. I shall lie down and pretend to sleep. You must leave me and wait for me in the courtyard.'

'But, my lady…'

Elaine put a finger to her lips and lay down on the bed, closing her eyes. A moment later the door opened and Lady Anne entered. She frowned as she saw Marion.

'Is your lady well?'

'She seems very sleepy,' Marion answered. 'She was awake a few moments ago, but seemed lethargic—as if she had no energy. I asked if she needed anything and she told me to let her sleep.'

'I see…' Anne's eyes travelled round the chamber, but everything was as normal. 'I shall let her sleep—and you must come, too. I would have you fetch Lord Stornway to my chamber. Tell him it is important.'

'Yes, my lady. I shall go at once.'

Elaine heard them go out and close the door. She tensed lest Anne decided to lock the door, for Elaine had heard an odd note in her voice that made her think she might suspect something. The door remained unlocked. Elaine waited a moment, then rose, took her cloak from the closet and pulled it on, bringing the hood up over her face. She went softly to the door and looked out. The stair was in darkness, but she could see lights in the hall below. Some were still at their supper.

Her heart beating wildly, Elaine crept down the worn stone steps to the bottom. If she could reach the side door to the courtyard without being seen... Her breath caught in her throat as she heard a man's laughter, but no one called out or asked who she was or where she went. The corner of the hall where she stood lay in shadow for the torches were flickering low. She heard Lord Stornway's voice saying that he had been summoned to his sister and dug her nails into her hand. Would he glance her way and see her?

Elaine was sick with fear, but there was no warning shout and no one ran to stop her as she softly lifted the latch and went out into the frosty night air. A moon was in the sky and it was light enough for her to see Marion waiting for her.

'Thank God you are come,' Marion said and caught her arm. 'I thought Lady Anne suspected something. Pray God she will not tell her brother. The night is too light and if they look for us there is nowhere to hide until we reach the woods.'

'Lord Stornway was called away to her. I feared he would see me, but I stood in the shadows of a pillar and he did not.'

'I did not summon him so she must have sent to him again,' Marion said. 'We must hurry, my lady. I am afraid she knows something.'

'If we reach the woods there are places we can hide. We must try to get home before the morning, because once they know I've run away they will come after us.'

'Why did you summon me at this hour?' Philip asked when he walked into Anne's chamber. 'Is Elaine ill? Have your foul potions made her sick again?'

'You blame me for her illness,' Anne said. 'I only did what you asked, Philip. You wanted her docile so that you could persuade her to wed you. I told you she would be difficult to persuade, but you would not listen to me.'

'Damn you, Anne,' he said and glared at her. 'I do not want a lecture from you. Be careful or…'

'Or what?' Anne asked, looking at him defiantly. 'You know that you need me, Philip.

She will never wed you if I do not make her subdued and easy to control. It might be years before you could have her.'

'Damn you, you witch. The priest will do as he's told or I'll have him beaten. As for you—if you harm her...' He advanced on her and Anne shivered. 'Tell me she is well or I shall wring your scrawny neck.'

Anne smiled. 'She is sleeping peacefully, brother dear. I gave her another small dose of poppy juice. Leave her to me and in a few days she will do whatever you wish.'

Philip nodded. 'You will do as I want if you know what is good for you.'

'When have I ever defied you?' Anne went over to her window and glanced out. She was in time to see two figures wrapped in cloaks disappearing through the side gate of the court-yard. She turned and smiled at her brother. 'Go and look at her if you will, but I dare say her woman is sitting with her.'

'The sooner that wench marries and leaves us, the better,' Philip muttered. 'You may tell her that she is dismissed in the morning. I want no one to serve Elaine who is not under your control.'

'Of course, Philip,' Anne said sweetly. 'I shall serve her myself—and one of my women may care for her bodily needs. You may rest easily, brother. In a few days everything you ever wished for will be yours.'

'It will be the worse for you if you do not keep your promise.'

He turned and strode from the room, shutting her door with a heavy snap.

'I shall keep my promise to you, as you kept yours to me, brother,' Anne said. She looked about her room, deciding what she would take with her. There were jewels enough of her own, but she knew where Philip kept some of his treasures. She would wait an hour or two until all was quiet and then she would go, using the same gate Elaine and her woman had used to escape. Once Philip knew they had gone, he would kill her, because he would know that she had lied to him.

Anne had only ever wanted to wed one man. That man was denied her, but she no longer craved revenge. Indeed, she cared not whether Zander de Bricasse was alive or dead.

Her brother Philip was a murderer and more than that she suspected that his mind was twisted—that he was insane. She had never been certain of it until now, but she could not forgive him for the terrible sin of murdering their gentle uncle. His sin was her sin, because without knowing it she had condoned what he did—she had schemed with him to murder and to force an innocent woman into a marriage that she now believed would have been hateful.

She would go to a nunnery and offer her life to Christ. She would pray for forgiveness and for the redemption of her soul….

Chapter Thirteen

'Can we stop running now?' Marion asked. She doubled over, her chest hurting so much that she could scarcely bear it. 'I have not heard anything since we left the castle. I do not believe they have discovered our escape.'

'Do not talk,' Elaine said, breathing deeply. 'We have escaped detection so far, but the sun will be up soon and we still have some way to go. We cannot rest long, because they will come looking for us as soon as they discover we are not in the castle.'

'At least Lady Anne did not alert her brother last night.' Marion sank down to the ground, her back against a tree. 'Have you any idea where we are—or how far we are from the manor?'

'I think if we keep going we shall soon be

through the woods,' Elaine said and sat down beside her. 'I do not recognise anything here— but once we leave the woods we may see a mile-stone or perhaps a church that we know. If not, we must ask the way.'

'We're lost, aren't we?' Marion said, her throat catching. 'We ran in such a blind panic that I did not take note which way we went.'

Elaine smiled at her. 'We must just keep going. In the morning we may see a farm cart and ask the way. Mayhap some kind soul will give us a lift home.'

Marion nodded and stood up. 'Yes, we must keep going. I wish Bertrand were with us, as he was when we left Howarth.'

'He was a good guide and I, too, wish he were here,' Elaine said, smiling at her. 'Have courage, my friend. I think God is looking after us. I was certain Lady Anne knew I was fak-ing my sleep, but she did not betray us. Luck is with us thus far. We must go on. When we are home we can pull up the drawbridge and resist all comers until my husband's uncle comes to help us.'

'I am ready to go on,' Marion said and reached for her hand. 'Forgive me for ever thinking of leaving you, my lady. If I had not been so deceived in Lord Stornway, we might have escaped before this.'

'His manner is always pleasant. Even now I find it hard to believe that he could be so wicked...and his sister...'

'You must believe me. If he were to recapture you...' Now Marion was urgent. 'We must hurry, my lady. We have to reach your manor before he comes after us.'

'What time do they open the gates?' Zander asked. 'We must do nothing to arouse suspicions.'

'Just after seven bells,' Bertrand replied. 'It is six bells in the summer, but at this time of the year it is later to allow for the sunrise.'

'Then we must make haste,' Zander said. 'We have yet to make our way through the woods.'

'Get beneath the sacks, my lord,' Bertrand said. 'There are others stirring already.' He pointed down the road towards two women. 'If you are seen...'

Zander was about to obey when Bertrand gave a startled cry. 'What is wrong?'

'My lord, I think...' Bertrand began to sprint towards the women and one of them ran forwards. He caught her in his arms and held her. Zander looked beyond them to the second woman. His heart thudded to a halt and he was turned to stone, as he knew her, his feet unable to move. 'My lord...' Bertrand beckoned to him. ''Tis Marion and my lady.'

His voice broke the spell that held Zander rooted to the ground. He took a step forwards as Elaine suddenly came flying towards them. She stopped as she reached him and he saw the uncertainty in her eyes.

'Zander...you are alive?' Her voice caught with emotion and he saw the tears trickle down her cheeks. 'I thought...I thought you were dead.' She was trembling, uncertain, staring at him in disbelief.

Zander's mouth was dry and the words he wanted to say would not come. How could he speak of all he felt? How could he explain the uncertainty that had made him linger with Janvier for weeks? How might he tell her that he had not believed himself capable of loving her as she deserved, but had fought his devils and won?

'What happened to you? Why did you disregard my message to stay inside the manor and draw up your bridge until I came?' His voice sounded cold and angry to his own ears, but he could not smile and, though his arms ached to hold her, he made no move towards her. 'We thought you might be a prisoner.'

Elaine lifted her head, a look of pain in her eyes. Zander knew that his cold manner had hurt her but he could not let himself tell her how much he had feared for her. Instead, he felt a roaring anger in his head. She had gone to Stornway of her own free will…and she had promised to wed the earl if there were proof of Zander's death—did she care for him? Had she come to realise that Zander was not worthy of her after all? He knew his suspicions were unfair, yet jealousy made him look at her with cold reserve.

'I never received your message, my lord,' she said and now there was pride in her eyes. 'There was a wounded man at Stornway Castle who claimed you had sent him to tell me you had been betrayed—but he said nothing of remaining at the manor. When we had no message for weeks I was anxious and feared you dead. I sent to Lord Stornway for help.'

'You went to him and then what happened?' His expression remained icy and he saw her look of pain, yet still he could not relent. Philip had sworn eternal friendship, but he had lied. Zander had trusted him—could he now trust her despite her avowal of love?

'My lady was very ill,' Marion said, speaking because Elaine was silent. 'Lady Anne nursed her and gave her potions that were meant to cure her, but I believe they sought to steal away my lady's will.'

'I will speak for myself,' Elaine said and now in turn there was anger in her lovely eyes. 'Lord Stornway told me you were dead. Your soldier saw you fall and it seemed certain that you were hacked to death. I became ill and when I recovered Lord Stornway said that I must marry him, because I should never be safe at the manor as a widow.'

'And you were content to wed him? You consented to marry him before Christ's Mass?'

'I said that I did not wish to marry at all— and I told him that I could not marry for there was no proof that you were dead. He said that our marriage was no true marriage and he did not need proof—that he would have it annulled. I told him that I must have time to grieve.'

'Annulled?' Zander's eyes narrowed and then nodded. 'He did not need proof, because I was called from home on my wedding night. It was a false alarm and now I understand what lay behind it. What a scheming knave he is…' He shook his head. 'We shall speak privately of these things, Elaine. Why did he allow you to leave?'

'He does not know,' Elaine replied. 'Anne tried to drug me again with her foul potions, but Marion poured the mixture away and I pretended to sleep. I thought that Anne might have guessed I was not truly asleep and feared she would alert her brother, but for some reason she did not. We waited until it was late and then slipped away when everyone was retiring for the night.'

'You must have walked all night.' Zander suddenly realised that she was exhausted. He saw her swaying from tiredness. 'I am a brute to question you. Forgive me…' Regret cut through him. She had exhausted herself escaping and he treated her as though she were his enemy. In truth he did not deserve her! He was beyond all hope of redemption.

Elaine sighed and stumbled as he moved towards her. He swept her up in his arms and put her into the cart and Bertrand did the same for Marion.

'We must thank God that we came upon them by chance,' Bertrand said. 'If we had not passed this way, we might have missed them— and, had we gained entrance to the castle, it would all have been for nothing.'

'I think this time God was on our side,' Zander said and glanced at the women as Bertrand turned the cart. He made the sign of the Cross over himself and felt the relief pulse through him. He had come very close to losing her. 'Once we have them safe there will be time enough to decide how to punish Philip.'

Elaine lay on her bed and wept. Her tiredness had soon passed once her women had brought her hot scented water to bathe and clean clothes. She had eaten soft bread and honey and drunk a little weak ale. After an hour or so had passed, she felt better physically, but still her heart ached.

Zander had looked so angry when he'd seen her. Her heart had soared with hope when she first knew him and she'd run to him, believing that he would catch her in his arms and hold her to him, as Bertrand had held Marion, but instead, he'd just looked at her coldly—almost as if he hated her.

How could he look at her that way? Even though he'd seemed concerned when he realised she was exhausted and lifted her into the cart, she could not convince herself that he loved her as Bertrand loved Marion.

What had she done to anger him?

She wiped away her tears and sat up. She was innocent of any crime, but it seemed that all men were the same—they all sought to dominate or use a woman for their own purposes. Women were used as bargaining tools, for power, land or money. Some men wanted to use them to satisfy their lusts, others only to breed their heirs. Elaine was not sure why Lord Stornway had tried to force her into marriage. He could surely have taken anything he wanted from her.

Elaine's heart ached, because she had believed that Zander was different. She'd kept his image enshrined in her heart, imagining that if only he would return to her, her dreams would all come true—but it seemed that she had deceived herself. He was no different from all the others.

The feeling of betrayal and disillusion made her want to weep again, but she refused to stay here in her chamber weeping. She was the chatelaine of this manor and Zander's wife—even if he had regretted their hasty marriage.

Did he imagine that she had gone to Lord Stornway because she secretly admired him and regretted her marriage? Was that why he'd looked at her so coldly?

Elaine had heard stories of women stolen

from their husbands and then disgraced by
their captors. When they were returned to their
homes they often found themselves reviled and
obliged to retire to a nunnery, because their
husbands could no longer bear to look at them.

If Zander thought so ill of her...

She heard a knock at her door and then his
voice, asking if he might enter her chamber.
Taking a deep breath to calm her nerves, she
bid him welcome and he opened the door, looking at her oddly as he entered.

'Elaine,' he said hesitantly. 'Forgive me if
I hurt you earlier. I had feared...many things
and seeing you apparently free...I did not know
what to think.'

'Did you believe that Lord Stornway sent me
back to you as spoiled goods?'

A tiny pulse flicked at his temple and she
knew that he had considered the possibility. 'I
am still the virgin I was when you left me to
take the Cross,' she said in a voice of ice. 'When
you did not come to me on our wedding night
I slept and in the morning I cut my finger and
sprinkled blood on my sheets, for I would not
have my ladies know I was still a virgin. I lied
to Lord Stornway and told him the marriage
had been consummated when he wanted to have

it annulled—but he bribed the priest to give his consent and would have forced me to wed him.'

'Marion and Bertrand have told me it all,' Zander said. 'I did not doubt your loyalty, but I know him now for the villain he is and he might have done anything. I thank God that you were not harmed when he had you at his mercy.'

'I do not know why he wished me to be his wife—unless it was because he wished to possess what was yours.' Elaine was thoughtful. 'I think he would not have bothered with me had I not been betrothed and then wed to you.'

'Why should Philip be so jealous of me? We were as brothers once.'

'Were Cain and Abel not brothers?'

'You speak truly,' Zander said and then held out a hand to her. 'Will you forgive me for deserting you?'

Elaine was not ready to give in so easily. He had left her and then, after he was attacked, he had sent only one messenger. 'Why did you not send word? Did it never occur to you that one messenger might not get through to me—that I might be anxious for your sake? Or did you think that I had betrayed you?' Her eyes widened in pain for the thought tore at her.

'How could I think so ill of you? It never

crossed my mind that you would play such a wicked trick.'

'Then why did you not come to me—or send someone to tell me you were alive?'

'I had so few men left to me and I did not know who I could trust. Janvier was badly wounded saving my life. He covered me with his body when they tried to hack me to death— and when my men finally drove them off he was more dead than alive. I felt I needed to care for him myself, for he has done so much for me.'

'I understand that you would nurse him, because he once saved your life—but had you no thought of me? Surely you knew I would be anxious?'

'I thought Eric would have told you. I was away for years at the crusades and you did not expect a message from me.' He sighed with exasperation. 'It was but a few weeks... Forgive me. I know you suffered. Marion told me that you were forever at your window. She said that you would not eat or sleep.'

Elaine tossed her head, angry that he needed her maidservant to tell him what he should have known. 'She would do better to hold her tongue.'

'She loves you, Elaine. I offered her land and

a pension, but she would not take it. She and Bertrand will marry, but they will not leave your service.'

'Lord Stornway offered them land, too,' Elaine said. 'Bertrand did not trust him. He suspected him of wrongdoing and it seems he was right.'

'I wish I had been as wary.' Zander frowned. 'Philip had you at his mercy at the castle. Anything might have happened. Yet I thought him my friend—how could I know he hated me?'

'I think Anne hates you, too. Does she have cause?'

Zander looked thoughtful, then nodded, 'Perhaps. I have learned that she loved a knight by the name of Sir Jonquil. He was the bloodthirsty brute who murdered innocents. When he was denounced he tried to blame his crimes on me and I fought him single-handed—it was his death or mine. I would have spared him at the end, but the King commanded that he die by the sword, as he had lived.'

'Then I understand why she hates you,' Elaine said. 'But I do not know why her brother should plot to steal your wife and have you murdered.'

'I believe it has something to do with my father,' Zander said. 'The only thing I knew for sure was that someone had him beaten to death—Philip told me it was the Earl of Newark, but now I think that may have been a lie… that he might have done the evil deed himself.'

'Why would Philip have your father murdered?'

'If I knew that…' Zander shook his head. 'I intend to call a truce with Newark. If he wishes for peace between us, he will return Howarth to us.'

'He killed my uncle and tried to capture me.' Elaine raised her head. 'I cannot forgive so easily.'

'I cannot fight two enemies,' Zander said, looking at her in a strangely defensive manner. 'You think I should avenge your uncle? I can see it in your eyes, though you do not demand it.'

'No, that is not so,' Elaine said. She wanted to go to him and tell him that all she wanted was to live with him in peace. 'I ask nothing of you.' She wanted so much! She wanted him to love her as he once had, with all his heart, but she was not sure that he knew how to love. He might at times call her by sweet names, but words alone meant nothing. Love was in the closeness, the sharing of all things good and bad that a true marriage entailed.

'I must deal with Stornway,' Zander said. 'What he did cannot be ignored. If he joined forces with Newark, I would not have enough men to defend you. Somehow I must make an alliance with one or the other.'

'I know,' Elaine said and her breath caught in her throat. 'Yet I would beg you not to leave me again just yet, my lord. Will you not wait until your uncle sends his reply to your request for help?'

'I have sent envoys to him,' Zander said. 'Christ's Mass is almost upon us and we should not make war at such a holy time. Besides, I would hear what Philip has to say. From what Marion tells me there is only her and Bertrand's word for what he intended. If I make war on the King's Marshal for no good reason, I should be an outcast. I must wait until I have proof.'

'Is my word not good enough for you?'

'You were ill. Who can say why? He would say he sought merely to protect you for your own sake. Philip has friends in high places. The king will return to England soon and he might choose to listen to his marshal above me. No, Elaine, I can only wait for Philip to make the next move against me. In the meantime…' He hesitated, then, 'We should celebrate the season of Christ's birth and…'

'And?' Elaine asked, because her heart was racing. She looked into his eyes and saw the heat of desire, her knees beginning to tremble as she read what was in his mind.

Zander took a step towards her. 'I think it is time our marriage was consummated. We must make certain that no one can claim it is no true marriage again. Next time, Philip will have to make certain that I am dead before he can claim you.'

Elaine's mouth was dry, her heart beating so wildly that she thought he must hear it. He was not telling her that he loved her—only that he meant to consummate their marriage. It might mean nothing to him, but it meant everything to her.

'Yes, my lord,' she said so softly that she could not be certain he had heard her. 'I think it is time.'

'I shall come to you this night, Elaine.' He smiled at her. 'Be ready for me and try to forgive me for leaving you to the mercy of evil men…'

'I never blamed you,' she whispered when she could speak, but he had already gone.

Elaine stared at the door he'd closed softly behind him. Her body was weak with longing and she wished that he'd taken her into his arms at once rather than waiting for nightfall, but perhaps the gentle side of loving meant less to Zander. To him it was merely a way of laying claim to his wife and her lands.

'If you are no true wife, you will be after to-night,' Marion said as she brushed Elaine's long hair so that it flowed loose on her shoulders and down her back. She brought her a gown of white gauze that showed the pale pink of her skin underneath. 'Lord Zander has made it plain to all that he longs to lie with you this night. He has vowed that nothing will keep him from your side this time—and if the village calls for help his knights must go alone.'

Elaine blushed. Some of the jests made in the hall that night had been so suggestive that she had felt uncomfortable. Instead of controlling his knights, Zander had joined in the laughter and she'd wanted to run away and hide, yet she knew why he allowed such coarseness. There would be no doubt after this night that Zander de Bricasse had claimed his bride.

Elaine had sat and smiled throughout the evening, though inside she had longed to run back to her chamber. Yet she had known that this was all a part of making her safe. Once she was Zander's wife in truth there would be no more talk of annulments—only his death would release her then.

A shiver went through her and Marion looked at her in surprise.

'You are not afraid, my lady?'

'Of my lord coming to me?' Elaine shook her head and smiled. 'No, I was thinking of… It does not matter. I refuse to think of anything but love tonight.'

They heard laughter outside the door and then Zander's voice firmly bidding his knights 'goodeven'. They departed with more jests and the door opened. Zander entered, his eyes moving over Elaine hungrily.

'Forgive me, my lord,' Marion said and made a hasty curtsy. 'I wish you both goodnight.'

She sent a laughing glance at Elaine and scurried away.

Elaine's heart was beating wildly. She rose to her feet, her mouth slightly dry, her knees feeling a little weak. He looked so handsome in the long black gown he wore, the hem embroidered with gold thread and beads. She noticed that the scar on his left cheek looked less inflamed and thought that perhaps it had begun to heal at last. Perhaps he had used the poultice she'd made for him. His mouth was soft and sensual as he smiled and walked towards her.

'Were you ready for me, my love?' he asked in a voice husky with desire. 'You are so beautiful. I dreamed of seeing you this way so many times while I was away, Elaine. When I lay close to death and Janvier cared for me so faithfully, it was my memories of you that brought me through.'

'Do you truly mean it, Zander?' Elaine breathed, moving towards him. Suddenly, any fear of the marriage bed she might have had had gone and she felt a surge of longing and need sweep through her. His anger and her doubts were forgotten as she held out her hands and he took them. 'I have always loved you—only you.'

'I know it,' he said. 'I am not worthy of you, Elaine. I was a foolish youth who looked for glory and revenge when I should have seen the happiness that could be mine was there for the taking. Can you forgive me?'

'Willingly,' she said and lifted her face for his kiss.

His lips were soft at first, touching lightly here and there as they caressed her, then his tongue flicked at her and she opened her mouth, allowing him to enter and taste her. The sweetness of the gentle probing made her tremble and she reached up shyly to run her fingers into his hair at the nape of his neck, stroking him. He moaned low in his throat and his arms tightened about her as the kiss intensified.

Elaine sighed and pressed closer to him, feeling the hard heat of his arousal through the softness of the material that divided them. It thrilled her to feel the urgency in him and she tipped her head back as he kissed her throat, her body arching into his as she felt herself swept on the crest of a surging wave of desire.

Zander bent and swept her up into his arms, carrying her to the bed and sitting her down; then he took hold of her fine night-chemise and pulled it up over her head, discarding it on the floor.

'You are even more lovely than in my dreams,' he murmured and knelt before her. 'I vow that I shall always protect and honour you, my lady.'

'I love you,' Elaine whispered, her throat tight with emotion.

'Lie down for me, my love,' he said and then threw off his robe. He was wearing some tight-fitting hose and long soft boots. Sitting on the bed beside her, as she watched, he pulled off the boots and then let down the hose by untying the strings at his waist. In another moment he was as naked as she.

Now it was Elaine's turn to gasp in wonder at the beauty of his body. Tanned by the years he'd spent in the sun of the Holy Land, honed to perfect fitness, it was not spoiled even by the fresh bruises and hardly healed cuts now revealed to her. Yet what made her draw her breath was the size of his aroused manhood, for he was a large, vital man in every way.

As he lay down by her side, she reached out to touch some of the fresh wounds. He had made light of them, but it was obvious that he had been severely injured in the ambush.

'Do these hurt?'

'I take no notice of them. Had Janvier not covered me with his body I might have died. He was so very ill. I could not leave him, Elaine. He has saved my life twice and I would not do less for him—besides, I thought it best to remain hidden while we were so weak. If my enemy had known where to find me...'

'I would never betray you. Surely you knew that?'

'But neither of us knew for sure who that enemy was...you understand my dilemma?'

'Yes, of course. I have forgiven you.'

Zander shuddered as a breath of air left his

lips. He reached out to touch her face, cradling it with his hands. For a long moment he simply looked into her eyes and then he smiled. He leaned down and kissed her brow, then the tip of her nose and her lips. His kisses trailed down her white neck, down to the valley between her small but firm breasts. His mouth sought first one nipple and then the other, sucking delicately and nudging at her with his tongue, licking her with firm strokes that made her arch and cry out in pleasure.

His tongue and lips continued their downward spiral, giving pleasure wherever they touched, until he reached the very centre of her sexuality. When his mouth sucked at her and his tongue stroked, she bucked and screamed with pleasure, her body shaking and trembling. Her hands clawed at his shoulders, her nails scoring little trails on his bronzed skin as she felt herself swept away on a tide of sensual pleasure.

When his body slid up hers and she felt his hot hardness probing at her, she opened wider for his entry. He slid into her warm moistness and for a moment stilled, but she pulled at him, wanting all of him, needing him deep inside her, her knees clenching his thighs as she offered herself to him.

For a moment there was pain, but it was

swiftly over and forgot as he surged into her and she rose to meet him. Zander moved slowly, with care, pausing now and then to allow her to feel the pleasure building deep down. Heat pooled low in her abdomen, feeding on the flames of desire until it reached a roaring flame and then burst into showers that ran all over her body, making her buck and writhe beneath him as he moved faster and faster to their climax.

When it was over, they lay still for a moment, totally spent, and then he rolled to one side, taking her with him so that she lay half across him, one leg curved over his body, her face against his chest. His skin was damp with sweat and she licked him, tasting the salt and smiling, as he looked at her, one eye half-closed.

'I am spent,' he murmured. ''Twill be half an hour at least before I am ready again, my greedy little wench. You've drained me.'

Elaine laughed, feeling a new confidence as she looked at him and saw the satiated expression, the soft loose mouth and heavy eyes that spoke of his satisfaction.

'Have I pleased my lord?' she teased and heard him growl.

'Carry on like this and you will get no sleep this night,' he murmured.

'No, no, I merely tease,' she said and snuggled into his body.

Elaine drifted into sleep and knew that Zander slept, too, his breathing shallow and even before she slept herself.

Chapter Fourteen

When Elaine awoke she lay wondering what was different and then smiled as she remembered Zander's passion of the previous night. Moving her hand across the bed, she discovered that the sheets where he'd lain were cold. He must have left the bed some time before.

Why had he not wakened her?

Fear ran through her. Had he broken his promise and gone off to meet with his one-time friend?

Jumping from the bed, Elaine ran to the window and looked down. She felt instant relief as she saw men training in the courtyard below. Zander was fighting with Sir Robert. The last time she'd seen them fight Sir Robert had looked the stronger, but this time he was being forced to retreat by the skill and deftness of his opponent.

Despite the icy cold morning, the men were wearing only leather jerkins over their naked torsos and tight leggings with long boots. Both used a shield to good advantage and the fight went one way and then the other, but after a few sharp thrusts from Sir Robert, Zander always attacked and advanced.

Even as she watched, Sir Robert cried enough. The two men were laughing, clearly the best of friends. They sheathed their blades and embraced, then Zander turned and glanced up at Elaine's slitted window, almost as though he knew she watched. He held up his hand and she waved back, smiling as she called for her ladies to help her dress.

When her sheets were thrown back the evidence of her night of passion was plain for all to see. Marion smiled and nodded, looking at her with satisfaction.

'If you were a maid before, you are a woman now,' she said. 'What will you have to break your fast today, my lady?'

'Bread, honey, some dates and a little cheese,' Elaine replied. 'I am hungry.'

Her ladies smiled and went away to fetch the food she'd requested. Marion remained to help her into one of her second-best gowns: a tunic of soft-green silk, covered by an over-gown of velvet in a darker shade. She brought a belt of gold leather set with studs of bronze and fringed at the ends. On her head, Elaine wore a band of green velvet rolled with white silk, and a veil of gauze hung at the back to cover her hair, which she had swept back from her face with combs of bronze.

Her mirror was small and of burnished silver, which gave her only a hazy reflection of her face, but she felt that she must look well for she had never been so filled with life and happiness.

'You look wonderful,' Marion told her. 'As a bride should look the morning after her wedding night.'

'Thank you, dear Marion,' Elaine said and laughed. 'I feel wonderful.'

Elaine did not feel like staying in her chamber or working at her sewing. Despite the frosty air, the sun was shining, calling her outside. She asked Marion for her surcoat and slipped it over her gown. As she walked down the stair of her chamber, she felt like singing aloud. Her body had surely never felt this good and her mind was free of the doubts and fears that had clouded it for so long.

A few servants were working in the hall as

she passed through. The great open fireplace had been made up with fresh logs and a fire was already burning. A housecarl was burnishing some armour and two maidservants were giggling in the corner as they swept the stone flags and sprinkled fresh herbs and rushes.

Elaine was aware of a feeling of happiness about her, as if her people knew that things had changed for the better.

As she went outside, she saw that some of the men were still training, others were watching, as were Zander and Sir Robert. The craftsmen were at work in the outer bailey and she could hear the ring of hammers as the blacksmith mended anything from a wheel to a sword or a ploughshare. The armourer was also busy making body shields, shaping helmets and sharpening the swords the blacksmith had honed in his fire. The cellarer was counting his barrels, while the saddle maker was busy stitching his leathers. The smell of bread baking and meat roasting were familiar smells, as was the sight of men and women going about their business with a laugh or a smile.

Perhaps it was just Elaine, but she sensed that the atmosphere was different. Everyone was in a good mood. It was almost Christmastide and some men were dragging in a load of greenery, which would be used to decorate the hall. The fresh sharp smell made Elaine think of the last Christmas with her father, when they'd exchanged gifts on Christmas Eve and roasted an ox, a whole sheep and twenty capons so that all their people could share the feast. She touched the silver cross that lay beneath her tunic as she went up to Zander.

If her husband continued to make love to her with the same passion as the previous night, she might have a child to share their celebrations the next year.

Zander turned and looked at her. For a moment he was frowning and her heart stopped. Was he angry again?

His frown disappeared and he smiled, making her feel as if her bones would melt with pleasure.

'Elaine, I told your ladies to let you sleep.'

'They did not wake me,' she said. 'I was ready to get up—but it is too pleasant a day to stay in my room and sew.'

'What would you like to do?'

Elaine thought for a moment, then, 'I should like to go foraging for herbs and berries. We dared not venture beyond the castle while you were away—but now, yes, I should like to gather a party of my ladies and your men and walk in the woods.'

Zander hesitated, then nodded. 'It shall be as you wish, my lady,' he said. 'Gather the ladies you would take with you. I shall assemble my men—and we will take food with us. It shall be a day of rest and pleasure—and this evening we shall feast.'

'Thank you.' Elaine looked at him shyly. Did he guess how much her heart fluttered when he looked at her like that? Did he know that she wanted to run and laugh and sing, because of the way he'd loved her the previous night? 'We shall not keep you waiting long.'

She ran back into the house, calling for Marion.

The woman came hurriedly towards her. 'Is something wrong, my lady?'

'No, everything is perfect,' Elaine said. 'We are going to have a day foraging. Zander and his men will escort us and keep us safe. Fetch Alice and Bess and Mary—and tell them to bring their baskets. I am sure Bertrand will come, too. Zander is arranging for food so servants will follow and we shall picnic in the woods.'

'A day of celebration,' Marion cried, eyes sparkling. 'It is but two days to Christ's Mass and everyone is excited. Shall I tell those who remain here that they may embroider or spend their time playing games?'

'Yes, why not? Zander's men who remain here will draw up the bridge after we leave, but those who have no duty may enjoy themselves, as they will.'

Elaine fetched her own basket and saw her ladies scurrying round to fetch cloaks, gloves and hoods. It was cold out, but the sun would make it a pleasant day. Some of the housecarls must continue to work, for the food must be prepared for tonight's feast, and a guard must always be kept on the walls in case of attack, but it was the time to be merry and enjoy life.

It was quite a large party that set out for the woods a little later that morning. Elaine rode her own palfrey, but the other ladies rode pillion behind a groom. Ten of Zander's men-at-arms were to accompany them and five servants followed with a cart. They would prepare food and set out stools and cushions for the ladies and knights to sit when they ate their meal.

Everyone was laughing and talking, and a piper sat on the cart making music as they travelled, his merry tune sweet on the frosty air. As they passed the village, the women came out to wave and smile and Zander surprised Elaine by stopping to speak with them. He took out a purse of silver coins and gave them to the village headman, who had come out to show respect to his lord.

'This is for your people so that they may enjoy Christ's Mass,' Zander said. 'On the eve of Christ's Mass we feast at the Manor and there will be food for those who come to the door.'

Cheers greeted his announcement and women called blessings on his name as the little cavalcade rode on. When they reached the woods, they dismounted, the grooms leading the horses while the women and some of the knights dismounted to walk through the woods.

Soon, they were pairing off and Elaine saw Marion walking happily with Bertrand. Every other moment someone called out that they had made a find: herbs, nuts and berries that would add flavour and variety to their food. All the ladies had been trained from girlhood to know which fungi were edible and which poisonous. The big flat mushrooms they occasionally found were just one of the delicious fungi to be discovered in the woods. One of the knights had brought a special dog with him, and his dog discovered a nest of truffles: two large and one smaller. Their pungent smell and the delicious taste would make a wonderful addition to their feast. Truffles were often hunted with pigs, but given the chance the pigs would eat them before the men had a chance to dig them up, whereas a dog would simply bark and scrape at the ground. Many roots found in the woods and hedgerows were edible and the rose-hips that still clung to the stems of dog roses were still of use, though perhaps past their best. Elaine found some nuts, which had fallen into the leaves at the foot of a hazel tree and, when she cracked one, the kernel was still sweet and full.

'We missed the best time of year, but just to be here wandering at will without fear is lovely,' she said and smiled up at Zander. 'It is what I have missed for a long time.'

'I truly hope that life will be happier for you in future, Elaine,' Zander said and took her hand. He carried it to his lips to kiss, his look making her heart thud in her breast. 'And for all of us.'

Someone had begun to sing. Elaine turned to look and saw that the women had set down their baskets and formed a circle. They were dancing while the men clapped and chanted the words of the song.

'Come and join us, lady,' Marion called. 'My lord, too.'

Elaine laughed and ran to her, then Zander came and took her hands. Now some of the other knights had taken the other ladies by the hands and they began to skip to the music and laugh as they enjoyed the spirit of Christ's Mass, which had come upon them all.

It was nearing the most holy night in the year—the night when the Saviour was born and God blessed mankind. This was surely the time to be happy and forget all the troubles that had beset them these past weeks...

Elaine thought that she would never forget her day in the woods. She always enjoyed foraging with her ladies, but this had been a special day and she was filled with a newfound delight in her world as they rode back to the manor house late in the afternoon. The drawbridge was let down to admit them, and though Zander questioned Sir Robert, who had been left in charge, nothing untoward had happened.

The men who had been in the woods were allowed to refresh themselves and then took the place of those who had been guarding the ramparts all day, just as the ladies who had been playing in the woods took up their duties at table. Everyone was talking and laughing.

Course after course of rich food was brought

to table. In the kitchens the housecarls were sharing the same delights as their lord and lady at the high board, which was not the case in every big house. They looked at one another and smiled, praising their lord for his generosity and congratulating themselves on having a just and fair master.

When Elaine said goodnight to her ladies and went upstairs to her chamber, she was feeling very tired, but determined not to fall asleep before Zander came to her. She hoped that he would not be too long, though she knew he intended to make a tour of the ramparts before he retired for the night. Just because it was a time of celebration they could not afford to relax completely. Zander did not wish to fight at such a holy time, but he could not know what his enemy was planning.

She did not have long to wait. Before the candle had started to flicker, Zander entered and came to her. Elaine went to greet him, lifting her face for his kiss. She gave him her hand and led him towards the bed, where they had found so much pleasure the previous night. Her heart was racing as she let her robe slither down over her hips and stood before him naked. He moved towards her, sweeping her up and carrying her to the bed.

Elaine gazed up at him, her lips curving in a smile of welcome. 'Last night you pleased me,' she said huskily. 'Tonight I would have you teach me how to please my lord.'

'You always please me,' he said and bent his head to kiss her lips. 'But I shall teach you all the ways we may please each other.'

'Will you teach me to dance, as your men did?' she asked and her eyes danced with laughter. 'I should like to dance with you that way sometimes.'

'You are a wicked wench,' he murmured and drew her close, his lips taking hers. 'And all that I could ever desire in my wife…'

Elaine smiled, welcoming him as he began to caress and love her—and yet there was a part of her that longed for something more. A sign that she was as important to him as he was to her. He wanted her, desired her—but did he truly love her?

'My lord…' Zander turned as he heard his servant's voice and smiled, going to greet him with outstretched hands. 'Janvier! You are well? I have been anxious lest Newark should refuse to listen and perhaps have you beaten or worse?'

'I think he was in two minds at first,' Janvier told him and smiled. 'Had it not been for an incident at table he might have sent me away or had me hung, but in the end he called me his friend and promised me anything I wanted within reason. I told him you would make peace with him and he said he would consider it.'

Zander was astonished. 'You must have done something extraordinary for Newark to be so grateful.'

'It happened as we supped that first night. A young man called Stronmar was sitting close to the earl at table, eating, laughing with his mouth full. Suddenly, he started to choke and could not breathe. Everyone was astounded, but I grabbed him by the stomach and thumped him hard in the back. A lump of hard bread flew from his mouth and he could breathe again.'

'You saved his life?'

'Yes, my lord. Some thought I was attacking him and they were all for seizing me, but Newark saw what happened and was grateful. He told his knights to stand back and, later, before we retired for the night, he thanked me privately and I would swear there were tears in his eyes.'

'You acted swiftly as always.' Zander frowned. 'But I wonder why the life of one man should affect him so powerfully—the man you saved is an ill-favoured brute, as I recall.'

'I believe Stronmar is Newark's bastard son—the child of a peasant woman. It is not acknowledged openly, but someone told me later that it was so.'

'Ah, now I understand. Newark's wives have given him only daughters.' Zander nodded. 'You have done well, my friend. I thank you. We must hope that Newark will accept my invitation to make terms. If Philip is biding his time, planning his next move against us, I cannot afford to be at odds with Newark.'

'All we can do is to watch and wait,' Janvier said. 'If Allah wills it all will be well.'

'I wish I knew what Philip was planning,' Zander said and frowned. 'It seems odd that we have heard nothing of him.'

Philip lifted the carved oak chest and threw it across the room. He'd torn down hangings and smashed anything that would break when he discovered the trick Anne had played on him that first morning, but she'd left little of value behind her. Her best gowns, her silver, jewels and trinkets had gone with her—as had a bag of gold coins and a silver chalice from his chest.

'Damn the bitch,' he muttered. 'If I catch her, I'll break her scrawny neck.'

At the moment his anger was directed at his sister. He'd trusted her to use her arts to break Elaine's will-power for long enough to make her his bride. Somehow *she*, her maid and his sister had all slipped away in the dead of night. Had they gone together? Had Anne helped Elaine to escape—or had she discovered the escape and panicked, fleeing before he could wreak revenge on her?

Philip knew that Elaine had gone to Sweetbriars. She was alone and vulnerable and he could take her when he chose, but he did not know where his cheating sister had gone. She'd robbed him of his gold and of his revenge on the man who had always been better at everything than Philip. Zander was stronger, cleverer and luckier in every way.

Yet for a time they had been friends. Had Philip not been seen murdering his uncle— had Baron de Bricasse not threatened to tell the king—they might have remained friends. It was the knowledge of what Zander might do if he discovered the truth that had made Philip realise that he must destroy Zander before he could rest easily at night.

In the Holy Land the Saracens had almost

done his work for him. He'd heard that Zander lay close to death and he'd believed himself safe, but then his friend returned and brought a fortune with him, some of which he'd sent to Philip for safekeeping until he returned to claim it.

Philip had been sorely tempted to keep the chests of gold, silks and precious items, but then he'd seen Elaine and he'd known that he must have her. She was what Zander prized most, far more than his gold and silver, which was only a part of the fortune he'd amassed over the years. If he wanted to punish Zander for all the nights of fear, when he'd woken in a cold sweat after a dream in which his one-time friend killed him, it must be through the girl. And she was lovely. Philip wanted to seduce her. He wanted to possess and hurt her—and she had almost been his.

She would be again. He would have her whether she liked it or not. When he was ready he would take the manor and he would take her. It mattered not whether she was his wife—he would use her, humble her and then…

'My lord…'

Philip turned and looked at the terrified housecarl in the doorway. 'I have news.'

'Speak, sirrah.' Philip glared down at the

wretch as he fell to his knees. The man was so terrified that the news must be bad. 'Speak or I will have your tongue.'

'Forgive me,' the man cried, almost weeping in his fear. 'We have found Lady Anne. She is gone to the Abbey of St Michael and the Abbess has given her sanctuary.'

'Damn her!' Philip kicked the man before him, sending him sprawling to the ground where he lay moaning. 'Get out of here.'

The man was almost gibbering when he looked up. 'There is more... Lord... Lord Zander hath come back. He and his men are at Sweetbriars and...he has been reinforced by at least thirty men this morning.'

A pulse was beating at Philip's temple and the pain was almost more than he could bear. He swung away from the cowering servant, his rage so great that for a moment he was close to falling in a fit, white spittle on his lips.

His sister was beyond his reach, for despite all his power the King's Marshal could not command her to come forth from the abbey. Even the king himself would not be admitted to that place of sanctuary if he demanded it—and Richard would never permit a House of God to be despoiled. If Philip raised a hand against his sister now, he would feel the king's wrath when he returned to claim his throne.

Yet even worse was the knowledge that Zander had somehow escaped death. Had the men he'd paid to do his dirty work cheated and lied to him? They swore that they'd seen Zander fall and a dozen sword cuts rain on his body. No man could live through that—could he?

Yet Zander bore a charmed life. Any other man would have died in the Holy Land, as Philip had hoped. He had cheated death too many times.

Philip swore several times and smashed his fist against the wall. He would have his revenge on both Zander and his wife—when he took the manor of Sweetbriars, he would have Zander chained, forcing him to watch as Philip took his pleasure with the witch.

His head was buzzing. The pictures went round and round in his mind, becoming fragmented and then shattering as he fell to the ground and began to twitch. He cried out for help, cursing his weakness. It was an affliction he'd suffered from since his uncle's death, perhaps a punishment from God for his evil deed.

'Anne, come to me…'

Whenever he was ill like this, Anne had

made him better—but his sister was no longer here to give him her foul potion.

Was he going to die? The thought was in his mind moments before everything went black around him.

'There is a message come from Lord Stornway,' Sister Eveline told Anne that frosty morning as she sat in her chamber sewing. 'Will you see him, lady?'

'I would rather not speak with him,' Anne said. 'I fear it is some trick of my brother's. He would tempt me from my sanctuary here and then...he would kill me.'

The nun crossed herself. 'God have mercy,' she said. 'If 'tis true, you must not leave these walls while he lives, lady—but the servant spoke of your brother lying prone on his bed and nigh unto death of some strange sickness.'

Anne frowned. 'My brother hath the falling sickness from time to time. I used to make him a cure that eased him, but...' She hesitated, then, 'May I use herbs from your gardens?'

'If it is for a mission of mercy, I am sure Mother Abbess would not object.'

'Then you may tell my brother's messenger that I will prepare the cure and he may return here tomorrow to fetch it. I will not deny Philip my help, but I shall not go to him, for as soon as he is better he would punish me.'

'God will bless you for your charity,' the nun said piously and went away to deliver the message.

Anne was thoughtful. Philip did not deserve that she should do anything for him, but he was her brother. She had sins enough on her conscience and had begun to repent them in this house of prayer. Yet because of Philip she was forced to spend the rest of her life here—and already she was bored with the routine of the nuns' days.

A part of her was tempted to send a herbal drink that would do nothing to ease her brother's fevered mind, but then she remembered that the mixture was strong. Had she not been there to oversee his illness in the past he could easily have taken too much and died.

His fate was in his own hands. She would prepare the mixture and send it to Philip, with the proper instructions—but if he chose to ignore warnings…then he could easily die. It would not be her fault.

Only God could decide what would happen then.

The twelve days of Christmastide were happy ones for all those at Sweetbriars. They danced, sang carols and played games, everyone enjoying the time of peace and plenty that had come upon them.

Elaine felt that Zander cared for her. He might not love her as she loved him, but he was passionate when he came to her at night and generous to her and her people.

For Elaine there was a chain of green stones that she knew were called emeralds set in silver, which she could wind in her hair or about her throat.

'This is beautiful,' Elaine said. 'I thank you for my gift.'

She gave him a pair of leather gauntlets she had embroidered with silks, using his initials and the crest of a flying eagle, which he carried on his armour.

Elaine had given small gifts of cloth to all her ladies, and Zander gave them five gold coins each, which would provide a dowry for any lady that wished to marry. She knew that some of her ladies had formed alliances with knights in Zander's train and some might wish to marry, but most would not leave her service unless their husbands won honours and could purchase a good house and land of their own.

After Christ's Mass was over, the household began to be busy once more. The men went out hunting to replenish their stores of meat. They brought back venison, hares and a wild boar. The boar's head was roasted, as was the hind they had killed, but the hares were cooked in rich sauces and the boar's meat was salted to keep a little longer.

Because of Elaine's industry in the first weeks she and her ladies were at the manor, they had several barrels of salted beef and pork, flour, preserves of fruit and dried fruits, but the time of winter was difficult and outside the manor house some of the common folk were starving. Every day they had beggars at their door asking for food and medicines for the sores that afflicted their skin.

Elaine was a generous chatelaine and she'd made good use of the herbs and berries they had gathered out foraging. No beggar was turned away without at least a piece of bread, perhaps a heel of cheese or a strip of salted beef to chew. If she thought her cures would help to ease their pain, she offered them freely, but often the only help she could give was to advise the sufferer to make a pilgrimage to a shrine and pray for the saint's intervention. Some had already visited several shrines, others spoke of miraculous cures brought about by holy water, but some took what she offered gratefully and said it eased them.

It was from one of the visiting pilgrims that they heard that the King's Marshal lay sick on his bed.

''Tis said that he was struck down with some kind of fit after Lady Anne ran away from the castle,' the man said and crossed himself devoutly. 'May God rest him, for he may not be long for this earth.'

'Do you know where Lady Anne went?' Elaine asked.

'I have heard she took sanctuary in the Abbey of St Michael,' the man said and crossed himself once more. 'It is said her brother threatened to kill her. May God protect and have mercy on her soul.'

Elaine told Zander her news when he and his men came back from another hunting expedition that night. This time they had taken only some wood pigeon and a small deer. The weather was bitter and the smaller game had vanished from the woods, either disappearing into the pot of a desperate villager or in burrows beneath the ground. It was unlawful for the villagers to hunt in the lord's woods, but Zander was lenient; he knew that many would starve this winter, especially on the lands of intolerant lords who gave their people nothing. Some barons would hang a man for taking a snared rabbit from his woods. Zander shared what he could, though at this time of year it could be hard to find enough food to exist, even in a house such as theirs.

'Do you believe that Lord Stornway is close to death?' she asked him. 'Or do you think it a clever ruse to put you off your guard?'

'I am not sure,' Zander said. 'I would go to Lady Anne and ask her—but I know she will never forgive me for killing the man she would have wed.'

'I could go in your stead?'

'No! Do not think of it,' Zander said and took hold of her wrist, his eyes boring down into hers. 'Promise me you will not defy me, Elaine. If you should be taken…we have heard nothing from Newark as yet, though Janvier sent word that he was on his way to visit him at Howarth.'

'Do you believe that the earl will restore Howarth to us?' Elaine asked. 'Why should he? You are stronger now and I know that every day men come to you and ask for service—but Howarth is not easily breached. It would not have fallen to Newark had he not used trickery.'

'We need more manors,' Zander told her and frowned. 'Sweetbriars hath supported us thus far, but the game is scarce and we need to move on soon, especially if I am to gather more armed men about me. I have asked my uncle to find me a house and land near his own, but Howarth belongs to you—and through you to me.'

'What will you do if he refuses to give it up?'

'I must settle with Philip first and then…' Zander frowned as he saw her look. 'I know you do not wish me to leave, but I have to protect your interests, as well as those of our people. As the lord of this manor I have my duties.'

'Yes, I understand.' Elaine smothered her sigh. Great lords had huge responsibilities to the people who relied on them for their living and the work of running a large manor went on from first light to dusk. She had been fortunate to have a period of some weeks settled at her dower lands. Sweetbriars was not large enough to support all Zander's entourage for the whole year; they must move on soon, and perhaps sooner than she'd hoped. 'You must decide for the best,' she said. 'Has your uncle found anything suitable for us?'

'He wrote of a manor not more than twenty leagues' distance from his own, which will soon be for sale. The land is sweet and there are extensive woods with plenty of game, also a small lake well stocked with fish. I think it may suit us—and I plan to visit my uncle to secure the property, as soon as I am certain you will be safe here.'

Elaine wanted to ask if she could go with him, but she knew she must not cling. Many knights left their wives at home while they went to court or to foreign lands to fight wars for their king. She had waited so many years for Zander to return and since then they had had only a few stolen hours of time alone together. He had his duties as lord of the manor and she had hers—but her heart protested at the thought of parting from him once more.

'When do you plan to leave?' she asked, but even as he prepared to answer there was a commotion in the hall and then one of his men came hurrying towards them.

'My lord,' he said. 'Will you come? The Earl of Newark is at the gates with a force of some thirty men. He claims he comes in peace to treat with you. Will you give him entrance?'

'If he hath no more than thirty men, he has no idea of making war on us. Ask him to come in with fifteen of his knights and they may retain their swords. The others must wait outside, but the gates will remain open.'

As the man hurried back to pass on his message, Zander turned to Elaine. His eyes were dark with concern as he looked down at her.

'Go to your room and lock the door lest it be a trick. There may be fighting and I would not have you harmed or kidnapped—though I think Newark must have come in friendship, because he would be outnumbered by my men.'

'I shall do as you ask,' Elaine said. 'Do not fret for my sake, Zander. I shall gather my ladies and we will work on our sewing until you send word that we may come down.'

'Then I must leave you.' He smiled and reached out to touch her face with the tips of his fingers. 'These past weeks have been the happiest of my life.'

With those words he left her and Elaine called to her ladies. They had hurried to her as soon as the news concerning the earl's arrival had reached them and flocked up the twisting stairs to her solar and the sewing room, where many of them slept at night. She could hear their whispers and knew that they were anxious and uneasy.

Elaine set them to mending torn garments or embroidery, depending on their talents. She went to the window herself and looked down at the scene below. Men and horses were mill-ing around and she could not tell whether they came in friendship or to cause harm.

'Sit with us, my lady,' Marion said. 'Read to us from the Bible. It will ease all our minds.'

'Yes, I must leave everything to my lord,' Elaine said. Her heavy Bible, bound in leather and embossed with silver, was set out on a lectern of good English oak. She opened it, looking at the pages of thick vellum on which monks had inscribed the words of God, each page beautifully decorated with bright images of gold, crimson, yellow and blue. It had taken several monks years to perfect this work of art, which was worth a small fortune.

Elaine read aloud the passage concerning the creation of mankind. It was writ in Latin and most of her ladies could understand a few words of the ancient language, but they all knew the story and were used to hearing it read by priests, for all religious services were conducted in the ancient tongue.

Her voice soothed them and they bent over their work, none of them speaking as she continued to read out loud. Some time had passed before a knock sounded at the door and then Bertrand's voice was heard telling them to open for him.

Marion got up and went to the door, looking at him anxiously. 'What news?' she asked. 'Is all well?'

'It seems the earl comes in friendship. He has brought documents for Lord Zander to see—some relating to the castle at Howarth, I think—and others to King Richard's return.'

Elaine closed her Bible. 'Does my lord send for me?' she asked.

'You and your ladies may come down now. My lord is satisfied that no harm is intended.'

Elaine breathed a sigh of relief, for Zander had taken a risk by admitting the Earl of Newark. She signalled to her ladies.

'Very well, we shall come down now.'

They gathered about her, still subdued and unsure, but she smiled at them. 'Zander would not send for us unless he was certain.'

She led the way down the stairs to the hall below. It seemed to be filled with men and she guessed that Zander had summoned his knights to give a show of strength. As she entered the large room a hush fell and every head was turned to look at her. She saw the earl, saw his eyes narrow and felt apprehensive. Would he truly submit so tamely to Zander's request?

Raising her head proudly, she walked to where he was standing with Zander. Outwardly, she was calm, though her heart raced wildly. She fought to subdue the trembling of her hands. This man had murdered her uncle, humiliated her aunt and done his best to capture her. Pride and anger banished the fear, her eyes beginning to spark with temper.

'Elaine, my love, the earl hath something to say to you.' Zander smiled at her.

'I have come to beg your pardon, Lady Elaine,' the earl said and his thick lips curved in what passed for a smile. 'Had I understood you were betrothed to Lord Zander, I should not have pursued my claim to your hand and lands.'

'You killed my uncle and banished his lady wife, sir.'

'Regrettably that is so,' he agreed. 'I considered that your uncle had cheated me and so I planned to take what was mine by force—but you escaped me. I have seen the deceit Lord Howarth meant to practise—he would have kept your lands himself and cheated us both, Lady Elaine. Since you are now wed to Lord Zander, your lands belong to him—and I shall restore them to him. I shall also make reparation of one hundred silver pieces to you for any harm that was done you.'

Elaine's gaze narrowed. The man's leer made her feel sick inside and she wanted to refuse, to throw his silver back in his face. He had murdered her uncle by a trick and it was a lie to say that he had been cheated, for he'd never had any right to her or her lands. She had refused his offer and he'd thought to take everything he wanted by trickery. It was on the tip of her tongue to tell him what she thought of him, but something in Zander's eyes warned her to hold her tongue. She was seething inside, but she said nothing and waited for her husband's lead.

'My wife thanks you for your offer,' Zander said. 'She was fond of her uncle, but like you she was deceived in him. Come, Elaine, set your hand to this document and the feud is ended. The Earl of Newark travels to his lands in Normandy, where he hopes to meet with Richard—and there must be no enmity between us, for the king needs all his friends when he returns to England.'

Anger flared into a roaring flame inside her. How could he demand that she allow this foul villain to flout the law? She wanted to denounce him to the king and demand satisfaction, but Zander's eyes narrowed and he looked angry.

'Elaine, come.' He held out his hand to her imperiously. It was a command, not a request, and she could only take the quill he offered to her, dip it in the ink and sign where the cleric pointed out. 'Good, it is done,' Zander said and signed himself.

'This seals our alliance, Newark,' he said. 'Tell Richard that when he comes I shall be at his disposal should he need my help.'

'Of course, it is no more than I expected,' the earl said smoothly. His tongue moved over his thick lips, making Elaine shudder, though she gave no outward sign. 'Richard was grateful for the generous donation, which made it possible to pay his ransom. He will no doubt show his appreciation when he returns.'

Zander stepped forwards, offering his hand. The two men clasped hands and smiled, as if they were the best of friends.

'You will sup with us this evening?'

'Forgive me, I must continue my journey,' the earl said. 'I have stayed too long, but I wanted this settled.'

'You may go with our good wishes. We bear you no animosity,' Zander said.

Elaine watched them go, then returned to her chamber. She was unhappy that Zander had come to terms with the earl so easily, for honour demanded that he should pay for what he had done to her uncle and aunt, and would no doubt have done to her had he caught her.

She knew that Zander had wanted the lands

of Howarth. Was it for that that he had betrayed her—selling her honour and her peace of mind for one hundred silver pieces? If he loved her, he must have known how hurt she was. He would have driven his sword into the earl's black heart.

Her uncle had never deceived Newark. It was all a lie to cover his wickedness and Zander knew that. How could he pretend to believe it and accept the earl's terms?

She paced the floor of her chamber, her soft slippers making no noise on the stone flags. Her heart ached, for she had begun to believe that Zander truly loved her, but now she was unsure. Why had Zander given into Newark's terms for so little recompense? Did he not see it was an insult to her uncle's memory?

Some time passed and then Zander came into her chamber.

'I know you are upset, but I can explain why it was necessary to accept the earl's apology.'

'I heard no apology.'

'It was as close as a man of his nature could come to an apology.'

'He is a murderer and a thief. I do not want his blood money.'

'I did not expect you to keep it. You may give it to the poor—distribute it as you please.'

'Very well, I shall use it to ensure that my people are well fed this winter—but I wish that you had punished him for what he did to my uncle and aunt.'

'You know that there was nothing else I could have done. Had things been different I might have challenged him—but he has Richard's ear and goes to meet him and bring his Majesty back to England. If Prince John hears of Richard's imminent return, he may try some treachery. I cannot pick a quarrel with a man of Newark's stature at this time.'

Elaine turned her head aside; the tears were so close that she could barely speak for emotion. It seemed to her that he cared less for her than his duty to the king, but she kept her hurt inside and said nothing.

'I have to leave you soon. I must speak with Lord Stornway—and then I must visit my uncle. After that I must prepare to meet the king. In the morning we shall hunt again, to make sure you have enough meat until we return. While we are away I would have you pack so that we can move on to the estate my uncle has found for us.'

'If you must go, you must go,' Elaine said.

'My women and I can manage here alone. There is enough food to sustain us for some months if we are careful.'

'I should not be away so very long and I shall leave sufficient men to protect you and your people,' he said and held out his hand to her. 'Will you not come down and dine now?'

She took his hand and went with him to join his men in the Great Hall. Clearly, he thought he had done the right thing in making peace with Newark, and perhaps he had. She found his attitude hurtful, feeling that she and her lands were merely pawns in a game of power play. Elaine held her sigh inside. He was leaving her again. Had he married her merely because he had thought it right to honour his promise made so many years ago—or because the acquisition of her lands and manors made him more powerful?

Once she'd believed he loved her as deeply as she loved him, but now she could not be sure.

Chapter Fifteen

~~~~~~~~~~~~~~~~~~~~~~

Zander did not come to her chamber that night. There was restraint between them and he merely kissed her hand and told her he would not disturb her.

'I intend to rise early in the morning for we must hunt and 'tis often better before the day is too far advanced,' he said. 'I wish you pleasant dreams, Elaine.'

She nodded, her eyes stinging with tears as she entered her chamber alone. Why was Zander so stubborn? Why could he not take her in his arms and tell her he loved her? Did he not understand how arrogant he'd seemed, commanding her to sign that infamous document? She knew that wives were supposed to obey their husbands—and he had the power to beat her if he chose—but she'd believed he was different from men like Newark and Lord Stornway. Were all her dreams of a gentle youth just the foolish imaginings of a young girl?

For a while at Christ's Mass, he had seemed almost like his old self, though there was always a part of him that remained aloof. Elaine had believed, hoped, that he would gradually return to her…become the God-fearing, devout man she'd loved and enshrined in her heart.

Now he seemed to have withdrawn from her again. Perhaps it was her fault, but he must surely understand her feelings? Had he explained the situation to her first rather than presenting her with the document to sign, she might have accepted it more easily.

Was she asking too much?

Rising from her bed as the first rays of morning light crept through her slitted window, Elaine went to look out at the scene below. Already the men were stirring. She could see the knights preparing to mount their horses, the runners and dogs, and the huntsman who was always the fleetest on foot and could keep up with the dogs. He would be there at the kill, to dispatch swiftly any prey that the knights might wound with their arrows.

Elaine saw Zander speaking with Sir Robert. The two men were laughing, talking easily. She felt hot. Were they talking of her? In another moment she knew she blushed for nothing. Their talk would be of more important things…alliances, the return of the king and the small matter of purchasing a new manor so that they might move on for a few months while Sweetbriars was cleansed and the stores could be replenished. A woman was just another possession; they would not waste their time in speaking of a mere wife.

As she watched, she saw other men come to Zander and ask him something; he gave each one his attention, as much to the lowest churl as to his knights. One of the women servants offered him a cup of water, which he took and drank, thanking her.

Elaine felt a spurt of jealousy as she saw how the woman looked at him. He was a tall, powerful man and, despite the scar, which had at last begun to heal, he was handsome. She ought to be proud that he was her husband instead of sulking.

Suddenly, as if he knew she was there, he looked up at her window. He seemed to hesitate, then lifted his hand. Feeling hot and foolish, she stepped back, not wanting him to think she had been watching him.

Had she been foolish to let him leave her the previous night? She had wanted him to lie with her, but pride forbade that she tell him so. In her heart, Elaine knew that she would always love him. Yet she wanted him to treat her as his equal, to love her truly and not just as a pleasant bedmate—a woman of good birth who had brought him her estate and would bear his children.

Was it ever possible for a woman to be treated as an equal by a man? Most would say not. Women were used to gain either power or lands. Elaine wondered at her own foolishness in expecting it. In her world women were often little more than chattels, to be bought, sold or given away as their fathers and guardians pleased.

She wanted so much more. She'd heard stories of women who inspired great love, like Helen of Troy. There were other fables, too, stories of women who had brought men to their knees. Even in the Bible there were women who could control great warriors, like Delilah, who had cut off Samson's hair, and Cleopatra, who held the hearts of two Roman emperors. Elaine had no desire to control—but she did want re-

spect and love from her husband. She'd thought
passion was enough, but now she knew quite
clearly that for her it would never be sufficient.

She was Zander's wife, nothing could change
that, but she wanted him to come to her in
love—and she wanted to share his life, to be
consulted before he made decisions that af-
fected their lives.

The hunting had not been good again. They
took three rabbits, five wood pigeon and a small
deer. It was hardly enough to feed the women
and servants, let alone the knights, and that
meant they would need to use more of the salted
meat from their dwindling stores.

Zander knew that he could not delay his
journey a day longer, even if Elaine begged
him to stay. He must find a larger manor with
woods that supported more game and fields to
rear sufficient livestock to keep them in meat
throughout the winter. Sweetbriars was a beautiful home in the summer and autumn, but in
the deep midwinter they needed to move on.
Castle Howarth had been restored to them, but
Zander knew that Newark would have drained
it of its stores. Its grain, roots and salted meat
would have been used, and though the game
might be more plentiful there, the estate needed

time to recover from being occupied by a man like the Earl of Newark, who took everything but put nothing back. Zander would need to speak to the steward, give him gold to replenish the stores—and then they might spend some time there next winter.

He frowned as he went into the house. Was Elaine still angry with him? God knew he'd had no choice but to accept the earl's terms. He was not yet strong enough to fight two enemies, and, though Philip had not come against him yet, he would. To make an enemy of the earl would have been folly and Elaine must know it in her heart. Surely she did? He had racked his brain trying to find some way of appeasing her without giving offence to his new allies, but could find none. She'd seemed reserved the previous night and so he'd left her to sleep alone, though he had lain awake thinking of her for hours.

However, as he entered the hall, he saw that she was already there, ordering the setting up of the boards for supper that night. Servants were bringing in the heavy boards and placing them on trestles; these tables were easy to clear away in the mornings so that the hall was empty and could be used for other things. The high table where he sat with his knights and Elaine was made of heavy carved oak and in one piece, but it was the only table that remained in situ all day and normally bore the huge silver salt and plates of pewter and silver. It had already been set with ewers of ale and wine, platters of bread and dishes of dates.

Zander walked to the table and took a date, biting into the sweet, firm flesh. He was hungry after a day in the saddle and thirsty.

'Will you have wine, my lord?' Elaine asked and he turned to look at her hopefully. Had she forgiven him for not consulting her? She was smiling and seemed to have forgotten their small quarrel of the previous day.

'Yes, thank you. It has been a long day with little to show for our labours. Our stores will last no longer than a month—and we must leave sufficient for those who remain here after we move on.'

'I know that you must go,' Elaine said and lifted her head proudly. The look in her eyes told him that she had not quite forgiven him for ignoring her wishes, though she'd decided to put it behind her. 'I shall do well enough here with my ladies.'

'I shall return as soon as I am able.'

'As you wish, my lord,' Elaine said.

He frowned, looking at her uncertainly. 'Are you feeling better now?'

'Much better,' she replied, her eyes icy. 'I know my duties as the chatelaine of this house, my lord.'

'And what of your duties as my wife?' Zander's voice was low and ominous, but she merely raised her head higher and turned away, as if she had not heard him.

Zander controlled the urge to take hold of her wrist and make her attend him. He resisted, though she pushed him hard. It was too public here and he would have time enough later to make her listen. Her pride was beyond bearing at times. He was tempted to put her across his knee and beat her.

The idea made his guts tighten and he realised that he would take no pleasure in chastising his wilful wife—for what he really wanted was to have her warm and willing in his arms. He wanted to kiss her, to stroke her soft flesh and feel her heat as she welcomed him into her body.

What did Elaine want of him? It was impossible to know a woman's mind. His wife was beautiful and he desired her, but she was also proud and tempestuous. He might indeed need to chastise her to teach her how she should behave!

He strode away from her, going to his own

chamber to wash the dirt of the day from his face and hands. This evening he intended to have things out with her!

Elaine was smiling as she finished overseeing the preparation of the hall for supper. She was aware of Zander's frustration and it pleased her. While she did not wish to be at odds with her husband, she was not prepared to become a mere chattel that he could order as he chose. She was the mistress here in her own right and he must respect her.

Would he also love her—or was she killing the affection she believed he'd had for her? She knew his temper; it came easily and usually blew itself out as swiftly, for he was a just man. He treated all his people as equals—so why not his wife?

When she was satisfied that all was in place for a celebration that evening—the last they would have for some weeks, until Zander returned or their stores could be replenished— Elaine knew as well as he did that they must begin to conserve what they had if they were to survive the winter. With the frosts so hard the game was all but gone and if they did not find new sources they would have to slaughter the sheep and cattle that should be kept to breed new stock in the spring. In a hard winter both the lord in his manor and the common-folk could come close to starvation if they did not manage their food stocks wisely.

Zander had to inspect the manor his uncle had found for them. Elaine understood and was ready to accept that it was but one of the absences she must endure over the years. He'd pledged himself to King Richard and, when his Majesty returned, must be ready to take up arms in his defence. A part of his urgency was to find a place where Elaine and her people would be safe if that should happen. A rich manor, well stocked with large woods and close to his powerful uncle's estate, was exactly what was needed. She knew it in her heart, but she needed to know that she was more to him than a mere possession, a chattel that became his to do with as he would when they wed.

Although she longed to give in and let him take her in his arms that night, she was determined to resist. He must learn to respect her views for unless he did, there could be no happiness for either of them.

Elaine might be asking too much, but it was what she wanted—what she needed—and if Zander were the man she'd believed him, he would know that.

* * *

Elaine remained calmly aloof throughout the meal that night. She smiled at those who served her, laughed at the jests Zander's knights made and graciously led the dancing that followed the meal. Then she bade them all goodnight and wished them a safe journey and swift return to their loved ones.

Zander watched her and brooded. He could find no fault in her manner, for she charmed his knights and treated her servants well. He knew that she was deeply loved by her people and returned their care for her diligently. Elaine was never idle and there would always be a poultice or a cure for any ill that she could ease with her simple potions. Neither she nor the physicians could cure many of the terrible ills that sometimes afflicted people; it was simply not possible to understand why people took the wasting sickness or died in terrible pain. Those that suffered from afflictions to their mind were dismissed as having been invaded by demons and chained or left to die in filth and poverty. Only God or a visit to a holy shrine might bring them to their right minds; the surgeons could do nothing. It was a fact of life and amongst the many mysteries that wise men sought to solve by studying their charts of the stars.

Why could Elaine not be as dutiful a wife as she was a chatelaine? Other ladies of her birth knew their place; they smiled and were obedient to their husbands. They expected to be told what to do and were grateful for what they were given.

At least Zander's mother had seemed that way to him. She would never have dreamed of challenging his father's decisions…and yet… there was a tiny part of him that admitted he did not truly wish for a submissive wife. One of the reasons he'd fallen in love with Elaine so many years ago was that she was full of life and playful…wilful…

A smile came to his mouth as he remembered a day they had spent together in the woods. Elaine's nurse had called to her that her father wanted her. She had been scolded and told to come in and tidy herself—but instead she'd taken Zander's hand and they'd run away to the woods. It had been early autumn then, warm and still with only the chattering of a red squirrel or the sound of birdsong to disturb the silence of the leafy glade in which he'd made a bed of his cloak. They'd lain there for hours, talking, laughing, and kissing…looking into each other's eyes as they talked of everything.

He'd shared his hopes and dreams with her then and she'd shared hers.

He'd wanted to love her so badly but he'd been too honourable to despoil his innocent lady. She'd been as pure when he left her that evening as when she had given him her hand in trust. He remembered her standing in the stream, her tunic up above her knees as she wriggled her toes on the sandy bed. He'd found her ripe berries, which she'd eaten greedily, the juice staining her lips—and he'd licked it from her mouth. Most men would have had her then, taking her in the privacy of their secret place, but he'd let her go—because he loved her. Because he had always loved her and loved her still, God help him!

It was these pictures and others that had sustained him in the years away, his dreams of returning and making her his wife. Then came the despair and grief of seeing so many die— and his own terrible injuries. He'd believed then that he could never wed her, but she'd seen the man she loved and not the scar. She was clever and beautiful and bold—and that was the way he wanted her. He loved her…and always would, no matter what she did or how often they quarrelled.

Zander felt the armour he'd built up over the

years crumble about his heart. Why had he tried to keep a distance between them? Why had he not told her how much she truly meant to him? Perhaps if she understood that she would know why he'd had to make that alliance for her sake.

With the realisation of his love came the knowledge that he had not changed deep down inside, despite all the suffering. He had denied God, but God had watched over him, waiting for him to return to His love and mercy.

Zander felt his eyes sting. He made the sign of the Cross over his chest as he whispered a silent prayer, thanking the Good Lord for the bounty he had granted in giving him so much. He knew then that he must make his peace with Elaine somehow.

Elaine had gone to her chamber. As Zander rose to follow her, he wondered if he would find her door opened or locked against him. He frowned. She must listen to him before he left her—even if he had to break it down.

Elaine had been thoughtful as she went up to her chamber. She hadn't been in the least tired, but she did not wish to go on with this restraint between them; it no longer soothed her pride to prick at Zander and see that look of annoyance in his eyes. Her chest had felt tight with tears and her eyes had stung. In the morning he would leave her for some weeks. All she wanted was to be in his arms, to feel his lips on hers and give herself up to the sweetness of his loving—but if she gave in now she would never be more to him than just a pair of warm arms when they were needed and a chatelaine for his houses.

She had told Marion that she did not wish for help just yet. Alone in her chamber, she sat down and removed her headdress and veil, taking up her silver brush and shaking out her long hair. Hearing the door open behind her, she did not turn until the voice spoke.

'You are just as beautiful as ever,' it said. 'I shall enjoy breaking you to my will.'

Elaine spun round, her breath catching in her throat as she saw the man standing in her chamber. He looked gaunt and ill, his eyes seeming to glitter as if with fever and yet there was an air of menace about him that chilled her.

'How did you get in here?' she asked and curled her nails into the palms of her hands as she saw the curving scimitar he was holding. 'You will never leave this house alive. My husband's men will cut you to pieces.'

'You are a proud bitch,' Philip said and

moved closer to her. 'Yes, it will be a pleasure to tame you—to teach you who is your master.'

'You came here alone?' Elaine was disbelieving. It was possible that one man might have slipped through the tight net that Zander had thrown around her to protect her, but she did not believe that his men were with him. 'You cannot expect to escape alive.'

'My life means little to me,' he said, 'though I bear a charmed one. I shall have what I want and that is the humbling of you and that husband of yours. He shall watch me as I bring you to heel—and then I shall kill him.'

Was he mad? Elaine had only to scream and…she'd told her women not to come to her yet. Down in the hall the men were still laughing, drinking and enjoying their last night at Sweetbriars. Could she reach the door and escape? She stood up and took a step forwards, but Philip moved closer, further into the room, his blade weaving from side to side, as if to threaten her.

Would he as soon kill her as ravish her? How could he imagine that she would submit to him? He must know that she would struggle and scream. She would fight until her last breath.

'You are mad,' she said, raising her head

proudly. 'I shall never submit to you. I would rather die.'

'Take her,' Philip called and two of his servants came from the shadows behind him, moving towards her menacingly. 'Bind the witch's arms behind her, but do not harm her. I want her alive…I want her to know what is happening to her and her husband. I want her to feel the pain.'

Elaine gave a scream of rage and rushed towards the door. The men leaped at her, grabbing her arms and trying to hold her as she struggled, kicking, screaming and biting like a wild thing. It took them several minutes to subdue her, but in the end their combined strength overpowered her. They thrust her to her knees before Philip, her hands secured behind her back. She could taste blood on her lips, but wasn't sure if it was hers or theirs.

'And now we wait,' Philip said, smiling at her in a way that made her feel sick. He was surely not sane. No one in their right mind could find pleasure in seeing someone humbled as he suggested.

'Are you mad that you come here?' she asked, lifting her head proudly. 'If you harm either my lord or me, his men will kill you.'

'I shall have my revenge first. Gag the witch,'

he ordered and one of his servants tied a filthy rag about her mouth despite all her efforts to dislodge it.

Elaine cursed herself for speaking out and angering him. Now she had no means of warning Zander—but perhaps he would not come? Her behaviour of late might have made him decide it was not worth the effort.

Even as she thought it, she saw a shadow darken the doorway.

'Elaine...' Zander's voice made Philip turn to look at him. 'What is this...?' His voice died away as he saw Philip and the two servants standing behind Elaine, forcing her to her knees. 'So, Philip, the rumours were lies to deceive us. How did you manage to enter Sweetbriars? Or can I guess...you came through the side gate when the men returned from hunting and were not noticed in the gathering gloom. Someone will be reprimanded for not keeping a more watchful eye.'

'You could not keep me out however I came.' Philip smiled and made a signal to one of his servants, who placed a knife at Elaine's throat. 'Throw down your arms and submit to being tied or she dies.'

Elaine tried to cry out but could only make a mumbling sound behind the filthy gag, so she shook her head violently. He must not submit. Could he not see it was the worst thing he could do? Once Philip had him secure, he would carry out his vile plan to despoil her before he killed them both.

She felt a surge of despair as she saw Zander unbuckle his sword and let it fall to the ground. He threw her a strange look she could not interpret before placing his hands behind his back.

'Tie him!' Philip cried gleefully and one of his servants rushed to obey. The man took out a stout rope and began to tie Zander's hands. Elaine did not see what happened next, but before she knew what was happening, Zander had the man on his back on the ground and a knife in his hand. The hapless servant was bleeding from a wound to his hands and lay whimpering with fright.

'Tell your servant to move away from her or this dog dies.'

'I care not what happens to the scum,' Philip screamed and pointed to the servant behind Elaine. 'Kill her…kill her…'

'Do you imagine you can leave this place alive?' Zander asked, addressing the servants. 'I shall give you one chance to get out and live. Go now, the pair of you, or you will both die painful deaths at the hands of my men. One shout from me and you are both dead—but my quarrel is with your master, not you.'

The servant holding the knife to Elaine's throat hesitated, then took the knife away. He began to edge closer to the door, then, as Zander kicked the other man, he ran past him and down the twisting stair. The second man rose to his feet at a jerk of Zander's head and fled as fast as he could after his fellow.

Philip was pale and sweating. He moved closer to Elaine, pointing his sword at her. Zander bent to retrieve his own blade. He moved steadily towards them, but Elaine was on her feet. They had tied only her hands and she could run now there was no one to overpower her. Philip tried to block her path, but Zander's knife went flying through the air and sliced into his arm, making him scream with pain. He turned to face Zander, who jerked his head at Elaine.

She needed no telling and went running past him, down the stairs to the hall where she screamed for help. Although only mumbled sounds came from her, men turned to look at her and she motioned frantically up the stairs with her head. As they ran past her, Janvier saw that her hands were tied and came to cut her free, easing the filthy rag from her mouth.

'My master?'

She pulled the gag away. 'Is fighting Lord Stornway. You must help him.'

'I think he will manage well enough,' Janvier said. 'Lord Stornway is soft and never as skilled as my lord. Come, lady, sit here and drink some wine.'

'I should go back,' Elaine said and started towards the stair, but Janvier held her arm.

'Forgive me, my lady, but your presence would only hinder Lord Zander. He must kill the man who was once his friend—and he will not wish you to see it.'

Elaine drew a sobbing breath. 'But I love him...'

'As he loves you, above all else. Why do you think he made a truce with a man he despises? Do you think it was easy for him to rein in his temper? It was for your sake, to keep you safe. There are times when a man must leave his lady and, if she is to be safe, he needs friends, not enemies.'

'Yes...' Tears were trickling down her cheeks. 'I know. It was just...just that he did not ask me.'

'A knight must be strong to win the respect of others. Any knight who asked his lady's permission would be laughed at behind his back.

Is that what you want? Or would you rather be protected and honoured—as my lord honours you?'

Elaine bowed her head, tears dampening her cheeks as she felt shamed by his scolding. She certainly had no wish to belittle Zander before his men. Suddenly, she realised how foolish she'd been, wasting the last few days she had with Zander—if he should be killed and they had parted in anger... A scream built inside her, but she held it back.

What was happening up there? She could hear nothing. It seemed eerily silent and her heart caught with terror. Had Lord Stornway killed Zander?

As she looked fearfully towards the stair that led to her solar, she saw Zander come down. He hesitated a moment, but she was on her feet and running to him.

'My lord, you are not hurt. He planned to make you watch as he despoiled me...and then he would have killed us both.'

Zander nodded grimly. 'I think he was mad. He lost his mind completely and screamed such things, obscenities...and he foamed at the mouth... I am glad you were not there to see or hear. I think his death was in the end a mercy and a blessing to him, for the thing he had become was not the man I once knew.'

'Forgive me,' Elaine whispered. 'Please forgive me for my temper and my obstinacy.'

A frown creased his brow. 'You should not ask for my forgiveness. I despise Newark as much as you, Elaine. Even though I know he was never my enemy, I despise him. It sticks in my craw that I must treat with men of his ilk—but it was the best for us, for you, my love. In life a man cannot always choose those he must befriend for the sake of peace.'

'I know. I was foolish but I wanted you to love me…to respect me for who I am.' She was weeping now.

Zander smiled and reached out to wipe the tears from her cheeks. 'Do you not know how much I adore you, my love? I have tried to show you in many ways, but words do not come easily to me these days. I am not the youth I was when I left to follow the king.'

'I know, but I love the man who returned to me,' Elaine said. 'Please forgive me. I shall try to obey you and—'

Zander sealed her lips with a kiss that took her breath. She pressed closer to him, wanting her response to tell him all that was in her heart, but he put her from him and took her by the hands.

'You cannot return to your chamber this night, Elaine. It must be cleansed and sweetened. You will sleep in my bed this night and in the morning—'

'Take me with you when you leave,' she begged before he could finish. 'Show me the new manor—let us make the decision of where we shall live together.'

Zander hesitated, then nodded. 'Yes, you shall come with me. I am not sure that I could bear to part with you.' A tiny shudder went through him and he clasped her hand tighter. 'I might so easily have lost you...had it not been for the mercy of God. Come, Elaine, let me take you to my chamber.'

Elaine held tightly to his hand as he led her towards the stair leading to his own chamber. She knew that it was bare compared to hers, the sleeping quarters of a soldier. He was a rich man, but he had been used to the rigours of war and had not bothered with the comforts he might have commanded, though he'd spared no expense for her.

Zander had given her jewels, silks and his protection. He'd shown his care of her in the only way he understood. He was a knight who had fought and suffered—and he had risked his own life to save hers.

She knew that a part of him must have found it hard to kill the man who had been his friend, but he had not shirked his duty. Had Philip stayed in his castle, Zander would probably have tried to make a truce with him, but he'd threatened Elaine and he'd paid the price.

Lord Stornway had been the King's Marshal—would that mean Zander must answer to King Richard for his death? She was certain it must and felt afraid for the future.

She was silent as they climbed the twisted stair to Zander's chamber, but once he shut the door behind them, she turned to him anxiously.

'Will the King be angry because you killed Lord Stornway?'

'Perhaps. I shall lay my case before him when he returns, but do not concern yourself with this now, Elaine.'

As she stood looking at him in wonder, Zander knelt before her. She gazed down at him, not understanding, but then he bent and kissed her feet, which were bare.

'How cold they are,' he said. 'Had I realised they were bare I should have carried you.'

'My feet do not matter,' she said. 'Why do you kneel to me, my lord?'

'I am not worthy to be your husband,' Zander said. 'I want you to accept my homage and know that you are more precious to me than all the world. I have ever loved you—and never more than when I understood what Philip would have done to you.'

'Oh, Zander, get up,' Elaine said and pulled at him, making him rise and stand. She looked into his face, then stretched out her hand to stroke his cheek. 'Do you not know how much I love and honour you? You could never be unworthy of my love. I know you for the honourable knight you are.'

'In war a man does terrible things. This night I killed a man who was once my friend—and there were women and children killed and despoiled when we fought in the Holy Land.'

'You told me,' Elaine said softly. 'The man who did these things was not you, my love—it was a soldier who did as he was told, who carried out his duty.'

'And must again if Richard should ask it of me, though I would not again go to make war on other people, but I must defend my king if need be.'

'I know, I understand. All I want is that you love me…treat me as your equal and tell me what you mean to do. I would be by your side in all things, sharing the good with the bad.'

'I see you as far above me,' he said and smiled. 'But I will promise now that, inasmuch as I can, I will share my decisions with you—though there may be times when I cannot, when all our lives might depend upon a quick decision.'

'I understand that, of course I do,' Elaine said. 'You are the lord here and you defend us as you see best—but in the things we share I wish to know that you value my thoughts.'

'You cannot forgive me for making a truce with Newark?'

'I have forgiven and I understand.' Elaine sighed. 'You are not the only one who realised this night that life is too short to quarrel. Had anything happened to you…I should not have wished to live.'

'You are always my first concern,' Zander said. 'Now let us put these things behind us.' He moved towards her purposefully and reached out to take her in his arms. 'You know I love you—you will not withdraw from me again?'

'Never,' she said and lifted her face for his kiss. 'I love you, Zander. I love you more than life.'

Zander moaned low in his throat, then bent

to sweep her into his arms. He carried her to his bed, which was big enough for the two of them, but much harder than Elaine was used to. Yet she made no complaint as he set her down, merely reaching out for him as he began to kiss and caress her.

'My beautiful, beautiful love,' he said. 'I have never been as afraid as I was of losing you this night.'

'And I of losing you,' she murmured, her lips against his as she drew his head down. His hands moved swiftly to remove her tunic and then her chemise, which were tossed to the floor together with his own gown.

They lay together, flesh to flesh, quivering and eager for the loving that both knew would be special. Elaine had always felt fulfilled and happy after lying in Zander's arms, but as he began to kiss and caress her now she knew that she'd never felt such pleasure in her life. Each kiss seemed to draw her heart from her body and she pressed against him, wanting more. His hands stroked and caressed, making her moan and whimper with need as the desire flared between them and became white-hot. Her hands stroked his back, her nails scoring his shoulders as he slid inside her and she shrieked out.

'Zander…' she moaned. 'Zander, my love… oh, yes, that is so lovely…so very good…'

She was lifted and tossed on the crest of a wave, carried with him to a place they had never been, their bodies moving in perfect harmony. His mouth caressed her while his tongue tasted and flicked, each stroke making her quiver and then cry out as the pleasure became so intense that it was almost pain.

'My beautiful, beautiful Elaine. I adore you…I shall never stop loving you…you must believe me…'

He was so intense, so imploring that all she could do was cling to him as the spasms shook her body and she felt such glorious sensation coursing through her. She was in an earthly paradise, loved and giving all the love within her freely.

'I shall never doubt you again,' she vowed and buried her face in the salty sweat of his shoulder.

When at last they were satiated, Elaine fell into a deep sleep while Zander lay beside her, one leg resting possessively over her and his arm about her as he lay looking into the darkness now that the candle had burned out.

She was his at last and he had returned to her in every way that he was capable of. He might not be the idealistic youth that had caught her young heart, but the knight who had come home in his place was determined to love and protect her all his life.

Epilogue

Elaine looked about her. The shelves in her stillroom at the Manor de Bricasse, as they had named the fine estate that lay no more than twenty leagues west of Zander's uncle's own estate, were filled to capacity with preserves and cures that she and her ladies had prepared. Bunches of herbs and wild flowers were hung up to dry and a bench was littered with the remains of their latest foray into the surrounding countryside.

Sir Roderick had chosen well for them and it was a rich manor, fertile and sweet, capable of supporting the growing army of men that had flocked to join Lord Zander.

Wiping her hands on a cloth, Elaine left the room where she often enjoyed spending her time and went through into the large hall. This manor house was more modern than Sweetbriars and the rooms were pleasant with bigger windows of leaded glass. She put a hand to her back for it had begun to ache a little of late, something she assumed was to do with the fact that she was carrying her husband's child.

Elaine sighed, wishing that her lord was at home. In February of that year, King Richard had finally returned to claim his throne. Instead of resisting, Prince John had promised allegiance to his brother and convinced Richard of his loyalty, though many doubted it privately. However, Richard had seen fit to embrace his brother and was even now making plans for yet another crusade. Zander had been summoned to meet with him and other knights and Elaine was anxious lest he had been asked to prove his loyalty by going with Richard on this latest expedition.

The king had accepted Zander's explanation of Lord Stornway's death. Elaine had wondered if Philip's sister would place an objection before the King, but a little to her surprise no word had come from her. Elaine had decided to write and thank her. The Abbess of St Michael had written to tell Elaine that Anne had decided to take her vows and would be joining their order.

Elaine had put the young woman from her mind, allowing herself to enjoy the following months. Having settled at their new manor, they were summoned by Sir Roderick to meet the king at his house and it was rumoured that he might be made the King's Marshal before Richard left on his next crusade. However, nothing was said and the visit passed without incident. She was not sure whether Zander's uncle was disappointed not to be named, because he had not mentioned it before her. Zander told her as much as he could, but his uncle was of the old school and believed that ladies must be protected from the truth for their own sakes.

It was in the June of that year that Elaine realised she might be with child. She waited a few weeks before telling her husband, but her physician had confirmed the signs were good and she was confident that she was at least two months with child.

'You are to bear my child?' Zander looked at her in delight when she told him and then kissed her hands. 'I can hardly wonder at it,' he said and smiled. 'We have been passionate these many months; it was bound to happen sooner or later.'

'Are you pleased?'

'Of course. Every man wants his heir—and you, does the idea please you, Elaine?'

'Of course. I am so happy in every way. I have always wanted children and they will make our life complete. Our new house is wonderful and the land is good. Why should I not be content?'

She particularly liked the new arrangement of their private chambers, which gave them a bedchamber that connected through a door and a parlour where they could sometimes be alone. It was so easy for Zander to come into her room and for her to go to his—and she'd made certain that his chamber now had the comforts that a lord of the manor should expect.

Yet now Zander was with the king and Elaine was anxious. She knew that if he was commanded to follow Richard, he must go and leave her. She would be well attended by her ladies, and with Sir Roderick close enough to visit often she need not fear attack or even loneliness, for Zander's aunt and cousin visited her each week.

It was just that she hoped Zander would be with her when she gave birth to their first child, which she was certain in her own mind would be a son. Zander said he did not mind, but she knew that all men craved a son. Her child was not due for some months yet and by that time Zander might be in the Holy Land.

She had made up her mind that she would not beg him to stay. Elaine hoped that he would not be called, but if he were she could not deny him. She loved him too much to put him in such an invidious position.

As she turned to mount the stair to her chamber, she heard a commotion outside the house and glanced back as Zander strode into the hall. He looked so strong and well, his scar still prominent, but much less vivid now. His eyes were bright with excitement and she feared the worst. Richard had asked him to join him and Zander had agreed.

Painting on a smile that hid her fears, she went to greet him. 'Welcome home, my lord. I am glad to see you.'

'And I you,' Zander said, looking down at her. She saw laughter in his eyes and wondered at it. 'Do not look so anxious—it is not the news you fear.'

'Richard has not asked you to join him in his crusade?'

'No. He asked something of me, but it was not that.'

'Tell me,' she said and aimed a little punch at

his arm. 'Do not tease me, Zander. I was afraid that you must leave me again.'

'I shall never leave you for a day longer than I must,' Zander said and smiled at her. 'Richard asked me if I would become his King's Marshal. He wants someone he can trust to keep the peace while he is gone—and I am to have the castle at Lanark and another at Rochester.'

Elaine caught her breath, as she struggled to take in the news. Zander was to be the King's Marshal! It would mean they must leave this house, which was dear to her, and spend time at the castles Richard had given them—but at least they would be together.

'What did you say?'

'I asked why he had not given the honour to my uncle. He said that Sir Roderick would be a warden of the peace here, but he needed a man who was strong enough to counter his brother's worst excesses—and he thinks I am the only one strong enough to stand up to the prince while he is away.'

'Oh...' Elaine breathed deeply. The king had bestowed an honour on Zander, but it was a two-edged sword. Her husband would be an important man, often away on the king's business—and if he made an enemy of Prince John he might be murdered. Yet if it was what he wanted she could not object, though her heart cried out against it. 'Has he made you an earl?'

'The earldom was offered, but refused,' Zander said. 'I asked that the honour of being the King's Marshal should go to Sir Roderick. If my uncle needs me, I am ready to support him and I have assured Richard of this—but I have no wish to spend my time at court or to play the king's games with his brother. I want to spend my time with you, Elaine. To watch our children grow and enjoy the quiet happiness we have found together here.'

'Ahh…' A breath of content left her. 'Was Richard angry?'

'A little disappointed, but not angry. I have served him well and he could not refuse my request to step back and let others take the honours.'

'Thank you,' Elaine said and moved towards him, putting her arms about his waist. 'Thank you for returning to me, my love—my gentle knight. I ask for no more than to have your children and live with you in peace.'

'For as long as we have peace in England I shall not leave your side,' Zander promised. 'Only if my sword is needed to protect that peace shall I take up arms again…and that, before God, is my promise to you.'

A promise she knew he would keep. She kissed his lips and was content.

* * * * *

A sneaky peek at next month...

HISTORICAL

IGNITE YOUR IMAGINATION, STEP INTO THE PAST...

My wish list for next month's titles...

In stores from 4th October 2013:

☐ A Date with Dishonour – Mary Brendan

☐ The Master of Stonegrave Hall – Helen Dickson

☐ Engagement of Convenience – Georgie Lee

☐ Defiant in the Viking's Bed – Joanna Fulford

☐ The Adventurer's Bride – June Francis

☐ Christmas Cowboy Kisses – Carolyn Davidson,
Carol Arens & Lauri Robinson

Available at WHSmith, Tesco, Asda, Eason, Amazon and Apple

Just can't wait?

Visit us Online You can buy our books online a month before
they hit the shops! **www.millsandboon.co.uk**

0913/04

Wrap up warm this winter with Sarah Morgan…

Sleigh Bells in the Snow

Kayla Green loves business and hates Christmas.

So when Jackson O'Neil invites her to Snow Crystal Resort to discuss their business proposal… the last thing she's expecting is to stay for Christmas dinner. As the snowflakes continue to fall, will the woman who doesn't believe in the magic of Christmas finally fall under its spell…?

4th October

www.millsandboon.co.uk/sarahmorgan

She's loved and lost — will she ever
learn to open her heart again?

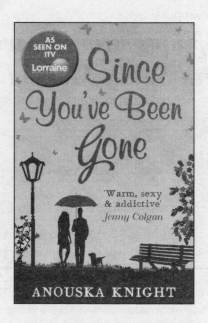

From the winner of ITV Lorraine's Racy Reads,
Anouska Knight, comes a heart-warming tale of
love, loss and confectionery.

**'The perfect summer read — warm,
sexy and addictive!'**
—Jenny Colgan

For exclusive content visit:
www.millsandboon.co.uk/anouskaknight

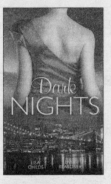
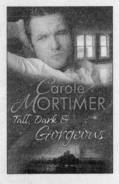